DRAGON POND

DRAGON POND

Vol III of the Kine Saga

A. R. Lloyd

ARROW BOOKS

Arrow Books Limited
20 Vauxhall Bridge Road, London SW1V 2SA

An imprint of the Random Century Group

London Melbourne Sydney Auckland Johannesburg
and agencies throughout the world

First published in 1990 by Frederick Muller
an imprint of the Random Century Group
20 Vauxhall Bridge Road, London SW1V 2SA
Legend edition 1991

Printed and bound in Great Britain by
Cox & Wyman Ltd, Reading

ISBN 0 09 969930 3

Contents

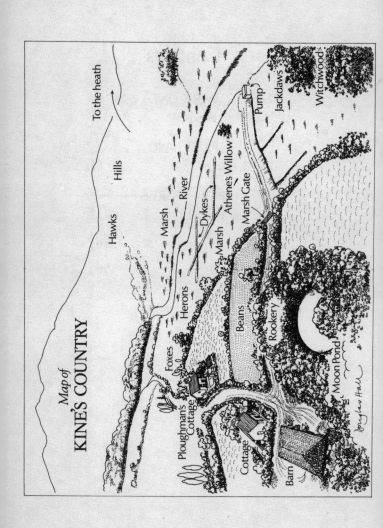

Map of
KINE'S COUNTRY

To the heath

Hawks Hills

Marsh

River

Herons

Dykes

Marsh

Foxes

Athene's Willow

Marsh Gate

Pump

Jackdaws

Witchwood

Ploughman's Cottage

Beans

Rookery

Cottage

Moon Pond

Barn

Douglas Hall

Part One

THE MOON POND

The pond in winter was eerie. Its turbid depths aroused fears, agitated the timid. The swims were deep, their brows veiled. It might have plumbed countless fathoms, a sump without bottom, so black was the surface. Only close to the side was the water transparent, where dark and leafy shapes wallowed.

Great trees bounded the edges. They formed a small but dense copse overhanging the banks, making caves with their skirts when the low boughs were burdened. Then the pond could beguile, its summer aspect seductive with flowering flags and water lilies. There would be song in the reeds, dragonflies, swallows skimming. But now the pond's face was daunting.

Against the sky pigeons wheeled, peering downwards, suspicious. At last, the birds filtered in, claiming roosts in the dusk, puffing up in the cold like balloons on the perches. Beyond the copse an owl fluted. In parts, the land had turned white and the molehills were stiffening.

There were four nights to Christmas. It was the feast of St Thomas and the countryside was silent. The valley sprawled in the frost; timbered slopes, marshy flats, an ancient stream flowing through them. Once wild oxen had roamed and flint-armed men prowled the region. Herons still fished the dykes; the marsh foxes were brazen. There were few human dwellings: the ploughman's home on the ridge and, nearby, a small cottage.

To the west the glow faded. A skin of ice glazed the water. It squeezed small sounds from the reeds, tiny moans, muttered protests. The voices came and went weirdly. Little creaks could be heard, a noise like foil being crinkled. There was a low, drawn-out groan and ice shattered, seemed to break for no reason.

Then something lashed, towered and sank, raising waves of black water – something from the pond's abyss.

There was a pier at the pool, a fallen tree from the shore with a hole in its topside. A shrew had dossed in the hole. Imperceptibly breathing, the manikin was asleep, its sharp snout in dwarf paws. It came to life with a jerk as the tree-pier vibrated.

Icy spray drenched the hole.

Soused, the shrew shook its coat then took flight through the hatch to the deck, along the trunk to the reeds, down an earthwork of roots to the bank, where it shivered.

Terrified, the myope squinted. In the dusk, all was dim but the shrew heard waves breaking, felt more spume and ran faster. The air was still, chill and breathless. Yet the pond was in tumult. The pigmy's legs beetled. There were laws in the valley, laws of large and small creatures, of hunter and hunted, of water and weather, and the shrew knew the pond law: beware of waves without wind, for all things had their causes.

Vague shapes patterned the evening, leaves of butter-burr, plantain. A hoary tree stump appeared and the shrew dived beneath it, landing slap on a snake – a school of snakes, hibernating. Disturbed, the reptiles writhed slowly. Again, the dwarf fled, still faster. Down a hedgerow it raced, across a path, past the cottage.

A white-winged owl prowled the dusk. It missed the shrew, floating on, and the midget paused, blinking. 'K-i-n-e . . .' it wailed, the call frantic. It was a squeak in the silence.

The ploughman turned his head, listening. On the frost, the sound carried but was something and nothing, and he shut up his chickens. His back was bad in the cold; it had ached on the tractor. He waved his arms with a wince. His two old geese were still out and he shooed them, blaspheming. They stirred like rags in the gloom, their dirty pallor unreal, then stood sentinel, hissing.

"Tis going to be a hard night.' The veteran spoke to the geese, a habit he had slipped into. His wife was dead; their girl wed, with a child down the cottage. It was the geese or the hens, and the hens could not hear him. Soon a chill moon would gawp, the ground freeze, beasts start prowling.

Goose and gander stared hard. With necks stiff, the pair cussed, their eyes fierce, heads aswivel. He could not say what they saw but there were things in the night, on the dark side of the wild, that geese detected like dogs: banshee wails, eerie movements. Geese were better than dogs, he sometimes thought, as night watchmen.

He held his back, the joints stiff. He was getting no younger. The darkening valley was gaunt and thin ghosts stalked the

4

marsh, the beds of sedge by the channels. He had no taste for the murk. Some might scoff; he knew better. Let those who smirked take his place, plod the lanes in the gloom, spend a night on the levels. Rancour tainted the dusk. Then the hedgerow clans roused, the rat squealed, stoat-kind rustled.

He steered the geese to their shed. 'Aye, *you* know,' Ploughman muttered. They sensed the fey, whiskered tribes, the teeth and claws in the brakes, bated breath, pad of vixen. 'Get you in and less fuss!' He took a step, grumbling at them. He had not spared them the chop to be robbed by marsh foxes.

On the feast of St Thomas . . .

He eyed the sky. A star twinkled. There was a countryside saying: the wind which blew on that day would hold its quarter till spring. There *was* no wind, the man thought. The only stir in the trees was down the track by the pond where, twice now in an hour, the wood pigeons had scudded. They did not take the night lightly – more sense, Ploughman reckoned.

A slender shape crossed the garden. It paused and sat on its tail, head held high, a slim goblin. The creature's white breast shone faintly. He knew the weasel of old – it bore a singular scar – but he had not seen it lately. He was surprised it had survived for wild things seldom lived long and it, like him, was past its heyday.

'Bah,' he wheezed, 'you wee devil! Push off or I'll have you.' It disappeared.

The man shrugged. The small beast had no pension; it took its chance in the frost. He gave a raw-throated grunt. Beyond the hedge the sprite glared. 'And merry Christmas,' the man croaked, then grinned, cackling drily. The weasel scorned the farm worker. Briskly hopping a ditch, it landed lightly in grass at a field's dusky margin.

'*Tchkkk* . . .' The weasel glanced back.

An old oak raised black arms, its bole bloated with ivy. '*Tchkkk-kkk-chk*!' The land belonged to its own, to the wildlife, not to Ploughman. So reckoned the weasel – Kine the weasel, the small one. What was the man but a drudge? The territory was Kine's; weasel country through history. All his life he had lived there.

The moon appeared and he danced, swaying this way and

that. Kine was small but astute, and he knew the deep places, the earths and sets, the mole's fortress. He knew the signs of the valley – the otter's seal, the hare's trod – and every scent of its creatures. He was Kine who missed nothing!

Many seasons had passed since the weasel first hunted. He knew the tracks and the runs; a hundred sounds were familiar. He knew the song of the wren, whose voice exceeded its stature, and the fox's sharp bark, which was harshly asthmatic. He knew the squeal of stoats fighting; the taunting laugh of the yaffle; the drumming wings of the snipe when March died and spring awakened. And, if he lived that much longer, the honk of wild geese returning would tell him summer was back, another winter behind him.

For now, the weasel was hungry. It was no time to be bragging; he was empty and cold, and the night would get colder.

From the gloom, an owl ghosted, quietly prowling the field, sometimes floating at hedge height, sometimes skimming the hoarfrost. Bristling, Kine watched his rival. The owl would glide for a while, white wings still, face downturned; then, with unhurried strokes, sweep and wheel in the half-light.

Stiffly, Kine hunted forward. '*Tchkkk*,' he churred as he forayed. 'Have a care, owl, I've seen you. I am Kine the formidable.'

The bird ignored him, still planing, keeping close to the shapes – the black thickets, a farm gate – which mapped out its domain. '*Tchkkk.*' The weasel's pace quickened. 'Kine is small but intrepid. Stay away from me, barn owl.' Indeed, the goblin was slight, little more than ten inches, but his dance was determined. He paused abruptly and listened.

There was a noise near the ditch. In the grass, almost hidden, a mouse was gnawing a nutshell, a relic of autumn. The mouse was sleek, yellow-brown, still plump on hedge berries. As it gnawed, its eyes twinkled: bright, protruberant orbs, the night sky in their brilliance.

Softly, Kine slithered forward. The valley lay in a trance. The moon burnished the marsh and, far off, voices whispered: the distant quacking of ducks, the low drone of an engine. The night was breathless with murmurs but they were lost to the sprite, who heard only the fieldmouse, the rasp on the cobnut.

Now the gnawing grew louder, now stopped – was resumed. The weasel tensed, whiskers twitching. His stomach was tight.

Then, out of space, the owl struck like a bolt, its wings lofted. The outspread talons came first, raking into the growth, their claws seeking the rodent. There was a lunge after landing, a squeak promptly stifled.

As Kine looked up, taut with rage, the barn owl crouched, its wings spread, its kill screened from the weasel. The bird's fierce glare was possessive. 'Kine is slow,' hissed the captor. 'You grow older, small hunter; your dance is stiff. Time is passing.'

'*Kine!*' the shrew called. 'Where are you?' The dwarf had stopped running, a frozen hoofprint for shelter. 'K-i-n-e . . .'

The shrew shuddered.

In the darkness a head rose.

'K-Kine?'

'Who's there?' Kine snapped.

'Scrat,' the shrew gulped.

Kine squinted. 'Old Scrat's dead, so's his grandson. Shrews have short lives. Who are you?'

'*Scrat* – Old Scrat's grandson's grandson.'

'Another doom-laden midget!'

There was a break. 'Doom it is, Kine.'

'*Tchkkk,*' the weasel said tersely. Slow and stiff! His blood simmered. Had he not slain the rat and danced rings round the adder? Had every rabbit that hopped not turned tail in his presence? Growing old! The sprite smarted. He muttered, scowling, 'I'm busy.'

'The pond, Kine – it's frightening.'

'All shrews are alike.' They stank, or Kine would devour them. Old Scrat's grandson's grandson! There was no end to their offspring, all twitchy, neurotic. He said, 'Kine lives by the pond.'

'You must move. You must run.'

'Kine the brave?'

'But the monster . . .'

'*Tchkkk.* What monster? We'll see.' Kine set off, Scrat

7

behind him. He eyed the dwarf, who was trembling. All shrews were alike, inedible and absurd. The pond was part of Kine's life. He had been born in the hole, the living womb of the wood, when the Life Tree stood upright. Ever since he had lived there.

'Waves,' wailed Scrat. 'Kine, I saw them.'

'On the Moon Pond?'

'Great waves!'

'We'll soon see.'

'Truly, Kine, it's the monster. It's been asleep in the depths.'

'We'll find out.'

'Kine, be careful.' Scrat held back. 'Doom,' he quivered.

'I can arrange your doom, midget, don't tempt me,' Kine answered. 'Ask the owl. I'm bad-tempered.' The bird had touched a raw nerve. In the copse, the sprite added, 'Me, with my reputation! Tell me, Scrat, am I slow? Isn't Kine still a spitfire?'

'Kine the bold!' gulped the midget. 'But don't g-go any closer . . .'

The pond was smooth, again frozen. The fallen Life Tree was ghostly. Kine paused briefly, remembering – recalling Kia, his lost mate, their dead kitts and his mother. All had graced the snug den which, in Kine's mind, was hallowed. 'Waves?' he rasped. It was quiet, the chill deep, cruel and stealthy. 'Monster?' Kine hissed. '*Where*, shrewmouse?'

***

Ploughman belched and sat back. He ate mainly from tins, never mind *her* opinion. The girl had plenty of those. She had cooked while she stayed, a sharp eye on his manners. Loneliness had compensations – he bet her young man was learning.

But they were happy together. He filled his mug from the pot and replaced the tea cosy. The thing was old now and stained. Once its patchwork was bright, stitched with love by a wife from the remnants of frocks he could still see her wearing: light, summery prints with full skirts that swirled round her.

8

He sighed. The kitchen was rough. Dirty crocks filled the sink and the stove needed cleaning. First, upsetting his back, he stooped and opened a cupboard, his hands reaching in it. The little tricycle shone, its seat red. The bell jangled. He put the trike on the table.

Next he fetched a brown bag – it had contained layers' bran, the mash he mixed for his hens – and applied it as wrapping. Over this, with more fuss, he tied the Christmassy paper he had bought for the parcel. It looked a seasonal gift, a gift fit for his grandson.

The farm man grunted his pleasure. The girl, he owned, had done well. She might have run a bit wild, a country girl with no mum, the harum-scarum young miss, but she had borne a fine son. The man picked up the fuel bucket. A lad as bright as a button!

He went outside to the shed. Freezing air stung his face, the grass white and unyielding. All those years – still alone. Now retirement was looming. He lit his pipe, squinting round. The valley scarcely seemed real; the copse was silvery, spectral. At least he had a warm bed. It would be tough on the wild side.

The weasel paused in the Tree, in the den of remembrance. The chamber echoed his exploits. 'Single file; keep together!' The nursery safaris. Life had thrilled on those outings; sun on kingcups, frogs croaking, breath of steers sweet and misty.

Later, Kine had met Kia and their own young had played there. Marauding mink had destroyed them – all but one tiny kitt – despite Kia's frantic fight, and her mate had sworn vengeance. Many battles had followed, Kine reckless, triumphant. But that was all long ago. In the Life Tree he shivered.

He thought he heard something move. Stretching stiffly, he listened. If the shrew had returned . . . there was a limit to patience, his toleration of pigmies. Kia had died at the pondside; it was a place sacred to him. He had no time for shrew stories and stuck his head out, ill-humoured.

The evening's silence had deepened, cold and deadly, unbroken. There was no knell for the weak – for the sickly wood pigeon, the toppled finch, its blood frozen. Just the moon's eerie shroud and galactic indifference.

The weasel glanced at the pond. Its ice was lifeless and void. There was no movement, no scent, and when he tested its strength it was rigid beneath him. Cautiously, he took stock then ran in bounds to the bluff, a small step in the bank where a tangled path ended. Again, he thought something stirred, a mere breath, but saw nothing.

'*Tchkkk*.' The shrew was a fool. Phantom waves and pond monsters! As if the dwarf's lurid tales impressed Kine the intrepid! Shrews and owls: *fools and liars*. Kine scorned both, his name famed, a woodland legend for grit (among those who remembered). He climbed the bank. A paw hit him.

The shadow curved like a scythe and Kine was swept to the ground, breath expelled, his legs flattened. The weight above held him fast. Sight had gone, the moon black; every rib seemed to snap, to cave in on his lungs. His jaws gaped, mute and helpless. Pinned, the weasel lay still, his coat rimmed with ice crystals.

There was a chilly hiatus. The fox had seen a faint twitch, a slight jerk in the grass, and pounced speculatively. A young rat would have pleased, or a vole, plump and tender. 'Kine?' it sniffed, peering down: it had been bitten by weasels. True, this captive was stunned, firmly squeezed underfoot, but the fox was judicious. It curled its lip slowly.

Kine tried hard to make sense, clear his head of its fog. He nuzzled into the frost. The icy shock brought him round and he stirred, the fox watching. Its ears were pricked, its snout toothy. Instinct kept Kine from struggling. Then, as the larger beast stabbed, the smaller twisted its neck, the move as swift as a snake's, and found the fox's soft nose where the whiskers were rooted.

'Kine the pain-bringer, fox!'

The fox yelped. Kine bit hard. He was whirled up as he leeched, the other hopping in anguish. The canine spun, ducked, reversed; it shook its head in dismay but could not lose the weasel. A foxy foot swiped an ear, scraped a cheek, achieved nothing, the weasel's hold tightening. At last the fox stood and whined. Kine let go and ran off. He was bruised but intact.

'Kine brings pain, learn the lesson; Kine is small but unyielding!'

He vanished into the scrub. None harmed Kine with impunity. At the edge of the copse, he took the track past the barn – the owl's tumbledown home – until drawn by a light. A warm glow bathed the frost from a small cottage window. Inquisitively, he stopped. There was a fire in the room and a Christmas tree twinkled.

Kine stood tall, his eyes sharp. The tree was intriguing. Often he came to the garden, for it was haunted by mice, but the tree was strange to him. Perhaps it presaged the spring, was a sign of revival. Perhaps its baubles were omens, indicators of fortune. He must hang on through the frosts. He knew that hunger would pass if he could see out the winter.

'*Pssst.*' It came from the eaves. Two cock sparrows were roosting. '*Pssst,*' said one, 'mind the light; you're very plain in the light, Kine.'

'The owl's about,' said the other.

'So?' said Kine.

'The owl's swift.'

'Kine is swift.'

'The owl's strong.'

'The owl is due for a lesson!' A thief and liar, thought Kine. 'I'm not afraid of the owl. *You* should know,' he reproached them, 'you've seen me in action.'

'When you vanquished the mink?' There was a shrug from one sparrow. The other said, 'Or the rats? It was a long time ago. You were a champion then, Kine.'

'*Then?*' he flared. 'I've just fought. Where were you?' he demanded. 'Kine has never been beaten. Ask the fox how I fared – and how its muzzle is feeling.'

The sparrows huddled for warmth. 'We mean a fight not a skirmish. We mean a fight to the death.' They peered down. 'Like the old days.' There was a pause. 'Mind the light . . . RUN,' they screeched. '*Kine – the window!*'

A pair of arms drew the curtains. Indoors, the girl said, 'Poor weasel, I saw him bolt. Poor cold weasel.'

'Poor *what?*' laughed her husband.

'You've no soul.'

A fire crackled. The low-beamed parlour was snug, merry flames in the hearth, a mantel festive with cards, strung with

tinsel and holly. The girl looked on as he worked, hanging
mistletoe for her. He was meticulous about it, his young and
handsome face earnest.

'*You*,' she teased, 'and your engines!' His job was minding
the marsh pumps. 'You're no lover of wild things.'

'I married one.'

'Poor old townsman!' She settled by the fire, smiling. She
was teaching him slowly: he knew a goose from a swan and had
learned about logs – that you could burn ash wood green but
that oak needed keeping, that larch would spit, pear was
scented. She could not teach him it all, for much was rooted in
childhood.

She looked at the mistletoe berries. Their pearly brilliance
bewitched, as did the curious leaves. One day when she had
been small, a speckled bird had flown down and wiped its beak
on a tree, an old scaly-barked apple. A sticky seed from the
beak, passing on to the bough, had eventually burst, tapped the
sap and made growth. In time, that growth was exuberant.

Each year since she had gone there and picked a small sprig
for Christmas. Speckled birds still arrived. Now they gorged
on the fruits, the tokens of the child's wonder: a mistlethrush in
a tree, the white magic of winter.

She could not teach him the magic, the vale was too
personal. She knew its lore and its legends, its secret glades
and their sprites; the haunts of bat, toadstool, serpent. The girl
had known the old poacher. The tramp had died some years
back but his yarns remained vivid, tales of woodland and marsh
which she would pass to her own child. Already, bedtime
meant stories: Flit and Farthing the sparrows, Scrat the shrew,
foxes, herons.

Her husband grinned. 'Well?' he asked her.

She smiled again.

They kissed where the sprig hung.

A cold, thin gleam slashed the east and something feathery
tumbled. Then again – it was snowing. The child's night-light
had guttered. On the chimney above, jackdaws crouched
seeking warmth, the hearth's embers still glowing. The hint of
dawn roused the sparrows. Flit-cat peered from his roost.

'Almost day,' he chirped, fluffing.

Farthing-feather sat near him. He stretched a wing. 'Snow,' he twittered.

'Another chilly morn,' Flit said.

Farthing said, 'Crisp and brisk.'

'A good day for a fight.'

'For a dust-up.' They fluttered.

By a flowerpot, Scrat shivered. 'Gutter urchins,' he moaned.

'What was that?' said the sparrows. They cocked their heads.

'We're doomed,' Scrat said.

'Speak up, pigmy!'

'I've seen the waves, the pond monster. I saw the *thing* in the Moon Pond.'

'Pah,' the sparrows said, sparring, 'the pond's not *our* problem.' They flapped and brawled. 'That's Kine's problem.'

'But he won't listen.'

'He's past it.' The sparrows rested, heads nodding, grey-capped in the shadows. 'Kine is yesterday's fighter.'

The shrew was swamped by a snowflake. 'Kine's still brave,' he piped loyally. 'My ancestors praised him.'

'Brave but old.'

'Still a hero.'

'In history, Scrat – life moves on.'

'Life will *end*, we're all doomed – doomed,' the mini-beast echoed. He made a ring round the flowerpot, trotting blindly, snow-smothered. 'Only a *hero* can save us.'

'Then you're all right . . .' Farthing answered.

'. . . since you've got one,' drawled Flit.

'Woe!' wailed Scrat from the pot, for was the weasel not heedless? Had the goblin not scorned him? From the gloom came the owl, swinging over the garden. It sailed the hedge, a snow-spirit. Then, as the light topped the hills, a flock of starlings took wing and the hunter sought stragglers. A frosty rabbit lay dead but the owl disdained carrion.

'Doom . . .' The shrew's squeak dissolved.

Everywhere it was grey, the sky and land without seam, the dawn's rayless face ashen. The white owl's kingdom was cloaked, field and lane snow-encrusted. Marsh and pumphouse were iced, scalloped drifts by the stream whose becalmed coves were frozen. The snipe had gone, and the duck. Above the vale, hungry kestrels, too impatient to fan, swooped and wheeled on the chance that some small bird would weaken.

But all life was concealed, like the vole in its vaults – hollows formed by dead growth where the snow made a ceiling. Fat and warm, the vole probed, found a green shoot and nibbled.

Overhead, the owl listened. It heard the rodent and paused, perching now on a fence spile. There was a howl from the marsh, a vixen's cry, loud and soulful, then creaking wings filled the murk, wild geese travelling, space-phantoms. As the owl watched the ground, a tiny snow cornice fell and the vole gazed up, startled.

The raptor crouched, cowled head tilting.

It was preparing to pounce when, from the frost-laden hedge, Kine emerged with a bound. '*Now* who's slow? Watch me, night bird!' He snatched the vole. 'Watch the dance. See the dance of death, barn owl.' He whirled his kill to the bush. 'Keep your eye on the weasel – learn that Kine gets his own back!'

The owl was stiff, face impassive. 'You'll pay for that, Kine,' it told him.

* * *

The toddler tired of the trike. It had been fun while they pushed, a helping hand as he steered, but they had gone indoors and the pedals were heavy. His dad had cleared off the path. There was snow on each side. It shone and flashed in the sun and the child's interest wandered. There was a face at the window. It was his mum's, framed by frost flowers.

'Don't get cold,' the face mouthed.

It disappeared from the pane and he kicked the trike mildly, enough to show it who owned it. 'I'm coming back,' he declared, testing the snow with a boot. He hesitated a moment, a little Eskimo shape in the hood and red parka. 'I won't be long,' he avowed, 'you're my best Christmas present.'

He crossed the snow to the hedge, scrambled through and

looked back. The trike was still on the path. Its meek obedience pleased and he trudged on, the glare dazzling. His father's van was outside. Snow had stuck to its legend, *River Board Engineers*. The roof twinkled. The whole valley was bright as the frost flared and sparkled. It was a fairyland world: crystal slopes, powdered woods, the barn a pillowy mountain.

Bursts of bird music tinkled. A robin sang in the sun and a dunnock was tweedling. With a full-throated shout, a wren beckoned then moved, scuttling mouselike ahead and the cottage-child followed. Again, the tiny bird trilled, loud and sweet from a fence, then whirled to the woodpile. The boy beamed, his nose pink.

Only the wren, which was charmed, could be at once here and there, but other marvels enchanted. By a gate, he saw gnats, silver-winged, dancing wildly. While water froze in the shade, such flimsy spirits could revel! Fantastic signs marked the snow, tracks of fabulous creatures. Where a stoat had bounced by, all four feet placed together, he saw the line of round holes and thought their maker one-legged.

Gnomish forts straddled fields. Like stepping stones in the snow, mounds of tilth had popped up – 'nunky-tumps,' the boy called them – one mysteriously moving.

The wren went off with a bob. It disappeared into holly, a tall and curious bush coroneted with ivy. He found its spiked leaves a puzzle. Unlike most in the wood they had no season of fall, always green, always polished. It was a mystical vale, his mother's stories proclaimed it so.

Down the field there was gorse, golden where its flowers opened. It never failed the year round, every month blooming somewhere, all a part of the spell, the magic life of the snow-realm.

The sun went in and the child paused. He felt suddenly cold but something moved in the copse and he lurched on through the trees. A pair of dog foxes fought, winter rivals, tails flicking. They ran away through the growth. The trees were grey, iced to windward.

Deeper in, the wood darkened. A bramble snatched at his sleeve and he said petulantly, 'Stop it!' A hollow stump caught his eye and squatting down on his heels, he peered in and saw snakes, a tangled mass of them, sleeping. For a while the boy stared then, bewitched, wandered farther.

He came at last to the pond. He was chilled, slightly frightened. The frozen surface seemed vast, a great snow-dusted void, its waste haunted by draughts, wraiths of icy white powder. His gaze was lured by the tracks. A set of crisp goblin prints crossed the ice to the Life Tree. The hulk was glacial, ghostly. The infant's face brightened. On one pale, frosted bough, gazing back, sat the weasel.

He knew the sprite from the garden.

'It's *me*,' the child exclaimed, beaming.

The weasel rose up on its haunches. It sniffed the air, its nose sharp, then skipped to the tree bole.

'Wait,' the boy cried, 'I'm coming. I'll come over. Wait, weasel . . .' He took a step on the ice.

'For God's sake!' Strong arms grabbed him. 'I told you – *don't wander off*!' He felt a shock of alarm. His mother held him, chest heaving. 'All right,' she soothed, 'you're not harmed; and no scenes, for it's Christmas. Just *don't* come to the pond – not alone. The pond's dangerous.'

'Why?'

'It is. You could drown.'

Her son frowned; it meant nothing. She sought a better deterrent. 'Besides,' she said, 'there's the dragon. You ask your grandpa, he'll tell you – when I was small he told *me*. We mustn't wake the Pond Dragon, it's fast asleep on the bottom.'

It snowed again as Kine forayed. He prowled the caves under drifts and popped up, his eyes beady. He probed the brakes and iced hollows. A flock of fieldfares took off, widely spread, calling tersely – '*clack-clack*' – and Kine listened. There was the faintest of sighs as the snowflake-host fluttered.

Virgin snow stretched ahead, Ploughman's dwelling white-mantled. The man had yet to get home and his geese were still out, growing restless, heads cranking. They seemed to mirror each other, slow and wary in movement, matched even in voice, which was low and unfriendly. Their powerful necks and bills threatened.

Kine held back in the hedge, gazing into the garden. The

16

rows of greenstuff were thin, their snow-burdened leaves drooping. When he moved the geese hissed, and he paused. 'Stay away,' growled the gander, 'this is private land, goblin.'

Kine drew off, well aware of their temper.

'*Far* away,' the bird grated. 'If you're wise you'll hide, weasel, for there's peril afoot.'

'*Tchkkk*,' scorned Kine.

'A *strange* peril.'

'Pah,' he said, 'Kine is field-wise.'

'A dire and alien peril beyond your knowledge, small dancer. We can tell; we can sense it.'

Kine looked back. They were hissing. 'You don't frighten the weasel!' He went with studied aplomb to make his point, but remained watchful. Geese had powers of perception; he did not despise them. Out of sight he kept low, lingering amid scrub – a clutch of thin, whippy masts – taking stock by an ash stole. It was dumpy, moss-covered. Kine peered round from its platform.

The snow whirled, cold and biting. There was no life in the poles, which afforded scant cover. He saw no owl, no small creatures. The birds had fled to the woods or to the shelter of farms, seeking warmth among buildings. He sniffed the air. It was sterile, stripped of scents by the blizzard. Only one smell, from the copse, reached his nose, faint, elusive.

He would have thought little of it had he not met the geese. The smell was odd, foreign to him. *Beyond your knowledge, small dancer*.

The odour went then returned and he snuffled, snout twitching. He could see nothing ahead. Flakes were thick, streaming at him. Again he caught the strange smell, his revulsion instinctive. It was unsavoury, evil, and it seemed to grow with each gust, to gain strength with the wind as if some rare beast drew close – as if the snowstorm's eye menaced.

There was a honk. The sprite froze. The geese were growing alarmed, their strident music like horns, primitive and blood-curdling. The smell was thick now, obnoxious, and Kine squinted, half-blinded. The storm of flakes batted round him.

Slipping down from the stump, the chilled weasel took

cover. The honks had stopped, turned to hissing. Goose and gander were spitting, their clamour aggressive. It reached crescendo and stopped, then the blizzard subsided, downy flakes tumbling gently.

He heard a tractor pull up.

In a while, a door slammed.

The stench had gone and one goose, now distraught, began bugling. Gingerly Kine crept forward, stealing back through the hedge and peeping into the garden. A splurge of blood dyed the ground, spilling from the dead gander. Snow and goose feathers mingled. Both were red and Kine ran, glancing back for a moment. He saw the man loom. Facing into the flakes, Ploughman flourished his shotgun.

It thawed soon after, then rained. Slush and mud swamped the fields under which land drains gurgled. Ditches brimmed, filling dykes; the pump below the woods laboured. The flow was fast and buff-coloured. Slabs of melting ice reared, sliding back in the flood; some revolved or turned turtle. More adhered to the reeds in thin, dwindling rafts.

In time, the fish would appear, the bream rise, the tench stir. From the sea would come trout, cleaving up through the flow, seeking gravelly shallows. In thousands elvers would writhe where the drainage pump spouted. In the past Kine had seen them, a mass of small squirming eels wriggling over the bank in search of dykes or the farm ponds.

He made for the pumphouse. It was of brick and held the motor. When the marsh levels rose electrodes switched on the power and then switched off when the flood fell. An earthy mound bore the structure, crumbling close to one wall where a dark gap had opened.

Kine slipped in and nosed round. It was dusty below. He was in the foundations amid a labyrinth of joists and thick concrete abutments. Here the mink had once bred, plundering from the stronghold. It was a charnel house now, a mausoleum of old bones, the brittle relics of slaughter. The weasel stopped, his neck tingling. The place repelled yet inspired, for old comrades had fought there.

He remembered the heroes – One-eye, Ford, other goblins

– the final fray of the Mink Wars. Here the fight had been won and they had snatched weasel vengeance. But that was all long ago . . .

The place was stale and neglected. He came, at times, to pay tribute, recall old friends, weasel martyrs. Kine would never forget them. He gave a sigh as he left, for that summer's spirit was dead. Now was the winter of thieves; it was each for himself now.

Well, Kine could play at that game – ask the fox and the barn owl! He saw the sparrows and crowed. 'Did you see the owl cheated? Did you see his prey purloined? That was justice,' he bragged. The sprite swayed, his eyes glinting. 'Tit for tat,' he exulted.

'You couldn't call it a fight.'

'It was a lesson,' said Kine.

'The gander *fought*,' declared Farthing.

'Huh,' said Kine, 'the fox killed him.'

'Fox?' mused Flit. 'Do you think so?'

'I was there.' The tone challenged. 'I saw the body,' Kine said, less convinced then he sounded. 'Who else kills a gander?'

The sparrows glanced at each other. They clung to reeds by the dyke, the dead stems creaking drily. 'You tell *us*.'

He flounced past them and turned in at the copse, gladly rid of their twitter.

'I'm Clary,' a voice said.

'Clary?' Kine said. 'Who's Clary?'

On the bluff by the pond sat a small female weasel. 'Me,' she said with a smile. 'They named me after the clary, a dainty flower of the wild.'

'Never mind your name,' Kine said.

'No,' she said, 'never mind.'

Kine frowned. 'This is *my* woodland.'

'It's a treat.' Clary beamed.

'And private,' Kine said, put out. He eyed her sternly a moment. She was young, a mere wand.

'It's so peaceful,' she murmured.

She was, he thought, sleekly graceful. He wished that he had not noticed. It took the edge from his anger.

'Normally,' Kine said darkly.

'I love the pond and the trees.'

'It's all *mine*.'

'Very grand!' Clary twinkled. She purred, 'I'm glad I met you.'

'You don't know who I am, do you?'

'Of course,' said Clary, 'you're Kine; everyone's heard of Kine.' Her face was bright. 'And the Tree – everyone's heard of that. A hallowed place,' she exclaimed, 'held in trust. Now, I've *seen* it!'

'Yes, well . . .' Kine was beguiled. He forced a grunt. 'You can't trespass.'

'I knew you wouldn't be cross.' Her voice soothed. 'Kine's a legend.'

The man pulled up at the pump. He had the child in the van, for the girl had gone shopping. 'Right,' he said, 'let's check up. Climb out, son, and keep clean.' Beside the dyke he said, 'Careful, don't run, you'll fall over.'

'In the mud!'

'And the puddles. You fall in and we'll cop it.' The young man grinned. 'See the water – there's the screw at the end. When that turns, she'll be pumping.'

'Make it turn.'

'Watch the splash, then . . .' The engineer tossed a stone. Its ripples touched an electrode and the pump rumbled. Swill entwined the impeller, sloshing loudly and foaming. Soon the channel was flowing, bilge and flotsam in motion sucked towards the housed engine. 'Come on now, to the river.'

They watched the outlet valve belch. Its water surged in great spurts, roaring, barging the current. It shook the sedges and reeds, making froth in its frenzy. Blobs of foam skipped and soared. 'Phew!' the toddler enthused.

'A ton of water a second.'

'Does the dragon live in it?'

The man looked blank and the child said, 'The dragon lives in the pond.'

'Ah, mum's story,' the man said.

'He's *huge*.'

20

'The pond's dangerous. So are dykes and the river. You mustn't go there alone, not near water. She's told you.'

'Yes.'

'Okay. Now the pumphouse.' He pushed the door.

'Wow!' the child said. It was like leaving a planet. The marsh had gone, with its views, and they stood in a space-cell. Fluorescent lights shone on dials; a sleek floor mirrored switches. At the centre, iron-clad, an immense motor whispered.

'There you are, how's that strike you?' The engineer advanced proudly. He checked the meters and beamed. 'That's one up on your dragon – strong as seventy horses!'

A tractor stopped and Ploughman entered. 'Brought a mate today, mister?' He eyed the lad. 'Left your trike home?'

'We made the pump start.'

'I noticed.' Ploughman coughed, his pipe fuming. At length he said, 'Something's thieving. Lost a goose, the old gander.'

'Killed?' The younger man frowned.

'In the snow. I just missed it.'

'Fox?'

'No tracks, the snow filled them. Didn't look like a fox job; didn't smell like fox, neither.' The veteran studied his briar. The bowl released a smoke spiral. He shook his head. 'Damned if *I* know; it's diabolical teasing. Mind, I'll have it, the brute.'

'I'll watch out.'

'Aye, it's lurking, the devil. I'd say it's something unusual; I've seen the work of most villains.'

'We'll keep our eyes skinned and tell you.' The young man picked up his son.

'Aye, you do and I'll have him.' Ploughman tousled his grandchild. 'Me and him liked that gander.'

* * *

It was true of the vale that you could always find flowers there, even deep in the winter. On worked ground bloomed dead-nettle with little purple-pink lips, and shepherd's purse, white and tiny. In the woods were larger blossoms: flowers of scented spurge-laurel beneath smooth, tapered leaves; clumps of snowdrops after Christmas, and – if you knew where to look – primroses in January.

That was a secretive, quiet month. Then with sudden to-do rooks returned to the copse, tired of wintering afield, and promptly set about courting. The air was full of commotion. Clattering in the oaks, they tumbled, cawed and displayed, patching up the old nurseries.

One bird sat apart, the colony's lookout. The watchman hunched on a branch, his gaze sour, his face grizzled. Age-ravaged and grim, he had no time for high spirits and less for lust's antics.

Sleek young corvids were preening, their iridescent heads handsome. He scratched his beak with a claw. They were, thought Watchman, all show, the libidinous strutters. Fawning paramours bowed; ogling partners coquetted. 'Wanton pea-brains,' he growled. No wonder conference ailed and debate was corrupted.

He could remember great meetings, solemn treetop assemblies. Rooks like Watchman had spoken and the senate was attentive. Then his wisdom was valued. Today, while fools discussed scandal, a luminary kept lookout! Such was life's march of progress. He turned his back on them, brooding.

Below, exploring the woodside, a weasel was dancing. Watchman flapped and hopped lower, perched at last on a thorn limb. 'Wait,' he wheezed, 'is that you, Kine?'

'No,' the sprite said, 'it's Clary.'

'Bah.' He saw his mistake: Kine was never so sleek. This was elfin, a pixie.

'Is Kine your friend?' she asked brightly.

'Kine?' he said with a shrug. 'The shrimp's an uppity fool, a vaunter and has-been. It's thanks to me he's alive; I've saved the braggart from scrapes. He owes his life to a rook.' He viewed the scene in the oaks, adding scornfully, '*This* rook – to Watchman the wise one.'

'I can tell you're wise.'

'A statesman,' Watchman said, solaced. The little beast was perceptive. 'I have to tell you,' he warned, 'Kine is less than well mannered. He's not a lover of strangers.'

'Are you sure?' Clary twinkled.

'He has no taste.'

'Is he suited?'

'*Suited?*' Watchman said fiercely. A younger rook with a twig was lewdly tempting a female. 'He may be brash but he's not loose. Kine keeps faith with the past. At least he scorns *that* obsession.' He eyed the courting and shuddered. Creation's oldest disorder! 'Kine's immune, he's reclusive. He hunts alone, on his guard. He has no time for intruders.'

Clary turned from him, smiling.

'But have no fear,' he went on, 'I'll keep watch, there's no danger. If the oaf shows, I'll warn you.'

'I have to go.' Her laugh tinkled.

Fitful sunshine teased fields, rainclouds scuttled. February was fickle, spring and winter in one: hail storms, aconites, lambs born. 'Pussy paws' decked the sallows. When the sun shone, the thrush sang and lesser chants issued. 'Tol-de-rol-lol-kiss-me-dear,' chinked the chaffinch, or so said tradition.

'Fools,' the rook snarled. 'Spring fever!' Not even spring – no one waited. It was St Valentine's Eve. Tomorrow, country lore held, the feathered world started mating, weeks before proper springtime. The virus would spread, pass from species to species until the whole valley caught it.

Then the songbird would fight, the timid hare punch his brother, the jealous moorhen do murder. In grassy tussock and dell tiny nibbling creatures, emulating the tiger, would roar and do battle.

'Libertines!' The rook ruffled. Glossy corvids were clacking, pairing high in the turrets. He squinted upwards with malice. Strut, flaunt and philander – what they needed was *work*. Watchman *cawed* and they hushed. As one, the rooks rose, their wings soaring, a dusky, straggling column, the 'dread' of the commune. As they toiled, he sat cackling. A false alarm did no harm.

'Go on, *sweat*,' he exclaimed. 'Take some healthy exertion!'

'Clary . . .' Kine tried her name. She had been lissom and smart, aware of fame, his distinction. That was rare now and

23

rewarding. *A dainty flower* – it was apt. He mooned a while by the pond. Clammy fog swirled about him. It came and went, thick and damp, blotting out the far shore so the pool seemed limitless and uncanny.

Like recollections, shapes teased. Like recollections of Clary . . .

The weasel stretched. He had duties. Fog encouraged the footloose, a cloaking licence to snoop, and many envied his holding. It was no time to be dreaming, he thought, there were guard rounds. Setting out he was cautious, for the covert had been transmuted. Gone from sight were far landmarks; near to hand objects crowded: a barren larder of nutshells, each chiselled and emptied; the bayonet point of an arum; a misty tussock of grass like a hill in the vapour.

Fog was full of surprises, abrupt apparitions. A spider's web made him jump, looming up like a farm gate. Spectral fungii lay in ambush. Small noises were startling, amplified and protracted. A droplet fell on a leaf with a *plop* that resounded.

The weasel paused, nostrils twitching. A mammoth hauled from the mist, became a hare and stood still, tremulous as it stared, its heart racing. Then it was gone to the lea where, like mountains in cloud, sheep were chewing the cud, stentorian in their rumblings. There was no harm in such wraiths and Kine turned to the warren. He was at home in the tunnels.

They took him down into clay, spacious underground pipes whose moist draughts smelled of rabbits. One bolted ahead. He ignored the dim scut; the beast would know the escape lanes. Kine's rummage was thorough. In earthy chambers and bores he nosed keenly for poachers, whether weasels or stoats, then, content, sought an exit.

His feet grew heavy, clay-burdened. He thought of Clary's lithe grace; she had been a bright dancer! Then the tunnel sloped up, rose through subsoil to loam, made a dog leg and straightened. At its end, he saw fog. He was back near the pond path.

'*Aheee* . . .' The squeal startled.

It pierced the mist, trailing off, and a clap of wings followed, magnified by the damp. The humid veil crawled and clung. In its plasma birds scurried, batting out of the covert. Kine could tell they were pigeons, disturbed at the Moon Pond. He cleaned his claws and advanced. He ran in brisk undulations, skipping serpentine briars, ducking low under thickets. Spooky columns towered round him, their wet lichen dripping.

Twice he paused, head up, listening. There was a baffling silence. Resolutely, he sallied. A moorhen burst from the mist. It passed in leggy retreat and the weasel grew chary. '*Tchkkk,*' he growled, lying prone, then jinked on like a lizard. He quizzed the fog. Something stirred. 'Who is it?' he challenged.

'*Doom!*'

'Where are you?'

'The b-bank, Kine.' There was a pause. 'Kine – I saw it!' The shrew was under a leaf. Leaf and shrew shook together, quailed like reeds in a draught, like a fly in a cobweb. 'D-don't go near, Kine, just listen . . .' From the murk came a pulse, the sock of water on earth, on the bluff. Suck-a-sock.

Kine crawled forward.

The pond rocked in the fog. It was subsiding now, rippling.

'Doom,' wailed Scrat. 'It reared up. It snatched a pigeon, I saw it. I heard its tail thresh the pond. I heard it splash – a great splash.'

'Like a bough?' Kine was pacing. 'Like a bough from a tree?'

'Yes, as loud – a great splash.'

'Over there, shrew, look hard!' A dark shape rolled and wallowed.

'*Aheee* . . .' The shrew goggled.

'A rotten bough, Scrat, calm down. You heard it fall in the pool.'

'But I saw it, the dragon!'

'You can't see anything, dwarf. You heard the pigeons take fright.' Kine was firm, condescending. 'All is well in Kine's purlieu.'

There was a cry. Something struck him.

He seemed to float, spinning slowly, then to hammer a tree bole. Kine lay still, his eyes rolling. In the fog the owl U-turned. It banked steeply, wings broad, and came back, stroking grimly. 'I said you'd pay!' its screech gloated.

'Fight you at the barn,' Flit said.

'You're on,' cried Farthing. 'A tussle.'

They shook their wings and fell to, the barn's roof a soft cushion. The moss was thick on the tiles and the incline was gentle. Sparrows sported there often. They liked to clinch at the top, rolling down in a bundle. As they grappled, they bounced, mops of twittering fluff, at last cupped at the eaves by the heavy-cast conduits.

'Rest . . .' puffed Flit, disengaging.

'You were whacked.'

'You are!' Flit chirped.

Sprucing up, they gazed round. 'Soon be dark,' observed Farthing.

'It's still foggy,' said Flit. 'Can't see what's going on.'

Somewhere frogs were awakening, their throaty overture drowsy, and toads stirred from slumber. There were mauve tassels on alder, red tabs on the hazel. All was hazy in vapour. Where the badger had house-cleaned, her sweepings littered the bank among fine ochrous diggings. From the copse came a bat squeak.

'What was that?'

'Scrat,' said Farthing.

'Something's wrong. Kine's in trouble.'

'Come on, Flit, a *real* dust-up!'

They launched themselves, gaining height, stabbing into the greyness. Their stubby wings made it swirl, stirred the damp exhalations. 'Can you see where we are?'

'No, keep close.' They passed ghost-trees. As they flew, phantoms flanked them. 'There,' chirped Farthing, 'the pond. On the bank – that's a weasel.'

'He looks bad.'

Kine was bleeding. They dipped and passed lower.

'Danger,' Flit yelled, 'the barn owl!'

'Are you ready?' cried Farthing.

'Ready,' Flit bawled.

'We'll mob him.'

The owl was streaming towards them, its eyes on its victim.

'Line ahead, Flit, don't flinch.'

'Don't *you* flinch.'

'You'll flinch first!'

The sparrows charged the owl headlong, bustling out of the half-light. Bemused, it raised its cowled face as they closed, Farthing leading. His line was true and Flit followed. As the predator jinked, they changed course, bearing in, just avoiding collision.

'Got him rattled,' whooped Flit.

Farthing climbed through the fog. 'Flit, I'm turning,' he shouted. The barn owl lumbered below. 'I'm going in again, diving.' They powered back down at the prowler, sweeping into its gaze, the narrow arc of its sight, and it swerved, yawing wildly. 'And *again*, Flit, he's flustered!'

Confused, the great bird made off, retreating clumsily now, floating back to the barn where it sought a dark corner.

The sparrows capered, elated. 'We mortified him,' screeched Flit.

'What a barney!'

'We trounced him . . .'

The pair calmed down. 'How's the weasel?' They planed to earth. Kine looked lifeless. A nasty wound on him bled and several creatures drew near, magnetised by the bloodshed. Scrat was there, his eyes popping. He was dumb for the moment. Watchman sat on a stump. Only Clary went close, alerted by the commotion, and nuzzled the victim. There was a hush. The shrew moaned. 'He's been killed, Kine the hero.'

'He isn't dead,' Farthing told him.

'He isn't bragging,' mused Flit.

'Doom,' wailed Scrat, 'we're all doomed. Only Kine could fight dragons!'

'He was mad enough,' Flit said.

Farthing said, 'He's done fighting. The owl caught him napping.'

'*Doom*, we're lost!'

'Oh, just stop it.' Clary turned on them hotly. 'Kine's in trouble; just stop it. One more wail, Scrat, and I'll bite you. Watchman, what shall we do? You're the sage. He's un-conscious.'

Watchman leered. 'I wish *I* was. Aches and pains. Let him perish.'

'Kine won't die,' twittered Flit. 'He's got more lives than a cat has.'

'More lives than sense,' the rook rattled.

'*Stop*,' snarled Clary, 'I warned you.' She stood her ground, small and fierce. 'A fine lot *you* are,' she snapped. 'A fine lot of friends Kine's got. I don't know why you talk that way.'

'Because life's hard,' wheezed the corvid. 'You're only young, you've not learned.'

'Oh, I'm learning,' she said.

'Because we know Kine,' the rook said. 'Because we know Kine the braggart.'

'Then you should know he's a legend.'

'All that's done, his prime's over.'

Clary snorted. 'So's yours.'

'And I'd be glad to be gone. He's not suffering, is he?'

Clary's eyes blazed. 'He'll fight. Kine's not done, he's a weasel. While there's life he'll fight, Watchman. I'll see he recovers.'

'We'll help,' Flit said.

Clary pondered the problem. 'I'll lick his wounds and stand guard. First I'll drag him to shelter, get him into the Tree. Rook, we'll need you as lookout. Sparrows, give us safe cover, watch for further marauders.'

'We'll beat them up,' exclaimed Flit. 'Mob whoever approaches.'

'Drive them off,' Farthing promised.

'Then here we go . . .' Clary toiled. Her mouth was clamped to Kine's neck, her back arched, her legs straining.

'Heave!' squeaked Scrat.

The load shifted.

'Bah,' said Watchman. 'Go on, then.'

* * *

Two youths sat on the bluff, the larger holding a rod. He was a big, lumpy lad with a ruddy complexion and his friend was pale and lathy. The wind was cold and they sniffed, their jackets up at the neck, shoulders hunched round their ears like a couple of herons.

'Heck, it's raw,' said the thin youth.

'Pike feed in raw weather.'

'You won't catch pike using paste.'

The float bobbed in the draught as the dark water shivered. They watched the red plastic dome, glancing fitfully round as if unsure of the venue. Through the trees the sky glared, a steely, infinite distance. The wood was quiet, blackthorn budded. Small, tight balls decked its twigs but had yet to grow starry. Where the water was smooth, the hard light rested on it.

'I'll bet,' the large youth conjectured, 'there's pike as big as sharks here.'

'Why don't no one else fish, then? No one comes to the pond.'

'Scared.' The angler grinned darkly. He eyed the other askance. 'Scared, like some I could mention.'

'I only said what I heard – that old Poacher's dad drowned here. And more afore him, they reckon.'

'That's why the pike growed.'

They cackled.

'You got a bite?'

'Aye, watch this.' A two-ounce roach swung aloft and the scrawny youth hooted. His lumpy colleague returned it. 'Them little roach never grow. See, there's hundreds,' he mumbled. Peering in they glimpsed movement, a shoal of small, muddy shadows. The shapes swung slowly and vanished. 'They're at the top. I'll fish deeper.'

'Where the *sharks* are?'

'The tench. I'll bet there's tench near the bottom.' They settled down. 'Big fat tenchies!'

'Heck, it's cold . . .'

The youths shivered. Reeds grew out from the bank, dense and huddled in wind-clumps. In June wild iris would flower there, and white water-soldiers. For now, the pond growth was bleak, swept in duck-haunted alleys, a dusky coot stealing out, sliding back, quiet and furtive. Only the coot knew what lurked there.

'In any case,' said the thin lad, 'you got to catch tench first thing with the dawn. Or late evening.'

'We'll find out.'

'I'm not stopping till evening.'

'Afraid of old Poacher's dad?'

'I'm not staying to freeze.' The angler's mate munched a sandwich. The meat inside was like leather. 'Waste of time, this old pond is.'

'You won't say that when they bite.'

They sat on, growing colder, brooding over the water. The languid float disenchanted. Across the pool a fish flipped. It mocked them, merely a tiddler. The tiny flash made them jump. The sky had darkened, rain threatening, and where the wind caught the swim, its dark and stony face furrowed. The ruddy lad reeled in glumly.

'Got a sandwich?'

'I've finished. There's only this. It was gristle.'

The big youth shrugged. 'Hook it on. It can't do worse than the bread did.' He made a face and cast grimly. There was a whine from the reel, a slight pause, then another. It screamed, spinning faster. The float had sunk without trace. 'Gawd . . .' The angler was struggling. The other rose. His eyes widened.

'You got a big 'un!'

'A big 'un?' The rod was bent like a coach-whip. 'I got a *whale* – flaming heck!'

The thin line strained and quivered. 'It's going down. Gawd, it's pulling!' The clumsy fisherman fumbled.

'You got to play it, it's running.'

'Flaming heck, I can't hold it!'

'The thing's beserk. Look at *that* . . .' Scummy bubbles were rising as if the pond's depths were boiling. The coot had burst from the reeds and made off, its voice scolding. The thin lad gawped. 'I don't like it.'

The other wrestled and slipped. The rod had dipped to the surface. 'Nor don't I, the bank's crumbling. I'll fall in and lose my tackle. Get your knife to that line.'

'Aye, hang on . . .' The youth cut it. They both fell back. 'Look!'

Reeds clattered. The whole bed of them rocked. The lads watched dumbly a moment then, 'Let's go,' gulped the angler. He gave the other a push. 'I seen enough, I'm not stopping.'

Kine awoke hearing voices. They died, the youths in retreat, and he forced his eyes open. He did not know where he was. A bright lens blinked, its glare blinding. Then, his vision adjusting, he saw the sky, round and brilliant. The space-filled hole was familiar: he was safe in the Life Tree.

Lying back, he slept on as he had when a kitt, the hole his first living sight, his day and night, his small cosmos. When next he stirred it was dusk and he stretched, his head clearing. He was not crippled, though sore, and he flexed stubborn muscles. He could remember the owl, a sudden blow, then no more. He must, he thought, have crawled home, somehow struggling to safety.

Life was new again, fresh. The clouds were pale, opalescent, the afterglow rosy. He put his snout to the hole and delicious air washed it. It brought a sense of delight, of having cheated on fate. He was Kine the fate-cheater, the owl-cheater – the charmed one! He felt euphoric and sat up, his pains vanished.

The wind had dropped and carp fed, making rings on the water. In the shallows a frog spawned, gently heaving, eyes goggling. Moths appeared, half-awake. He watched their frail, prayerful wings, his pulse quick. Kine was living! The owl had failed, as they all failed. Kine survived and he danced, lightly skipping ashore, showing off on the bank where he leaped, his bib flashing, chased his tail and somersaulted.

In the trees rooks were roosting. Watchman yawned, his eye jaundiced. 'So you've returned from the dead, then?'

'*Tchkkk*' said Kine, 'that was nothing.'

'That's all *you* know.'

'A scratch! Am I harmed?' Kine asked, dancing. 'The owl can't harm me, he's nothing.'

'He almost killed you. He should have.'

'Do I *look* hurt?'

Watchman grunted. 'You look a fool and you sound one. How d'you think you were saved?'

'I'm resilient, Watchman. Weasel grit and guts saved me.'

'A weasel saved you, all right. You were carrion, shrimp. I'd have left you to rot but the small female saved you.'

Kine looked up from the bank. A single celandine flowered, a glossy star in green growth amid dog's mercury and plantains. He gazed at the bloom. '*Clary* saved me?'

'She must be moonstruck,' the rook rasped. 'She must take pity on braggarts.'

'You mean . . .?'

'She dragged you to safety; she nursed your wounds.'

'I don't see her.'

'She went off home. She left when you were past danger. At least she had *that* much sense. She didn't wait for the boasting.'

'I've got to find her.' Kine turned. 'Where's her home, rook? Where is she?'

'Let her be.'

'I must find her.' He started rummaging, snuffling, and a pair of snakes was disturbed. He said, 'Where's Clary, the small one?'

'We weren't awake,' said the adder.

'The weasel woke us,' his mate said. 'Bite the shrimp.'

They were sleepy. 'It's not yet spring,' said the first. 'He'd no right.'

'Bite the goblin!'

'I only asked.' Kine danced sideways. 'Besides, it's *my* land you sleep on.'

'Fill the weasel with poison!'

Kine bounced on. '*Tchkkk*, I'm busy.'

The she-snake hissed. 'And I'm tired. I'd kill you now if I weren't. Another time, Kine,' she threatened.

He spat and called, 'I'll be ready!' He was not frightened of snakes. Kine was ready for all things. Not that he was deluded: the odds against him had lengthened; the dance grew sterner each season. In his youth death had flirted; now her steps were in earnest. Deadly earnest.

But Kine survived – thanks to Clary! He might have guessed she would care. She had the manner of Kia. She had respected, admired him.

He reached the wood's edge and paused. Nearby a thrush was rehearsing, its evening anthem cascading. Once he had stood there with Kia, roused to pride by the setting. 'Kine's land,' he had claimed and she had said, 'Yes, I love it, this weasel wood.'

'Then we'll share it.' And so they had, all too briefly.

32

He could see Kia in Clary. The little female had *feeling*. She had sensed the Tree's history. 'A hallowed place,' she had called it, 'held in trust,' which was right. She had felt the peace, sensed the spirits. For one so young she was wise, and now he owed her his thanks.

Across the vale stormclouds mustered. Low as yet, they formed groups, tightly bunched, black as crows' wings. There was a flicker of lightning. Though far away it was bright, hurling forward the hills for a glaring split second then gone, leaving twilight. Something rose to Kine's front and he snarled, scenting weasel. Its shape drew close, a young male, strongly built, boldly looming.

'Halt,' said Kine. 'Come no further.'

The stranger paused, almost careless. His condescension was vexing.

'The wood is Kine's. This is Kine's land.'

'I've heard,' the newcomer answered. A supercilious lip curled. 'The famous copse with the pond, the famous Tree. I've been hearing.'

'And I am Kine the unconquered, whose fame is wide – the death-dancer.'

'So I've been told, a great *legend*. I've heard a screed about Kine.' The brazen male ambled closer. He was tough-necked and agile. 'Kine the creaking campaigner, the bold geriatric.'

'For that,' said Kine, 'you'll be sorry.' He started stomping, his back up. 'Let me sing you my war song.'

The other circled, unhurried. 'I've had an earful of Kine, heard it all,' he said, flexing. 'I've heard enough for a lifetime.'

'You're well informed, then,' spat Kine. 'For a *brat*,' he said quietly. 'We'd better see how you dance, brat.'

A sparrow stirred in the trees. A second joined it atremble. 'A weasel fight!' Flit was thrilled. 'We're in luck.' Farthing nodded. 'A proper treat, a blood tussle. A first-rate fury. Kine's seething.' They watched the goblins shape up. The younger weasel was powerful.

'It's on yourself, Kine,' he growled. 'I didn't come here for this – to waste my strength on old bones.'

Kine's teeth snapped. He was whirling. 'Save your breath and dance, bratling; dance with Kine the death-dancer!'

'She wouldn't want me to kill you.'

The light was dim, ebbing swiftly. Pausing, Kine could hear thunder, a throaty roar in the clouds as they climbed the sky darkly, their loury vanguard like smoke driving wild air before it. Twigs and scrub started twitching. Kine was still. 'She?' he panted.

The sparrows groaned. 'He's stopped,' Flit said. 'He isn't fit, the owl drubbed him. He needs more time.' Farthing ruffled his wings. 'We were right, the sprite's past it.'

Beneath them, Kine had drawn back. A sudden veil had dropped, an umber pall as the storm struck. The younger weasel glanced upwards. He said, 'I can't fight you. I can't tell Clary I hurt you.'

The sky exploded, rain pelting.

'Clary?' Kine said. 'Where is she?'

'Where she belongs – where I've come from.' The storm unloaded its burden. Gleaming sheets hid the woods and the beaten clod shivered. They stood and stared through the deluge. 'I'm not stopping in this, Kine, I only brought you a message.' The torrent hissed, washing branches, lashing grass and young nettles, and both weasels recoiled.

'A message?' Kine said. 'From Clary?'

'No, from me, Kine, a warning.' The other glared, his flanks streaming, flushing rills to his belly. 'Kine,' he shouted, 'forget her. I've staked my claim. Clary's mine.'

'You'll have to fight for her, brat. You'll have to fight Kine the steadfast.'

'I've many rivals to vanquish, brash and lusty young hopefuls. I can do without veterans. Be your age, Kine, stop mooning. Clary's young and you're bewitched. Let it go, don't be foolish. There's no excuse for an *old* fool.'

Thunder roared, dull and deafening, raging off round the valley.

'I'll find her, brat, I'll come looking.'

'Find her, Kine, and you'll suffer.' The words were drowned in the rain which flung from bucketing blackness. Lightning stabbed. 'You'll be crushed.' Kine was blind, his eyes stinging. All he saw was the gloom, the white bolts as they flashed; all he heard was the storm – then, receding, 'Be warned, Kine!'

'A fiasco.' Flit shuddered. The sparrows shook, shedding water.

Kine took shelter.

He mumbled, 'You wait, bratling, I'll find her. We'll see who Clary prefers. You'll learn who is the fool, brat, and why Kine's a legend.'

*   *   *

The spindle grew by the copse, a straggling shrub of the woodside. You could quite easily miss it. Its wands were thin-leafed and green, put upon by the briars while thorn and thicket browbeat it. Save for a few weeks in autumn, when its fruit claimed attention – a shocking pink, orange-centred – few noticed the spindle.

In winter, aphids lived on it. Moving off in the spring, they drifted down to the docks where they bred in profusion in wave on summery wave, a virgin birth for each mite, a maleless greenfly conception.

Perhaps because it was quiet the spindle bush drew the shrew, who foraged urgently round it. His hunger seldom relented. It was a chronic condition induced by rapid digestion and it made the dwarf restless. Now, in moist, sun-flecked shade, he searched the honeydewed dock plants.

The copse was warm, splashed with flowers, spring's traditional palette. White and yellow prevailed, sloe, wood sorrel and primrose, a few anemones out, one or two bluebells opening. Upside down in a bush a dormouse hung by its toes, hibernation concluded. Chessel-crumb the girl called it, a country name for the creature.

The beast was plump, contemplative, neither true mouse nor squirrel. 'Another spring . . .' it reflected. It hung a while, munching quietly, then watched the shrew catch a beetle. 'Another spring,' yawned the dormouse. 'Tell me, Scrat, what's been happening?'

'Don't ask me, Chessel.'

'I just have. Unless,' mused Chessel, 'I dreamt it.'

'You wouldn't thank me for telling. It's been a nightmare,' said Scrat. He gulped and added, 'Most of it – almost all of it, Chessel. Except that Kine pulled through safely. He nearly died.'

'Kine? He should have.'

'No,' cried Scrat.

'He's a weasel. All weasels should die. They eat dormice,' drawled Chessel. He drowsed a moment. 'That's logic.'

'You're wrong,' sobbed Scrat. 'The vale needs him. Times are bad, woeful, Chessel.'

'Naturally,' sighed the dormouse.

'It isn't natural at all.'

'Woeful times are *quite* natural, they're like sleep,' Chessel brooded.

'Well, it's awake – the Pond Dragon!' Scrat twitched, the dread uttered. 'The thing's astir and there's carnage.' Again, the urge to eat seized him and he foraged. 'I'm hungry.'

The dormouse scratched in his store, fetching out an old filbert, part of winter's iron rations. 'Try a nut,' he said vaguely, 'they're somewhat dry but quite filling. I find them good for most problems.'

Scrat had fled, his gut churning. He needed food and protection – to know that Kine was on guard. At the Life Tree he halted. 'Kine?' he called. No one answered. The pond was smooth and he gulped. The slightest swell kissed its rim, dark and slick, an enigma. He called again. The squeak echoed.

Something lay on the bluff. Fighting fear, he moved round until the steely scales glimmered. It was the corpse of an eel, about the size of the adders. Its head was torn from the trunk, which sprawled limply, discarded.

'Doom!' he shrieked and ran blindly.

There was an alien smell, a bane to minuscule nostrils. Bolting on through the copse, he blinked at dim, towering columns, his midget legs scrabbling. The ground grew soft and he sank, hugged at first and then smothered. A pile of feathers engulfed him.

'Woe,' he cried. Where was Kine?

The shrew sniffed. Pheasant's feathers: a pile of buff, hen-bird feathers, a monument till the wind blew. 'Double death!'

He squirmed out, racing on to the warren. Brilliant blood drenched the diggings. The blood was fresh, like the fur, a few grey tufts plucked from rabbit – the grey-lagged buck. The shrew gaped. There was no sign of a struggle.

'Woe,' he wailed. 'Triple slaughter!'

Where was Kine?

'K-Kine?' he whimpered.

Watchman stirred, a nap broken. The sun was warm, soporific. He squinted down. 'Silence, pipsqueak! Kine's decamped, quit the covert.'

'He can't have done . . .'

'Left this morning.'

'We didn't wait – we lit out. We've not been back since it happened.'

'Did you run?' asked the toddler.

'We kind of scrambled,' the youth said.

'*He* run,' said his comrade. 'That old fish wasn't natural.'

'Nor's the pond,' said the first.

The girl laughed, bringing snacks. The lads were piling up logs and she enjoined, 'Stack them neatly, I want this yard nice and tidy. They won't be used till next winter.' She held the tray for them. 'Scones.'

'They look good.'

'I've been baking. They're hot – mind the butter.'

'Me!' the child cried.

'Take care, then.'

The infant scoffed, his chin greasy. 'I want to go to the pond.'

'Not alone,' said his mother.

'Your mam's right, it's unhealthy. We've done with fishing the pond.' The youths munched gravely. 'It's spooky. There's something *big* there.'

'That's the dragon,' the child said.

They caught the girl's wink and grinned. The big lad straightened his face. 'I wouldn't know about that. I've heard tales about pike, though; old Poacher told stories. Afore he died, he once told me . . .'

'Told *me*,' claimed his crony.

'Told us both.' They munched dourly. 'He wouldn't let his dog swim there as this old pike was so big. It took a fox, Poacher reckoned, and mallard. It was old – old as Ploughman. More'n fifty years old.'

'More'n sixty,' his friend said. 'I told *you*. It was sixty. More'n sixty, he reckoned. A pike'll live to hundred.'

'The Queen sends telegrams to 'em!'

'It isn't funny, a pike. A pike's got teeth like a saw: on its tongue, round its mouth. *Banks* of teeth,' said the thin lad. They licked their lips. 'Pointing backwards so things get in but not out.'

The child gorged, his eyes bulging.

'Clear a pond, an old pike will, a big old pike on its own. It grows huger and huger then, when the food's gone, it starves. Its body withers and shrinks till there's just this old head, this great ugly head swimming.'

The child's mum smiled. 'There's more scones.'

'Thanks,' they said. 'They're good, missus.'

The toddler took one, his fingers shiny with butter. 'Can we look for a pike?'

'Not today, dear, I'm busy. In any case,' said the girl, 'we couldn't see through the water.'

'The sun can see . . .' His eyes narrowed. The sun could see into pools, to trough bottoms, through puddles.

'Another day, child.'

He brooded. He bet the sun had seen pike; there was not much the sun missed. It found things out, showed him secrets: like tiny motes in the air, cobwebs hiding in corners. His mother's face, in the sun, was flecked with soft, golden down. So were bees while the sun shone.

'It might be raining,' he sulked.

'Tosh!' the girl said.

'*They'll* take me.'

'You're going nowhere, just hush.' She strode indoors and the youths smirked.

'You'll get us sacked, you will,' one said. 'We're here to work, not go jaunting. There's two ton of logs waiting.'

The infant poked in the wood. An old birds' nest lay broken, a little ball of dead moss, strands of sheep's wool and grass. It came apart in his fists, almost nothing when handled. At last he said, 'Did you see it?' He wiped his fingers. 'The pike's head.'

'We saw damn all, mate.' Logs rattled. 'That's just a tale – we don't *know*. It could've been something different.'

'What?'

'Just *something*.'

'What something?'

'By the heck . . .'

'A pond dragon?'

'Aye, if you like, a blamed dragon. We don't know. Ask your grandad. It could've been a giant eel. They say they're partial to flesh, especially nosey young lads. Especially them who ask questions while logs wait for stacking!'

Kine had trekked to the ridge, hunting there as spring lengthened. Behind the valley had greened, reaching wide to the hills. Perch had spawned, bluebells opened and woodland floors matched the sky-dome. On the marsh dunlin rallied, great flocks flashing their wings while snipe drummed and gulls floated.

Ahead new vistas unfolded, lands strange to the weasel. His rival's trail was long cold but Kine had not given up; doggedly he sought guidance. None had spotted his rival; sheep and steers had stared dumbly. Herbivores were dim creatures. The ridge was barren of signs and Kine's search had solved nothing.

Now, at rest on the rise, he was scolded by skylarks. High above they reviled him, clamouring as they hovered. 'Move on, weasel,' they shrilled, 'leave the ridge, you're unwanted.' Their twitting vexed and he glared at them crossly.

'Tell me which way the brat went.'

'Brat?' they sang. 'What do *you* care?'

A host of fields stretched ahead but the paths were strange to him. Reaching out between woods, skirting small, dumpy hills, they trailed off into mist, the first heat-haze since autumn. There was a summery feeling. The sun was warm, its touch bold, not the crone's kiss of late but recharged with old passions.

The green of hedges was brilliant. Youthful leaves shone

39

with life, beamed and fluttered on larch, spread their spring skirts on chestnut. Elsewhere, shy like the streams, lanes cast secretive glances, lady-smocked, pink with campion. Kine smelled cowslips and balm, the aroma inviting.

'Tell me which way, which path!'

'Just move on,' shrilled the skylarks.

'When you tell me where Brat went.'

'How should *we* know? Who cares? Anyway, he would kill you. What's your interest in Brat, Kine?'

'He's my lead to the female.'

'Ah,' they cried, 'to the small one! Suppose we knew where she lived?'

'Then,' said Kine, 'I'd be off.'

'Good,' the larks screamed, descending. 'Take the lane ahead, weasel; take the tunnel of shade; cross the bridge – that's her holding. That's her apple-land, Kine. Clary lives in the orchards.' As he left, their song changed. 'Clary-ary,' they warbled. 'Another suitor for Clary!'

The lane was leafy and dim, arched by trees from both sides. Hazels pressed at each flank; holly thickened the hedges. The narrow roadway was rough. Crumbling shoulders formed traps, pitching steeply to ruts while old stumps guarded ditches. As it wound through the woods, the green tunnel shelved down, became dark, small springs trickling.

Then, as slowly, it rose, sunbeams piercing the roof so the tarmac was dappled. Here the rays drew young rabbits, little goggle-eyed starters, or, catching squirrels midleap, made their silvery tails shine.

'Take the tunnel of shade . . .'

Kine pressed on, undistracted. His hankering had grown fierce, an old obsession revived, at once vital and blinding. All he thought of was Clary. Such mindlessness was absurd, yet he felt young again, bold, the Kine of old times, immortal.

'Cross the bridge . . .'

It drew near: three broad planks side by side. Beneath the planks a brook clacked and on the far side Kine halted. The lane had gone, a view opening. To his front billowed blossom, the snowy whiteness of cherry with creamier plum flowers. In the sun it was dazzling, cloud on cloud of pale petals, orchard rising from orchard.

One led to another. Now the blooms became pink, warmer, shell-like and fragrant. The rosy awning was bliss, the air heady, bees humming. Apple-land – Clary's country.

* * *

Kine regarded the scene, the frothy clouds of sweet blossom. Scented air teased his nose, bees worked luminous petals. Clary's apple-land smiled, flushed and sunny. And yet his bones said, 'Trust nothing.' Such was the rule of the wild and did not exempt orchards. 'Least of all, trust temptation.'

Warily, he went forward. There was no truce in spring's warmth, nor safe conduct in perfume. In cool green grass could lurk ambush. The lure of Clary beguiled but instinct told him to be careful. There was, he noticed, no sound; no bird sang where he ventured. Beware of silence, the law said.

Be not complacent, it warned. Kine took heed, his eyes beady. He had survived by the law, the rules of large and small creatures, of hunter and hunted. *Beware of danger downwind!* He whipped round, his nape tingling.

They came upwind at him, quietly. There were two, both strange weasels. One was bald round the ear, an old battle scar, Kine thought; the other dusky of coat, smoky-brown as a scoter, the duck of the winter.

Scoter snarled, his teeth showing. 'Where,' he asked, 'are *you* going?'

Kine held still. 'That's my business.'

'Who are you?'

'A fighter!' He eyed the ground, his glance practised. The grass was lush, the trees squat in long ranks with low boughs. He stored details.

'Pah, an old one,' rasped Scoter.

'He's after Clary,' growled Bald-ear.

'Aren't we all!' said the first.

Kine said softly, 'Who'll stop me? For I am Kine the unbeaten. Stand aside or dance, riffraff.' Scoter sprang, the lunge signalled. Clawing air, he peered round. Kine had gone

41

with a leap, his toes bedding in tree bark, clinging fast like a squirrel. 'Too late, dark one,' he mocked then, relaunching, plunged back, landing squarely on Bald-ear.

They rolled together, teeth snapping. Wildly Scoter piled in and all three were entangled. The mass of squealing fur bristled. A whirling storm, it spun wildly, legs kicking, heads spitting. '*Eeoow!*' screeched Bald-ear. 'Let go!'

'Who?' hissed Scoter.

'*You*, Scoter!' They broke, the third weasel missing. Kine had slipped from the scrum and now wheeled, charging swiftly. Bowling Bald-ear aside, he upturned the dark goblin, found his neck and bit grimly. Scoter shrieked. 'Get him off!'

Bald-ear snatched their opponent. The patch-marked weasel was strong but Kine slipped him and sallied. Kine the will-o'-the-wisp! As he danced, Bald-ear blinked. This was no common skill; this was artistry, foot-craft. Feinting, Kine stabbed then sidestepped. It was a lesson in movement.

A voice apart showed approval.

'Bravo . . .' Brat was watching. 'Keep it up,' he applauded, 'I'm with you, Kine, we'll confound them. We'll be rid of two rivals.' He glanced askance. 'I was wrong in the rain by the copse. I was wrong, Kine.'

'Yes,' rapped Kine, 'but you're learning.'

Scoter charged. '*Tchkkk*' he shouted. 'Skin them, Bald-ear!' Brat hit him. As they tumbled and clawed, Kine ducked Bald-ear's defence and all four reeled together. Fur flying, they battled, their curses resounding. Their cries of wrath were bloodcurdling, thrown back by the blossom. For several minutes they echoed then stopped, a dog barking.

'Break it up,' Brat said, freezing. 'Run!' he breathed and they bolted.

A long-haired terrier capered. Tail wagging, it yelped, racing to and fro madly, sniffing the apple trees and barking.

Alone in one, Kine climbed higher out of reach, then lay panting. He heard a woman's command – 'Come to heel!' – and things quietened. The other weasels had vanished. At length, relaxed in a crotch, he took stock, growing thoughtful.

The tree was knotted and rough, one of scores spaced in lines, long anonymous ranks, each branch laden with flowers, the whole ceiling unbroken, a rosy sun-suffused roof without end from his viewpoint. At home he knew every growth, every oak, thorn and shrub; here each tree was the same, every vista a puzzle.

The trek and tussle had tired him. He had no plan of advance and no den in the orchard. Even his rivals had fled and there was no sign of Clary. He knew what Watchman would say – a lot of effort for nothing, a passing passion, spring fever! Was Kine no wiser than Brat? As raw as Bald-ear and Scoter?

To leave the Life Tree for this! He viewed his pruned refuge glumly. It might raise blossom like clouds but he would swop the whole lot for the copse and a clump of wood violets.

'You make a fine bird,' a voice said.

He jumped. 'Did you fly here?' laughed Clary. She banished gloom, her spell instant, and Kine's doubts were routed. Scrambling down, he felt shamed, her frank pleasure abashing.

'Kine, you're here, this is lovely!'

He found his wits. 'You surprised me.'

'I thought *I* was surprised.'

'There was a dog . . .'

Her eyes sparkled. 'I'm glad you came, Kine, so glad!'

'Not only came but fought for you,' he growled, guilt retreating. 'Fought callow rivals who trembled. They'll remember me, Clary.'

'Kine is famed!'

'Yes,' he boasted, 'a fitting mate and protector. A legendary opponent. Let them come. Kine will shock them, shock them all for you, Clary – Kine the bold, the mink fighter! Kine who cheated the owl, scorned the fox, awes his rivals. I'll vanquish Scoter and Bald-ear, kill Brat if I have to.'

'No,' she said, 'no more fighting.'

'They must learn.'

'I'll decide, Kine.' She laughed again. 'It's *my* life.'

'Yes, but . . .'

'Hush,' she said, waltzing. 'There's more to spring, Kine, than squabbling. You've not come this far for that. Smell the flowers and rejoice. Let me show you the orchard.'

He followed, drawn by her charm as she danced, bright and

43

supple. She was a flame, he thought, chasing – a tongue of fire in the breeze. Wildfire sprang with such speed, leapt with just such elation. He had a job to keep pace. 'Wait,' he gasped, 'I've been tussling.'

'Poor old thing!'

She sped, chortling, bounding high and volplaning. A hundred fruit trees whisked past, geometric in order, every view making files, fore and aft, right and left, grassy avenues shafting. Everywhere perfume hovered. A yellow butterfly winged, lightly threading the trees. Then, at last, the path spread and a hedge loomed beside them. Kine saw thorn and wild plum, a lank windbreak of poplars.

Clary paused and glanced back. She said, 'It's dense round the edge, full of bracken in summer. The orchard's crawling with rabbits; they even climb in the trees.'

Kine admired her: sleek Clary. Her throat was petal-white, dazzling.

'And there are apples,' she said. 'Every size, brightly coloured. At first a few tumble down, the small green ones, and then the ground fills with windfalls, red and yellow, fat, juicy. Birds and voles come to gorge; the wasps gather. They make their bikes in the hedge and the badgers uproot them. And there are fieldmice galore. It's a banquet,' she burbled.

Kine was resting.

Her eyes shone. 'It's safe and quiet,' she went on, 'seldom darkened by danger. We'd build a den in the fern – me and the partner I chose – and rear our young in the orchard.'

'*Here?*' said Kine.

'But why not?'

'That's impossible,' Kine said.

Clary quizzed him. 'It's easy.'

'I can't live here,' Kine protested, 'my home is back in the valley, the land of martyrs and heroes. I couldn't live in the orchard.'

'I'm sorry, Kine . . .'

'My home's ready: the sacred place of my forebears, my mother's den. I was born there. The Life Tree's hallowed, ancestral, a weasel place down long years. My *first* mate reared her kitts there; I offer it to my next. It's my heritage, Clary, you have to see what that means. It's my trust and my duty.'

'I understand.'

'I'm glad, Clary.'

'But so must you,' she said gently. 'I couldn't live by the pond, Kine. You didn't say your kitts died there.'

'Long ago.'

'Yes,' she murmured. She nosed the ferns, sorry for him. 'But has it got any safer? You know the word, it's all round. You must have heard what they're saying.'

'*Tchkkk*,' he snorted. 'Shrews' gossip!'

'It's more than that. Ask the pigeons, ask the pond fowl, they'll tell you. Oh, poor Kine, the news travels; the news of fear, of strange killings.' She stepped away, moving slowly. At length, she turned. 'The Pond Dragon.'

There was a sigh. '*What* pond dragon? There's no dragon,' Kine told her. He gave a heave of impatience. 'Make sense, Clary, I live there – am *I* frightened by rumours? You've seen my province, it's peaceful.'

'I like it,' Clary admitted.

'The best of realms.'

'Yes, I thought so.'

'Well?' he snapped.

'Kine, I'm sorry. I wouldn't care for myself but, don't you see, there'll be kitts. I have to think of their safety.'

'Nowhere's *safe*.'

'It is here. At least,' said Clary, 'at most times. I really am sorry, Kine, for I like and admire you. You stand alone in achievement and the others *are* callow. You'd be a mate of distinction.'

'Then trust me, Clary, come with me.'

'Slay the Pond Dragon first, Kine!'

'*Aaak!*'

The farm man looked up. A heron rose, its legs dangling. Above the wood it wheeled twice, grey on grey as dusk thickened.

The smuts from Ploughman's blaze drifted, sailing down the wood's fringes. In the gloom the field glowed, freshly sown,

45

earthy-smelling, the fragrance mingling with smoke from the bonfire of seed bags. Ploughman stamped on the ashes. A good day's work, neat and thorough. Could a young man do better?

'*Aaak*,' the bird screamed, upset.

Ploughman leaned on his tractor. The fowl had towered from the pond and he watched its flight, puzzled. Not much worried the heron. He stretched and envied its grace: *it* did not suffer with backache. Those strong wings spanned six feet and the long bill was powerful. Something, though, had disturbed it.

He recalled his geese cursing. The gander's death still perplexed and he eyed the copse darkly. Lighting his pipe, he strolled over, quietly treading the pond path.

The sun had gone from the pool, leaving fine wisps of vapour. Ploughman swiped a mosquito. It was a gesture of habit, his weathered skin insect-thwarting, long immune to the brutes which grew large in the valley. An early bat prowled the glade, jinking darkly among them. Underfoot the growth crunched, shadowed banks thick with plants, stuff he thought of as weed, jungle-green, poison-berried.

In tepid shallows life scurried. Tiny pond monsters paddled, raising silt, jaws voracious. Farther out than the bugs a black slime rose in blobs, an unpleasant Sargasso drawn by warmth to the surface. He saw no heron-molester, no predator lurking. Indeed, the pool seemed deserted. The dusky emptiness sagged, hung like dewy grey sheets and the man felt uneasy.

He never had liked the pond, a place of moods and old drownings. The girl might speak of its charms, for she was one for the wild like her mother before her. The girl would goggle at ducks and spend hours on the marshes. She spoke with awe of pond lilies and what he called 'them horse-stingers', the dragonflies of late summer. The pond bewitched her – but not Ploughman.

Like the youths he felt edgy, though sceptical of their story. There were no fishes so big as those which could not be landed. Besides their bait had been wrong, especially for a pike. He thought an eel was more likely. An eel could grow mighty strong. On the marsh, in his day, he had known eels of five feet weighing twenty pounds, easy. He reckoned that was what had scared them.

The man went back to the field. The damned old heron had hoaxed him. He guessed its day had been bad and it had cussed out of pique. He viewed the scene from the tractor. His own day's work had gone smoothly. The bare, drilled soil ran in lines, rolled with trim corrugations. The bonfire was ghostly. As he watched something shifted, and twilight yielded a weasel.

The goblin came from the field, scrambling on the crumble. It had a slow, weary action, unalert, out of spirits. It seemed dejected, past caring, heedless even of Ploughman, who watched it toil to the covert. He pushed his cap back, surprised. It must have come from the ridge – from the orchards, the man thought.

* * *

The cottage door was wide open. Looking down from the oaks, the rook could make out the doormat and see the pot on the step with a geranium in it. On the shed at the back a piece of string through a hole made a pull for a latch, and a ringdove was sunning. An ancient tree nudged a wall whose bricks were mellow with age. The tree would soon fill with walnuts. Below the child rode his trike, the bell's jangle spasmodic.

One eye on the child, Watchman took in the rook nests, a Babel now, with the other. From masts tumultuous with young, the parent rooks flew to fields, toiled for food and straggled homewards. Dawn to dusk the birds slaved, the demands on them ceaseless. Watchman leered. Just deserts! Their days of strutting were done, their philandering chastened. This was the cost of their lust – an aptly gluttonous harvest!

He could have told them as much, and more, he thought, for it would worsen, the ground grow hard, worms infrequent. But he was only a lookout. 'So much for wisdom,' he wheezed. They might have learned had they listened. The same applied to the sprite, who had returned unrewarded. 'I know you're back, Kine,' he croaked and eyed the Life Tree. 'Stop moping.'

A head popped out. 'No one's moping. I had a long trip, I'm resting.'

'You had a wasted trip, shrimp. You wouldn't listen. I warned you.'

'It wasn't wasted; who said so?'

'Where is she, then?' the rook answered. He sneered and said, 'She rebuffed you.'

The weasel glared. 'You know nothing.' He left the hole and slouched round, scowling up. '*Less* than nothing.'

'I know this, shrimp, that you're lucky. You could've ended as they have.' Watchman's gaze raked the corvids. 'Fetching, carrying, slaving. Thank the stars you escaped; thank good fortune she spurned you!'

'You're wrong,' said Kine, his eyes shifty. 'She's coming later.'

'Haw-haw!'

'In her good time.'

'That's an old one. We've heard it, sprite, say no more, you're well out. Thank your blessings. There's no rest with the fever. It can prove fatal at our age.'

'*Your* age, rook,' Kine said glumly. He shook his head; life looked bleak. 'There *is* a snag,' he confessed. 'Clary's made a condition. I've got to slay the Pond Dragon. The trouble is . . .' He felt foolish. A drop of rain struck his nose. The sudden shower spattered leaves, which twitched, seeming to snicker. He said, 'The dragon's a myth; I've to slay a myth, Watchman.'

The rook's beak gaped. 'To win Clary?'

'She's set the task.'

Watchman cackled. His shoulders shook, shedding rain, and he whooped, coughing hoarsely, 'Slay a myth? Haw-haw-haw!'

Puddles formed, their brows twinkling. The cottage door had been closed and child and trike bundled in. Roof tiles beamed, wet and shiny: water gurgled in gutters.

'Haw-haw-haw, that's rich, weasel!'

'There it is . . .'

'Kine, it's *killing*! Haw-haw,' the rook hooted. He rocked his perch, almost tumbling, and flapped his wings to recover. At length, in fear of a stroke, he held still, gasping feebly. The shower had passed and he stared out at the marsh while regaining composure. Oyster-catchers were piping. A pair of swans thundered up, winging over the channels. 'Slay a myth,' the rook croaked. 'You'll slay *me*, Kine, I'm aching!'

On the track by the copse Flit and Farthing were bathing, flicking spray from a puddle. 'You like a fight, you two ruffians,' said Watchman, sharing the joke. 'A legend versus a myth. That's a thriller,' he cackled.

Kine ranged the deck of the Tree, turned and counter-marched, brooding. He paced in sullen frustration, vexed by Watchman's behaviour. The lookout was senile. Kine had not been amused; there was a fire in his mind, the bright flame he esteemed, the spry elf that was Clary. 'Slay the Pond Dragon, Kine!'

Her demand drummed within him.

Among the reeds a duck nested. The mallard's head was drawn in, ten warm eggs tucked beneath her. She thought her secret unknown but Kine knew where she sat, as Kine knew most things (or claimed to) save that which now mattered: how to reassure Clary.

There was a way, for there *must* be; all was possible, always. Such was the creed of the sprite. It had not been disproved. He had, at points in his life, performed improbable feats, the near-impossible sometimes. He would do no less for Clary – climb the clouds, pluck the stars for her!

A tendril twitched on the bank. Pinhead eyes quizzed him vaguely. 'Is that you? Are you back, Kine?'

Kine looked round. 'Come here, shrewmouse.'

'Me?' squeaked Scrat. His nose puckered.

'About those tales . . .'

The shrew blinked.

'The so-called dragon,' Kine prompted. 'Tell me more.'

The shrew beamed. 'You're going to fight it. You'll save us!'

'Hold still, shrew, and pay heed.' Kine placed a foot on Scrat's tail warning him. 'No inventions. I want the facts and no nonsense. I want no lies or tall stories, rumour, gossip or visions, doom or woe; no hysterics. Just the facts of the matter – and make them convincing.'

Scrat cringed. 'But I've told you . . .'

'Phantom waves, wails of horror!'

'*Deaths*,' snapped Scrat. 'You ignored them.' He paused, appalled by his boldness. 'The waves were true, Kine, all true. You should've listened,' he shrilled. 'You kept dodging the issue, kept avoiding the question. T-tell me this,' the shrew blurted: 'What lives in a pond, p-plunders woods, crosses fields? What defies the P-ploughman, kills a goose and takes rabbits? What reeks of nothing on earth? Tell me, weasel, or can't you? What water creature kills pheasants? N-none that's normal, that's certain. Only – *doom* – the Pond Dragon!'

'A guess,' huffed Kine. 'Supposition.'

'I've seen it, Kine.'

'Then describe it.'

'You know my eyes . . .'

'That's the point. We *all* know your eyes, midget.'

Kine took a hop to the bluff, lapsing into reflection. A wistful heart voiced his thoughts. 'It *could* exist,' he allowed, 'it's not impossible, Scrat. We've no *proof* there's no dragon.'

'You'd fight it, Kine?'

'That's my duty.'

'I knew you would!'

'Kine is fearless.' He thought of Clary and added, 'Don't think I'd shrink from a dragon – Kine flies high, ask his rivals. Ask Bald-ear and Scoter, ask young Brat, shrew, they'll tell you. Ask who dazzled with speed and whose brilliance dumfounded. If they've the words, they'll inform you. Ask who Clary admires and implores to fight for her.'

'Kine, of course!'

'Just so,' Kine said. He eyed the shrew. 'Will you help me?'

'Proudly, Kine.'

'Listen, shrewmouse . . .' The goblin hunched, his glance sly. 'I've a plan: we'll *entice* it. If this monster exists we'll entice it to the surface.'

'Entice it, Kine?'

'Set a bait.'

'A b-bait?'

'Some small creature.'

'S-some s-small . . .' Scrat's eyes popped.

'Don't fret, shrew, I'll be with you. I'll do the hard part, the ambush. The bait's the easy part,' Kine said.

He searched the growth – Scrat had gone.

'What a friend!' Kine was scornful.

'What a *plan*,' the growth echoed. The voice was high in the scrub, high enough to be candid. Chessel drawled, 'Bait a dragon? You'd not catch frogs with a shrew, it wouldn't tempt a blind toad. Where's your mind, Kine, your thinking?'

'*Tchkkk*,' snarled Kine.

Chessel yawned. 'You need to cogitate, sprite, get your brain working sometimes.'

'Careful, dormouse . . .'

'You've got one – you've got a brain in that skull. It's full of threats, crude responses. Give it space, let it think. Let intelligence blossom.' Chessel closed his eyes lightly, yawned again and said, 'Dragons. That's a good abstract subject. Just relax and think of dragons.'

'*You* think. You're the thinker. Tell me how I can slay one.'

'Find one first,' said the dormouse.

'Just supposing there is one.'

'If not, then it's harder. You'll have to think upside down, invert the logic,' mused Chessel. 'Night-time's best, you'll need moonshine.'

'Pah,' said Kine.

'By the pond. You'll find the moon upside down there. Stretch the mind, let it float. Just relax and be patient. Remember, Kine, topsy-turvy.'

'And *you* remember,' Kine told him, 'next time, dormouse, I'll eat you.'

'Threats,' sighed Chessel.

Kine left him.

The copse was quiet; Scrat had vanished. A weepy sky washed great trees. In their vaults it grew dim, the light uncannily green, colouring massive columns and tinting piles of old brashings. Faintly now, from the crowns, the cry of rooks reached the weasel.

Was Watchman right after all? A larval doubt gnawed the weasel. Could he be under a spell, the whole thing a delusion? Was Kine the hero bewitched? Some very odd things were happening: a crazy shrew half-convinced him, he let a fool dormouse twit him. Was this, indeed, the spring curse, or merely pent-up frustration?

What he needed was *action*, the dash and thrust of his kind, the blood tonic that lifted. Summon dragons to fight and let him leap like a weasel, do or die, dance with glory. Let the Fury consume him; let the war cry be with him!

The rain fell, one more shower. It drubbed the top of the copse, trickling down from young leaves and spattering on the loam, or on sappy ground cover, doubly green in the wood-light. Spatter-splat. The sprite listened. The rooks were suddenly quiet, the silence heightening the dripping. Its steady thud made him tense.

Splat-splat-splat.

Kine's snout lifted. There was a smell in the air, a smell the weasel remembered. A reek of 'nothing on earth', as the shrew had described it. It raised the hairs, soured the nostrils.

Splat-splat-splat.

The sprite waited. The splash of drips aggravated, seemed to grow till it pounded and Kine's heart pounded with it. And then the rain must have stopped, for the beat was abating, slow now, more erratic. There was a vast sense of stillness.

'Aaeee!'

Kine whipped round.

It was a cry of stark fear, thin by even Scrat's standards. The echo died as Kine charged. The weasel's rush was impulsive, a spurting, gut-churning reflex, its thrill ousting caution. He flew in leaps for some yards then stopped suddenly, flummoxed.

'Scrat?' He needed a guide. 'Call again, shrew, where are you?'

The wood was quiet.

He surged forward. Through scrub and thicket he thrust, dodging trees, hurdling logs, less sure now of his course, seeking signs, his ears straining. *'Tchkkk,'* he cursed. 'Are you there, Scrat?'

In the silence, he paused and then, baffled, changed tack. He stepped, this time with more care, probing nooks as he ran, quartering with a system. A sombre edginess gripped him, a sense of close and dire danger. He felt a strong hostile

52

presence and, doubting Scrat had survived, grew increasingly chary.

Back where Chessel had climbed he saw a branch on the ground, the thin limb freshly torn so the white wound was raw, stripped of rind at the fracture. Nearby, strewn around, lay the remains of the nest in which the dormouse had wintered.

Kine called, 'Chessel?' and waited. The weasel's voice trailed, unanswered. 'Are you safe?' Shadows brooded.

Nothing moved and he turned, making tracks for the pond. There was a mood, a strange tension. It was as if the whole wood – the trees and plants – held its breath and Scrat's absence reproached him. The midget's shrill rebuke haunted. 'You should've listened . . . I've seen it!'

The weasel peered forward. An awesome swell rocked the pool. It heaved and fell, slowly settling. He watched the reeds; some were flattened. The mallard's eggs had been smashed, the shells in yolk-besmeared fragments. All he saw of the duck was a fan of wing feathers, brown and flat like a raft, adrift close to the bluff. Their blue speculum glittered.

* * *

The weasel crouched by the hole, staring out at the water. Save for the cold, brilliant moon, it was black as a mole, the mirrored globe wobbling slightly, now a shimmying blob tossed and teased by small waves, now as still as a lamp. Stars were out, the night mild, and Kine struggled with tiredness.

Earlier, about dusk, the sky had rung with wild cries, the first swifts of the year racing over the valley. Then, by and by in the murk, owls had sailed darkening rides where, as though wraiths were lurking, pale sprays of may glimmered. Now the weasel took stock; it was no time to feel drowsy.

There was a rat on the bank. It paused then scuttled away and, soon, the weasel heard steps, clumsy sounds drawing nearer. A badger trundled the path, broad and squat, striped snout questing. Here and there it sought worms, making scrapes, rooting in them. An odd, preoccupied beast, it turned at last for the marsh, leaving Kine to stretch tiredly.

A tiny moan reached the weasel. The moon had slipped

from the pool, briefly screened by thin clouds. Quietly groping and fumbling, a small and dirt-matted form stole on deck, where it trembled. 'Doom,' it groaned with a twitch.

'Scrat! I thought you were dead.'

The soiled mite gave a heave.

'Kine, I thought so myself. D-did you see it?'

'I caught the smell.'

'Kine, we're doomed. I felt its breath burning on me.'

'You're in a mess.'

'I ran blindly. The rain left mud.'

'You're still living.'

'Just,' the shrew said then, flinching, 'what was *that*?' he gasped, frightened.

'Only the moon.' The orb startled. In the pond it swam back, its white nakedness dazzling. Fascinated, Kine watched. Only the moon in the Moon Pond – his first worldly vision! For quite a while, as a kitt, he had believed that fish flew, that the stars grew like daisies. Topsy-turvy . . . He pondered. At length, the weasel said, 'Chessel?'

'Ch-Chessel perished.'

'I guessed. I mean – how much did he know?'

The shrew blinked. 'About what?'

'About the moon.'

Scrat looked vague. 'He spent a lot of time dreaming.' He thought and added, 'All the winter.'

'About the moon and the *dragon*. He said to watch the moon, midget.'

'I'd best be off.'

'To keep vigil. He said to watch in the moonshine.'

'The p-pond's doomed, I'm not stopping.'

'Go, then,' Kine snapped. 'I'm staying. I'll watch all night, if I must.' He eyed the wallowing disc. 'Push off, Scrat, Kine's on guard. A weasel doesn't desert; a weasel's vigil is steadfast.'

'A shrew's a shrew.'

'Run and hide.'

'Kine – take care.'

The shrew fled, a fleeting shade on the bluff, and the pond-watcher settled. Lean grey clouds hunted north. Leaping up from dark hills, they took the copse in their stride, stretching out in great packs so the moon shone less often. Shapes dissolved, shadows spread; everywhere form was swallowed.

A little owl caterwauled: the fierce and unloved *Athene*. Deepest night was approaching, that still, black space at time's heart when nothing moved, all was silent.

Kine lay flat. The air was colder. It was a time for the den, a time of fear in the vale when prey and hunter called quits and the rabbits had vanished. In deepest night the hare froze; the quiet fox fled the woodside. Only the mole took no heed, and the mole could see nothing. In deepest night, strange things happened: tides paused, planets halted. It was no time to be out and even worse to be watching. To look away was much safer.

The weasel gulped but stood fast.

He thought of Scrat in the dark and felt a twinge of compassion, for even Kine shuddered now, his fear as old as the hills, primeval and chilling, the age-old fear of the small hours. He wished the moon would come back. The fallen tree had grown dim. It groped the void with its limbs and they were lost, sucked in by it. Even the hole was obscure, a mere hop from the post where he sat, peering grimly.

As he tired, weird shapes loomed, chimeras of the murk mocking overstrained eyes with a shadowy mischief. The more he peered, half-deceived, the more they teased and he stared. He looked away, his head cocked, better served when he listened.

There was, he thought, a faint splash. It died at once in the hush, a quietness now so profound the wood itself might have fled. And yet his sixth sense was roused. He had a prickly skin, a strangely icy awareness he was no longer alone. In the blackness he crouched, still as the hulk of the Tree, and breathed in. The stench reached him.

It fouled his nose but passed off.

Nothing happened.

He seemed to wait for an age before he heard the pond stirring. It was, at first, a soft slurp, an eerie slavering rasp as the dark banks were jostled. *Suck-a-sock*. It grew louder, the rhythmic pounding persistent, as if the pool sought escape, impatient of its restraints. The cloud had thinned, making gaps, and now where starshine returned a rising swell caught the glow, slick and lumpily threatening.

The tree had started to shake; Kine could feel the waves breaking. As they slapped the old hulk, they pitched spray and swamped branches. The whole black reach seemed in ferment, heaving up, sliding back, glowering greasily at him. On the crests he saw sludge and knew the depths were ascending. The weasel's gaze slewed and stopped. A frothing wave held his eye, the water sluicing and gleaming.

What happened next was quite slow, a kind of lazy eruption. A massive hump reared and sank. As it rose it made foam, shedding spume from its flanks, the thing shiny and dark leaving whirls when it vanished. It broke the surface again, now two humps in the gloom, and Kine strained to see better.

Through the bubbling and froth, he could just glimpse a tail like a thong, lashing fiercely. The humps, he saw, had deceived: they were no longer great dorsal mounds but curves in one twisting length, a monstrous worm. The brute squirmed. It was an eel of such size, so grotesque, that Kine froze. Drenched by spray, he felt nothing, incredulity numbing.

The thing's travail was bizarre, a writhing ballet of wrath. The coiling giant seemed possessed, doubling up, threshing air, exacerbating the waves until the pond was in tumult. Only when the head rose, thrusting clear of the foam, was the brute's ire explained – there was another beast present.

Fastened near the eel's throat hung a fiend with wild eyes, the wedge skull thick and streaming. Cruel claws tore at its foe. It had a deep, powerful chest, a coat slicked to the bone and a strong, sodden tail. Violently, the tail whipped.

If the eel had dismayed, its adversary dumfounded. Kine looked on in chill awe as the prodigies battled. Down they plunged as he stared; up they heaved, their toil frenzied. The weasel thought of the shrew, the inscrutable riddle. What lives deep in a pond, plunders woods, crosses fields? The truth was shockingly simple: nothing did – no *one* thing.

The 'dragon' did not exist. In its place were *two* fiends, the great eel and its foe, either of them a nightmare.

More clouds passed, vision thwarted. The awful splashing

went on, the grim heaves and wild dives fearful sounds in the darkness. Kine could feel the black waves, sense the coiling and writhing. He thought his perch would be drowned so mountainous was the water.

Then, again, the light teased and he could just see the toilers. Still the awesome brutes raged but the serpent was tiring. The massive, snake-like fish rolled, hauled now by its tormentor. Moiling backwards through mud, the latter wrestled and tugged until the eel was ashore. There it threshed, streaming water, before its ultimate spasm. At last the great coil was still and the victor shook briskly.

Flecked with faint incandescence, the pond seesawed gently. There was a noise in the wood. It made the eel's killer stare. It seemed crazed by its effort, huge of neck, spiky-tailed, then the creature had vanished.

Kine kept low, stiff with dread. Presently, gaining nerve, he stole down to the bank and approached the eel's carcase. The vast round trunk made him quake; the brute's teeth glinted cruelly and daunted even in death. The monster's fierce round eyes glared.

He did not dwell on its slayer. He needed sleep, calming sleep. There were thoughts he did *not* need.

He was still tired when he stirred. The barest hint of dawn gleamed and he curled himself tighter. Somewhere over the vale a single blackbird gave voice. It threw a few random notes and, next thing, the sun roused him. He must have napped as it rose. His head was ringing with song, such a paean that it deafened. Every bird seemed possessed.

Blearily, Kine sat up.

There was a scratching above and a snout sniffed the Tree hole. 'Kine?' piped Scrat. 'Have you rested?'

'Oh, *you're* back.'

'Were you sleeping?'

'Huh,' said Kine, 'with that din?'

'It's a glorious morning.'

'I had a harrowing night, Scrat.'

'They want to hear from you, Kine.'

'Shut them up, my head's aching.' He climbed on deck, out

of sorts. A tractor roared past the wood, its cab radio blaring. *A sunny day in the south . . . scattered clouds . . . pressure rising . . .*

A score of birds joined the noise. Pheasants crowed, pigeons cooed, moorhens clucked. The wren trilled like a diva. Even its tail seemed to sing, beating time with each note. A yaffle bawled, finches piped. Staring down through the trees, rooks gave voice from the crowns while the first cuckoo shouted.

Sparrows cheeped as they roistered. 'Great news, Kine, but a cheat. You might've done it by day. The fight of fights and we missed it!'

'I heard it all,' cried the wren, whose nest was nearly complete, a mossy, spherical den on an ivy-clad stump. 'It woke me up in the night. I thought the pond would flood.'

'It's like the old times,' chimed Flit, 'like the days of the heroes. Another giant-killing epic.'

The sparrows fluttered with glee, brawled and romped round the eel whose vast trunk caught the sunlight. It lay as Kine had last seen it, beady-eyed, dark and shining, as if its coils were embalmed. 'What a triumph,' cheeped Farthing, 'what a weasel sensation!'

Flit put in, 'What a comeback,'

'Kine's a hero,' squeaked Scrat, 'he's our saviour. I told you.'

Farthing said, 'That's a weasel – you think his best days have gone and he slays the Pond Dragon. That's a champion for you!'

Kine's head swam. 'But . . .' he muttered.

The pond was flat, its face blank.

Watchman said, 'It's a fluke. Don't inflate him, the shrimp, he'll never let us forget it. He'll have the female here next; we'll have a brood of young braggarts.'

'But . . .' said Kine.

Ducks were dabbling, complacently dunking. A heron fished from the reeds. Round the copse hawthorn bloomed, its cream sprays sweetly scented. Clary? Kine thought and dreamed. His mind went back to the orchard. Apple blossom and Clary – Clary bright as a flame. 'Slay the Pond Dragon, Kine!'

He regarded the revellers. 'You gave me up,' he declared, 'thought me past it. *She* didn't.'

'Not me,' Scrat shrilled, 'I told them.'

'We knew you had the skills,' Flit said.

Farthing chirped, 'And the courage.'

'Kine's a legend,' cried Scrat.

'Kine the bold,' Kine said, warming. 'Kine who's never been beaten, the scourge of rats, the mink fighter . . .'

'The dragon fighter!'

He hushed.

'Tell us how you fought,' Flit said.

'Was it fearsome?' asked Farthing.

'The waves were high,' cried the wren.

'The waves towered,' Kine remembered. 'The monster lashed and they thundered. The monster writhed, its teeth flashing. It dived and heaved, snapped and twisted. There never was such an ogre.'

The shrew said, 'Kine never flinches.'

'A weasel fights to the death, Scrat.' Kine stood tall. 'That's his creed. A weasel does what he must.'

'And has the luck of the devil.' Watchman viewed the eel darkly.

'Luck?' growled Kine.

'Was it ailing?'

'Ailing?' Kine snarled, indignant. 'The giant was strong as a steer and fought like a demon. You would've shuddered to see it.'

'Weren't you scared?'

'Am I ever?'

Part Two

THE BERSERKER

The girl lifted her child and swung him over the brook. 'Mind, it's soggy, take care.' He wobbled in the red wellies. The little stream joined the pond, running out the far side. Everywhere bluebells flowered, a dense mat in the wood. Ladysmock flanked the rill along with pendulous sedge, sulphur-hued, the heads fuzzy.

At the pool she called, 'Wait, come round here where it's safer.' A grassy creek caught the sun and its shallows were limpid. The toddler crouched, peeping in, his excitement contagious. It was an overdue treat. 'You *said* we'd visit the pond,' he had accused till it shamed her. Now she watched him, absolved, purged of guilt by his pleasure.

'A snail, a snail!'

The girl looked. It moved, shell-down, in the pond, the surface film for a foothold. 'A water snail,' she agreed. 'And look there – what are those?'

'Tittlebats,' he exclaimed.

The little spike-backed fish gleamed. 'Watch them fight,' the girl murmured. 'They fight like bulldogs for wives. The brides wear silver and gold, the grooms are dressed in red waistcoats. They can swim backwards,' she said.

'How d'you know?'

'Poacher told me.'

'He's dead.'

'Yes, he is. He told me when I was small.'

'And what else?'

'Well, let's see. Sticklebacks? They make their children behave. If little sticklebacks stray, their dads get hold of them quick and pop them back in the nest. Now – *keep still* – what's that creature?'

'It's got four hands.'

'It's a newt.' It caught the sun as it overturned, its underside brilliant orange. The tail was dotted with spots, the stripe of blue on it dazzling. A tiny monster, the child thought.

'They're what your granpa calls merrows. They live mostly on land but take to water in spring. Shall I tell you a secret?'

'Yes!'

'Then listen,' she told him. 'From time to time,' she averred, 'they take their skins off like coats.'

63

'With their hands?'

'With their hands.'

'Why?' he asked.

'They need new ones.' His mother laughed. 'Same as you.'

'Can we go round the pond?'

She straightened up. 'Then take care.'

'To the tree?'

'But keep off . . .'

The child galumphed ahead. 'It's a boat,' he called back. His eager charge was unsteady. 'The tree's a boat in the pond!'

'You keep off.'

'The weasel lives there, I've met him . . .' He had gone on past the bluff and stopped, suddenly silent. The girl could see his jaw sagging.

'Oh, my God.' She caught up.

The monster shone in the grass.

'It's quite all right,' she forced out, 'it's not alive. It's quite safe.'

'It's *big*,' her son said, in doubt.

'Big and dead.'

'The Pond Dragon?'

'No, it's an eel.'

The boy listened. He heard a tractor pull up and waved his arms, spotting Ploughman. 'Granpa, look, it's an eel!'

'By the heck . . .'

The child beamed. He said. 'It's dead, it's all right.'

'Aye,' wheezed Ploughman, 'by heck. You won't see many like that, lad.' He tipped back his cap. 'I've not seen many myself, not *that* size. It's a beggar.'

His daughter smiled. 'It's a fright. I reckon that's what the youths saw.'

'I reckon so. I was right. I said it wasn't no pike.' The man examined the coils. 'Be damned, that's big, that's a weight.' He stuck a boot out and toed it.

'Can we keep it?' the child asked.

'I'll tell you what, we'll weigh it.' The farm man stooped with a grimace. His back was still giving pain. He raised the eel, the trunk drooping. A glassy eye met the child's, dead and living

64

both brilliant. 'We'll take it back to the farm and put the brute on the scales. Want a ride in the tractor?'

'Behave,' the girl said. 'I'll walk on back.' She paused, frowning. 'What killed it, dad?'

Ploughman shrugged. 'What killed the gander?'

'You'd best find out.'

'Too true, lassie.'

That night there was fog. It filled the levels like milk, muffling marsh frog and owl, gagging even the vixen. It made the farm man's hens cluck. They were secure in their hut but huddled close, sensing prowlers.

Something dark left the marsh.

Amid the vapour it paused, then drew up the field's margin. It was a beast of the murk, of ditch and shadow, a night fiend. In the gloom it looked ghoulish. It might have stepped out of time, out of the pliocene mists its fierce forebears had haunted.

Had Ploughman ventured outside he would have seen the thing moving. It must have been two feet long, large of claw, neck and skull, the coarse outer hairs spiky. As it slipped through the hedge roosting starlings erupted.

'The thing!' they shrieked. 'It's the thing!' The beast was alien to them.

In Ploughman's beans it stood listening. It heard the hens and the goose. Their smell was strong round the huts but sturdy bolts forbade entry. The creature snuffled, frustrated. It sniffed the doors, scraped the earth, clawed the woodwork. Its lust thwarted, it grunted.

Inside the hens cried, 'Who are you?'

There was no sound from the night; the beast was quiet, salivating.

One plump chicken felt weak and hit the slatted floor, squawking. Again sharp claws scraped on wood.

The hens knew one thing for sure: the brute had murdered the gander. It had the same baneful stench, the stench of nothing on earth. It reeked of hatred and fury. It lacked the fox's sly fear, Reynard's prudence. The man indoors did not scare it. It was, the chickens thought, crazed, a respecter of nothing.

65

They huddled closer and clucked. It was a seeker of blood, of warm flesh for the rending.

Another scratch ripped the door.

The fog had climbed from the marsh and wreathed the ridge, growing thicker. It made the darkness intense. The night was dense, claustrophobic. The fowls were scared of the strangeness, a new and faceless marauder. It had not entered their lives until it ended the gander's.

They eyed the door. It was quiet and one repeated, 'Who are you?'

'You'll find out,' the voice answered. 'The night I enter you'll know me. Call me Lord of the Night. Call me Hob the Berserker.'

May bugs swarmed by the oaks and Kine watched pheasants courting. The cockbirds fanned out their wings, showing coppery feathers. They seemed to hide behind shields as if the females were gorgons. Some had two or three partners. Most birds now went in pairs, preoccupied with their own. It made Kine feel neglected.

He sat a while on the bluff, his reflection beneath him. Overhead the leaves rocked, dense in growth if still pale, mossy-yellow on the oaks. They framed the weasel's pond image. It was imposing enough but not the warmest of partners.

'*Tchkkk*,' he told himself sternly, 'a weasel hunts on his own.'

'Sometimes, Kine.'

He was startled. The pond reflected two goblins. The other laughed. 'You're surprised?' She danced away. 'Aren't you pleased? You *did* mean what you said? You killed the Pond Dragon for me.'

'They told you that?'

'News travels.'

'It wasn't . . .' Kine shut his mouth. She was a dream, a bright blessing. 'You're here,' he said, 'it's you, Clary!'

Her chortle teased. 'Wonders happen. All things are possible, Kine; a flower may answer a cloud, a stone may move. May I join you?'

It was a marvel, he told her.

'I don't see why, now it's safe. What other choice would I make? There's Brat but Brat isn't Kine, nor are Scoter and Bald-ear. They're not distinguished or famed and none has slaughtered a dragon. I want to live in the Tree, share the copse. Will you show me?'

'Of course,' he cried, 'come and look.' She disappeared in the hole and, while he waited, Kine preened. He had done nothing pernicious. Good luck was hardly a fault; they had just jumped to conclusions. In any case, she was wise. It was quite true, all she said. She could find no better partner.

'Kine, it's perfect.'

'An ancient lair.'

'A fine nursery.'

'Come on,' he cried, 'now the wood. You haven't seen it all yet.'

They bounded off side by side, the day bright, Kine elated. The lakes of bluebells were deep and down the paths, like confetti, lay fallen wild cherry petals and scraps of bloom from the thorn. There was a sweet southern zephyr. He felt as spry as a colt.

'I'll take you first to the cottage.' The sun was warm in the garden and spotted flycatchers danced, flitting up to the gnats then tumbling back to their perches. He said, 'The lawn's stuffed with voles. We'll come again when it's darker.'

'We'll hunt *together*?'

'Of course.'

'I thought . . .'

He laughed, running on. 'The rules are made to be broken.' He showed the way, bouncing lightly. The track was flanked by cow parsley, here and there a great hogweed. It was like butter and cream: kingcups, stitchwort, archangel. Whitethroats gabbled in hedgerows; the candles blazed on horse chestnut.

'I love it, Kine.'

'There's much more.'

He took her into the warren, twisting down through the roots. Bobbing scuts fled before them. 'A feast of rabbit,' he told her. 'You'll not go short, it's good country.'

They paused in clay-laden chambers.

'Kine's country!' she burbled.

'Kine's and Clary's . . .'

They lingered. In the dark they were close and he exclaimed, 'Weasel country – a kingdom fit for young weasels.'

'A dandy pack,' Clary answered.

'Yes,' he said, thinking back, recalling Kia the ill-fated. Five immaculate kitts, all but one of them lost, and it had started like this – just like this, one spring day, the great geese honking home, streaming back up the valley. He said no more for a moment. At length, 'The best,' he declared; 'they'll be the very best, Clary.'

'They'll be bold hunters, don't worry.'

He nodded.

'The finest, Kine, in the land. They'll have a legend to guide them.'

He said, 'That's true, you're quite right. Come on, I'll show you the brook.'

It chattered where the wood ended, spreading out into bog, a sea of snowy wild garlic with purple orchids on banks, little rills winding through them. The masts were tall, lightly leaved, and sun dappled the footing. A fallen pole blocked the path. 'Clary?' Kine said. 'Where are you?' He stopped and called, 'Are you coming?'

There was a hiss. 'Kine, *I'm* with you!' A painted head towered and pointed. 'I'm with you, Kine, I've been waiting . . .'

The weasel glared.

'. . . a long time.'

His back rose.

The snake swayed. 'All spring,' lisped the she-adder, 'to keep our tryst. I was patient. The adder keeps her word, weasel, her solemn promise. Don't move. A single move and I'll strike.' She watched him coldly. 'No hurry. I swore I'd kill you and I will. But pause a bit to reflect, recall the insults I've borne, the fool you've made of me, Kine. You got too big for your skin. You thought you lorded the covert.'

'The wood is Kine's.'

'One last boast!'

'The wood is Kine's and his partner's.'

The serpent sneered. 'Who'd want Kine? You're just a boaster, a has-been. Where would Kine find a partner? In any case, she's too late. You've had your final word, weasel. She's missed the death, Kine, where is she?'

'Behind you,' Clary said quietly.

The adder turned and Kine sprang. He knocked the head to the ground and leaped back, skipping briskly. Clary pranced. 'Well done, partner!'

'Shall we dance?'

'Like the wind.'

They whirled in rings round the snake, small eyes fiery, bibs flashing. Like elves they circled and swayed, as weasels will when provoked, until the reptile's head swam. Still, the war dance continued. It had a sly, malign rhythm.

'You'll rue this, Kine,' hissed the snake.

'Aren't you stopping?' he answered.

The serpent fled. 'One day, weasel . . .'

'Run!' mocked Kine.

The sprites rested. Lithe and sleek in the glade, they regarded each other. 'I'm glad you came,' Kine said, breathless. She was a cool one, unruffled. 'We made a fool of the adder.'

'You've got nice neighbours.'

'That's nothing.'

'Not after slaying a dragon.' The female beamed and Kine gulped. She said, '*I'm* glad I came too; we'll make fine partners. You're tired?'

'No,' he lied.

'Good, let's hunt. Kine, I'm hungry!'

* * *

The pond had come about this way: long ago in the valley, when the forest was dense, men had dug for iron ore there, felling trees for the smelting. When the smelters moved on they had left gaps in the woods, glades with cavities in them. Some of these became pools, the wildlife taking over. Such was the Moon Pond's beginning.

Many years had passed by and the pond served no purpose.

69

Now and then to its banks had come groups of tired troops, fugitives, bands of gipsies. Now and then maids had bathed there, country girls on the loose, or footsore pilgrims had paused to immerse stinging blisters.

Later, foot travellers dwindling, the pond had slipped into fable. When spooky myths had evolved it had played the part with conviction. A home to things of the wild, it kept their secrets with guile, a brooding, loury-browed host. 'A special place,' Kine maintained, 'a place of weasel tradition. I drew my first breath here, Clary.'

They sprawled at ease in the sun, lying out on the Life Tree. A dreamy peace stretched above; swallows swung back and forth. From somewhere nearer the barn, a spanner's 'clank' sounded faintly: Ploughman fitting his mower. The grass was high, purple-green. Soon the cutting would start and they would hunt the hay meadows.

'It's hot,' said Kine, 'almost summer.'

'The time of plenty,' sighed Clary. She felt a twinge of nostalgia. 'The fruit at home will have set; there'll soon be little green apples.'

'Your home is here now.'

'I know. And, Kine, it's all I could want.'

'It will be, Clary.'

'It *is*. But I can't help looking back.'

'You were born in the orchard?'

'Yes, life was fun growing up. I knew a lot of young friends.'

'Including Brat?'

'Yes, poor Brat.' The female laughed at Kine's scowl. 'You'd like him, Kine, if you knew him.'

'I know him, Clary, he's brash.' The male snarled. 'It's time you . . .'

'What?'

'Thought less of him.'

'*Tchkkk.*' The female sprang up. 'And what of Kia?' she inquired. 'You think enough of the past.'

'But Kia's dead.'

'That's no help. I can't set to with a ghost. Not that that's what I want for I've respect for your history. Mine,' said Clary,

70

'is short, less fulfilled, but still mine. Don't tell me what I should *think*.' She paused, softening. 'Poor Brat.'

'If he comes round . . .'

'Let him be. Poor old Brat had no chance; you've no cause to be jealous.'

'Huh, jealous!'

'No reason.'

'When was Kine ever jealous?'

The female purred. 'Then that's good. I like my friends to be friends, to be generous rivals. Oh, Kine, the sun is such bliss, the whole valley is splendid. And just look there – a white swallow.'

There was, indeed, an albino, purest white, with its fellows. It skimmed the pond then soared high, as bright as crystal, and paused. For a split second it swayed, strung aloft like a star, a magic sign in the blue before the oak crowns concealed it. 'Kine, that's a marvel!' cried Clary.

He eyed her, thinking, that *she* was – she was the marvel. 'A swallow?'

'A lucky augury for us. It shows our partnership's blessed. It's a hero's reward.'

'A what?' he said.

Clary laughed. 'You've not forgotten?' she joked. 'You did do battle to win me? You did demolish the dragon? I'll start to think I've been hoodwinked!'

The sharp-eyed hen rook was vexed.

'Slouch,' she cawed, 'go and help.'

'Help yourself,' replied Watchman. He had been hen-pecked too often.

'You dried up slouch, help my young. The turf's hard and they need worms. You were my mate once. Go and help.'

'I'm no one now, just a lookout.'

The female pecked him and glared. 'Still the gallant,' she rasped. 'It's plain to see why I left you.'

'As I recall,' Watchman leered, 'for a greasy young strutter. They're not *my* offspring. It was *your* prurient folly. Get your lewd mate to help you.'

He cocked a glance at the ground where oxeye daisies

winked up, wiry symbols of summer. They were prepared for the drought and would flourish in concrete. 'I'm just a watchman,' he told her.

The hen chastised him again. 'I hope you starve!'

'Bah,' he gritted.

She should have learned, lustful crone. It always came, the dry season. There were fat worms beyond count, tens of thousands an acre, the oldest ploughs in creation. Each few years in the vale the topsoil passed through the worms, every hummock and grain. There was a feast in the turf – until the ground dried and hardened. You could not stab through dry clod and young rooks knew few tricks. They had not learned how to search, to be resourceful and forage.

It was age-old, the crisis; they never learned, went on mating. It was their problem, not his. He had no part in the folly.

'Procreation!' he huffed. The whole hog's hash was a scandal. 'You dunderheads, try the marsh; don't mope here, try the marshland!'

They rose in clouds, looking pleased, as if each one had hit on it, and Watchman followed. The blockheads! '*Caw*,' they cried. 'To the marsh – the marsh is moist still and soft!' No hint of thanks for the tip, no gratitude. '*Caw*, the levels!' They pitched in families, digging, while lapwings screamed, their peace broken.

Watchman perched on the pumphouse.

'The very bird,' a voice cheeped and he saw Flit and his comrade. 'We need your brains, rook, we're stumped.' The sparrows were sitting near him. They had been sparring and now preened. 'The point is,' Farthing explained, 'that, having missed the great fight, we want to fix up another. The problem is how to match him.'

'You see,' said Flit, 'Kine's so famed, we'll have a job to find takers. We thought you might . . .'

Watchman grunted. He viewed the dark, strutting corvids. Now they had food they forgot him. A redshank buzzed them, protesting – '*teuk-teuk*' – and made off. It dropped, at length, to the stream. He was neglected, a lookout!

'We thought you might think of something.'

'Think?' he rasped, disenchanted. 'The shrimp's a fool, that's what I think.'

'Kine's the champion, Watchman.'

'Pah!' A strutter, they all were! Gorging now like starved sheep. Well, they had best make it quick, for the marsh would dry too, and then where would they turn? Already wild bees were working, a summer sign; insects droning. Pairs of reed buntings stuttered. The rook could hear the sedge warblers. The rainy season had passed and when the marsh dried it *dried* – baked as hard as the high ground.

'We thought,' said Flit, 'of his rivals. There's Brat and Scoter and Bald-ear.'

'But then,' said Farthing, 'they're out. They wouldn't fight the champ now.'

'Now he's slaughtered the monster.'

'*That* nonsense,' wheezed Watchman. 'I never heard such a fuss. In any case, *did* he kill it? Who says the creature was dead?'

'You saw it, Watchman; we all did.'

The lookout sneered, squinting sourly. 'We saw its coils, a large trunk. It didn't move. What does that prove?'

'It didn't move all day, Watchman.'

'But it was gone by next evening.'

'So someone took it,' said Flit. 'The girl was there, so was Ploughman. The thing was dead – the rook's quibbling.'

'I know the shrimp.'

'Kine's unbeaten.'

'You're fools,' the rook snapped then sulked. 'You're like that lot on the marsh – pick my brains but don't thank me. No "Thank you, Watchman, good point". No "Well done, Watchman, we're grateful". It's just a bleat, "The rook's quibbling"! Well, *you* trust Kine and *I'll* quibble. A champion, do you call him? There's not one beats him at bragging.'

'With cause,' cried Flit. 'What a victory!'

'I know it's cost him his freedom.'

'He once fought *here*,' Farthing said. 'He beat the mink at the pumphouse.'

'Another mink, now,' dreamed Flit. 'Another mink would do nicely.'

'Or something bigger,' said Farthing. 'More fearsome, to stretch him.'

'Fools!' the rook groused.

They smirked. 'You'll be there,' they exclaimed. 'The day we fix the next scrap, you'll be cawing him on. You're just a crusty old fraud. You know you like a good fight.'

'I know Kine's taken a mate.' The rook looked shrewd. 'See what *she* thinks. She'll give you "good fight", I'll warrant.'

The marsh could charm when the sun shone. Then wagtails danced by the dykes and the willows were silver. Even the pumphouse, by day, was not bereft of appeal, incongruous as it was, like some eccentric gazebo, a waterside folly.

But come the night and it changed. As bats skimmed its roof the black pile was a dungeon and where the reedy stream flowed shadows floated like corpses. At night the bog grasses bristled, dark spines in the mire, and cold and close-set eyes stared whenever fitful stars glistened.

The moon went in and Scrat cowered. He had no love for the marsh but found its beetles seductive. At times his stomach took charge and then, as now, he felt frightened. The river's dirge did not help, an eerie drone on the flats. Nor the owls in the scrub, for their screams pierced like talons.

There was, as well, the frog gossip, a throaty chorus of fears, a consonance of marsh horrors. '*Brek-ek-ek*' and '*Kroax-kroax*'. They sang from sedge and from milfoil, from naiad and crowfoot. You could not tell where they were since each frog threw its voice, a throbbing croak from the dark. The chant pulsated with warning; it made the dwarf jumpy.

'Beware the marsh' (sang the frogs) 'when night is dark and dykes whisper.

'Beware the slumbering pump, the streaming, moon-clawing clouds and all unspeakable sounds.

'Beware the trembling reed, breath of stoat, moaning culvert.

'Beware of talon and fang, of ghoul, bat's wing, marsh demon.

'Beware above all, of Hob, for Hob fears none and is vengeful – Hob the crazed, the night demon.'

Terrified, the dwarf listened.

'*Brek*,' they sang, and, '*Kroax-kroax*.'

Shaking, Scrat reached the path. He should have left before dark, fled the levels by dusk; he should have conquered his belly. He paused to stuff in a cockroach. 'Doom,' he mouthed, 'woe to gluttons!' He munched in haste as the moon flared. It cast the pumphouse in black, the flood bank silhouetted, castellated with tufts, a lone sentinel on it.

Scrat peered up at the creature.

The big buck rabbit stood tall, shadowy on its haunches. It had formidable limbs, its strong kick well respected. To Scrat the sentry was huge and he blinked, munching quickly. It seemed – he questioned his sight – that near the rabbit a tuft stirred. Then something leaped from the murk.

Its whirling speed was confusing; it was demonaic, a thing possessed. The shrew goggled. There was moment of frenzy, a threshing scrum, then a scream. The scream was short, lacerating, and that was that, it was done – the rabbit limp in the grass, the other hunched, its tail bristling. The sound of lapping ensued and Scrat smelled something warm, sickly.

'Doom!' he howled and ran blindly. He struck a stone and was dazed. With a shake, he raced on, anywhere in the darkness. Only once did he turn and they were moving in tandem. Against the moon they stood out, the demon hauling its kill, dragging it to the pump.

'*Kroax*!'

Frogs sang as Scrat fled, his coat soaked, tumbling, scrambling. He did not stop till the woods, then only to gulp and rush onwards.

'Kine . . .' he piped. 'Kine, where are you?'

Beneath the pumphouse Hob heaved, toiling through the foundations. Ancient bones and skulls crunched, dragged along with his kill in the dry, musty lair. The earth was littered with relics, charnel left by the mink. In the bunker he listened. Distantly the frogs croaked, their lay faint in the labyrinth.

The vale was teeming with life, a living store, thought the demon. A single guard – the old man! A valley made to delight, for Hob's indulgence.

For carnage.

* * *

The youths came up the stream laughing, flicking stones at the water. A cuckoo cried from the copse and they recalled cuckoo stories. As little boys, still wide-eyed, they had one day come on Poacher. He had just dropped from a wall, out of breath, his coat bulging. Why, the boys asked, intrigued, had such a high wall been built? It contained only woodland.

'Ah,' the villain had breathed, 'do you hear that old cuckoo? He comes and goes every year and when he goes he steals the summer. That's why the squire built the wall – to keep the cuckoo from thieving. I'd say a foot more might do it.'

They chuckled now. 'It near killed him, he was too old to be climbing. He was a stubborn old rogue.'

'D'you know he had these war medals? I saw them once, they were brilliant.'

'He knew the valley all right, every thicket and brake, like her up at the cottage. He used to tell her his stories.'

'He told the *magistrates* stories.'

They laughed again and their dog pulled. It was a terrier type, not enamoured of dawdling. The creature lunged on its leash, stopped to choke then strained on, every now and then whining.

'Let her off.'

'No, she'll run. She'll have the bullocks stampeded.'

They reached the pump in good spirits. The engineer was outside, his van parked by the dyke. He had a Flymo and was trimming grass round the bricks as if in some city garden. It gave the youths a fresh laugh and the dog barked.

' 'Morning, mister.'

He was all right, the girl's man, but still a greenhorn they thought, a foreigner with his ways – his old dials and his clipboard! And little bits of cut grass! Not country-bred, like his missus.

Now, *she* could show you the vale: every wild flower and warren. She knew where kingfishers lived and the water voles swam. She knew the old vixen's lair and where, at any time now – perhaps the next balmy evening – badger cubs could be seen. She knew the heart of the valley. They held the man's wife in awe. She could be wild herself sometimes.

The engineer stopped the mower.

'You selling teas?' jibed the thin lad.

'I'll give you teas, you two tramps!' It was conveyed without malice. 'Not everybody's bone idle.' He viewed his handiwork keenly. 'I'd say that's better, it's *neat*.'

'You need some paint on that door.'

'You volunteering?'

They grinned. 'I guess you heard,' said the lean one, 'that the pond mystery was solved?'

'I heard – an eel.'

'Ploughman took it. Not *any* eel, a damned giant. He oughta stuffed it and kept it.' The youths fell silent, remembering. At last the big one said gravely, 'An eel like that could do harm; you should've felt the brute pulling. The thing had teeth like a croc. I read about those old giants. They say they like human flesh. I read this Japanese tale: they say that eels become dragons; they're really dragons disguised. I'd say we got away lightly. We might've lost more than tackle.'

They eyed the dog, which whined quietly.

The thin youth said, 'Her, for instance.'

'If we'd took the dog fishing. Or someone might've fell in . . .' The bitch pulled and was scolded. 'It's got the old fellow worried. The question now is what killed it?'

The pump man smiled. 'You're the experts.'

'We might be that but it's strange. I mean,' the big lad explained, 'the way it done for that eel. There was the gander as well, and marks on Ploughman's old coop. It's got the old fellow anxious.'

'You're right,' the engineer told them. 'That, and facing retirement.' He cleaned the Flymo with care and lifted it on the van. 'That's what nags him.'

'Packing work up – a problem?'

'Not to you. It's his life. That and one or two fowls. You wouldn't know about work, though.'

'Flaming heck, poor old Ploughman!' They watched the terrier strain, snuffling under the pumphouse. It had its nose to the hole where the earth met the brickwork. The scrawny youth jerked the lead. 'Something's there, she can tell. Hear her growl? She's sniffed something.'

The dog was drawing great gulps, sucking dust in. It clamoured.

The other lad said, 'Good dog!'

'Aye, she's keen,' said the first. 'Isn't that where the minks lived?'

'They've long since gone,' said the man. 'It's several years since mink lived there.' He drew his coat on, reflecting. 'The year old Poacher packed in, that was it, his last summer.' He saw the doubt on their faces. 'I'm not *that* thick,' he exclaimed. 'I know a mink when I see one.'

They nodded, granting the point. He would have seen the mink hunting; the creatures moved during the day and he was down there so often.

The scrawny lad rolled his eyes. 'Perhaps *it's* in there, the killer.'

'Nah,' his pal drawled, 'it's rabbits. There's rabbit fur on that brick. There's plenty of them around. He's got them in those foundations. We'll let the dog dig.'

'You won't.' The engineer stepped in firmly. 'I've got that grass looking trim. She'll make the bloody hole bigger.'

They yanked the dog from the wall. It stood and quivered, its hair up. 'Tell you what then, how's this: we'll stick a ferret in for you. We've still got Poacher's old ferrets. You don't want rabbits to breed, they'll *really* dig up the works. We'll bring the ferrets and clear them.'

'When?'

'One day, before dawn.'

'You two loafers?'

'We'll call you!'

The wind came out of the blue, the sky bright and deceiving. Above the hills to the south great white clouds puffed their chests. They had a matronly air, dignified and benign while below the wind rampaged. When the woodlands were bare it blew through them unchecked, but now dense leaf blocked its progress. Like men o' war under sail, brakes and copses did battle.

On the slopes oak trees tossed, the ash swayed, its boughs bending. Cracks and groans came from spinneys; arms snapped, hanging broken. In the thick of the fray leafy twigs hit the ground and white wounds flashed on branches. The birch poles squeaked as they lashed, grinding one on the next; and where pines marched in ranks the weak lurched, caught by comrades.

Round the barn the gusts swirled, plucking straws out of bales and ballooning tarpaulin. Dusty earth flew from paths and scattered over the fields. In the yard whirlwinds formed; sheets of tin roofing clattered. A heavy door swung and creaked. Now and then it crashed loudly. There was scant sign of life save for the wind's living presence.

A nose appeared by a gatepost. Not far off lay a plough, out of work for the season. The weasel ran to the plough and hid under its shares, then peered out, the nose questing. The yard was foreign to Brat and he viewed it with interest. Vast and shabby ahead, the old barn moaned and rattled. As the door banged, he bristled.

'What's the game?'

Brat glanced up. Two grey heads topped a gutter. 'What's the game?' said the first. 'You're off bounds,' chirped the second. Flit and Farthing stared down, the gusty air at their tails so their underplumes fluttered. 'This is Kine's patch,' said Flit, 'you're off bounds on this manor.'

Farthing brightened. 'It's Brat!' He nudged Flit.

'So it is.'

'*There's* a thing . . .'

'Would you ever?'

A boisterous draught howled them down, eddying round the building. On the ridge at the back a bunch of heifers cavorted, kicking out, their heads tossing. A hare got up, loping off, and they paused to snort at it.

Brat looked at the sparrows. He said, 'I'm not here for trouble.'

'You're not?' said Flit, disappointed.

'We'd hoped,' said Farthing, 'you might be. It's good rumbustious weather.'

'Fighting weather,' Flit added. He watched the yard's rubbish flying. Above the copse young rooks struggled, oaring hard to stay put. 'You wouldn't care for a dust-up?'

Brat frowned, his coat windblown. He looked vexed by the question.

'No,' cheeped Farthing, 'you wouldn't. I don't suppose your friend Bald-ear . . .?'

'He's not my friend,' answered Brat. He smiled, amused by their glumness. 'He might, though. Bald-ear's a brawler; he's always good for a barney. In the orchard, he might.'

'We'd not get Kine to the orchard.'

'Then you're unlucky,' laughed Brat.

'We missed the fight of a lifetime.' Flit shrugged. 'Now he's matchless. That's our luck! You're all scared.'

It drew a grunt of disdain.

'They'll not face him,' said Farthing.

A plastic sack crossed the yard. Wind-tormented, it bulged, writhing out through the gate as though rats tussled in it. The strong young weasel said, 'Scared? Nothing ever scared Bald-ear. He's not the brightest of sprites but he'd take on a milk cart.'

'What of Scoter?'

'He's sharp. I've fought Scoter, he's quick. Don't tell Scoter he's frightened – and don't tell *me*! We don't frighten. The weasel kind doesn't flinch.' Brat's tail twitched. He said sharply, 'It's well you're up in that gutter. Come down *here* with your insults.'

'No offence meant,' chirped Farthing. 'It's just that Kine has excelled.'

'Granted,' Brat allowed coolly. 'Kine's a master, I'll grant. All the same, no one's frightened. I'd have fought him before; now there's no decent reason. Clary's made up her mind.'

'Ah,' said Flit, 'but you're *here*.'

'Yes, to check that she's settled.' A cloud of dust stung Brat's face. 'You see, we always lived close, both grew up in the orchard. I'd like to know she's all right.'

'Well, of course . . .'

'You could tell me.'

'Could we?' Farthing dissembled.

Flit looked artful. 'Who knows? Hard to say,' he lied gravely. 'Better, Brat, that *you* ask her.'

'Kine might mind.'

Farthing beamed. 'Kine? Why should he?' he simpered. 'You mean no harm, Brat, we'll take you. We'll brave the storm, Brat, how's that? We'd like to be there, eh Flit?'

'Be a privilege,' Flit said. 'Couldn't ask for more, Farthing.' A fight arranged just like that! 'Wouldn't miss it,' he promised.

The tempest howled, the door crashing. Rusty downpipes were fluting. The wind had numerous voices. They droned and piped with wild mischief. '*Brat's been warned*,' proclaimed one and Kine stepped from the dust storm.

'Perfect timing,' hissed Flit.

Farthing quivered. 'Eureka!'

They watched the weasels square up. Straws took flight, whirling round them. Scraps of Brat's protest drifted. 'Kine, I came here in peace . . . I've no argument with you.'

'I'm not *arguing*, Brat.'

'Kine, it's truce . . .'

'Run or fight!'

'*Fight*,' the birds chirped together.

Kine looked up and Brat sprang. 'If we must . . .' He drove fiercely. Locked together, they rolled, fur on end, dust-enveloped. Grit flew by as they fought; wind-tossed leaves spun and hurtled. In the gale's frenzied eye the small animals struggled.

'Kine to win!' Flit was thrilled.

'Fight! Fight! Fight!' twittered Farthing.

'Stop,' a third voice commanded. A snarling form passed the gate, a typhoon, and they hushed. Clary charged at the brawlers. 'Fools,' she cried, 'stop at once!'

Startled, Kine and Brat paused. 'Fools!' she snapped, jaws agape. They stood back. 'It's disgraceful. You're worse than Bald-ear,' she blazed. 'The pair of you are thick-headed. I've told you, Kine, Brat's a friend. And Brat, things here are fine. You'd better listen and learn. I'm not having *this* nonsense.'

They looked ashamed.

Clary turned. 'As for them – those two birds . . .'

Flit and Farthing had vanished.

* * *

He had left before daylight. 'Go,' the female had yawned, 'I'm not hungry this morning. Hunt alone, I'm not coming.' She was, he thought, still annoyed, for Clary's hunger matched Scrat's, insatiable until then. 'Leave me, Kine, I've got business.'

'You'll need to eat.'

'Kine, get on!'

Kine had looked back as he went. The Tree was dim in the gloom and he had almost returned, oddly dismal without her. A weasel hunts on his own! And so he had for too long, until the advent of Clary. That seemed moments ago and yet, already, he missed her.

Had he become so attached, his young partner so vital? Was Clary's spell so complete? A single foray alone – surely that was no upset! He shook his head, now, bemused. He had been drawn by her charm but there was more, a power in her. She was a force, like the spring. She was the earth and the sap and Kine was young again with her.

The wind had died, the air calm. To the east darkness thinned, the wraith of predawn ascending, and Kine heard a whimper. 'Kine,' the shrew sobbed, 'where are you?' The ground was littered with twigs. A large branch sprawled grotesquely.

'Kine . . .' wailed Scrat.

'Over here.'

The dwarf clambered the debris. He was soiled, his coat matted. 'Kine, it's bad!'

'The gale's passed.'

'Not the gale, Kine, far worse. Far, far worse – a disaster. I saw it, Kine, on the marsh.'

'Hush, keep still . . .'

The owl ghosted. On silent wings, it swept by, fading into the dimness. Twice each day the owl prowled, dusk and dawn, seldom missing; and twice each day dropped two pellets, one small and one large, the grisly chaff of its victims.

'He's gone,' said Kine. 'What disaster?'

'A terror,' Scrat breathed, 'a fiend – a demon worse than the dragon. I saw it plain by the moon, Hob of frog lore, a monster. Kine, he's crazed, a berserker.'

82

'That's enough.' It was terse. Kine had heard all he wished. He had tried hard to forget, to dismiss the pond nightmare. Irate at being reminded, he cursed the dwarf. 'Frogs – frog gossip!'

'But Kine, I saw him. I saw him kill the buck rabbit.'

The weasel scowled. 'A mere rabbit.'

'We'll *all* be killed.' The shrew blinked. A caterpillar looped by, a refugee of the winds, succulent and green-bodied. Scrat's jaws snapped and he chomped. 'Hob the Night Lord, we're doomed!'

Kine was tense.

'Dead,' the shrew howled. 'A fiend from the past, Kine!'

'*Quiet!*' It burst from the weasel. 'I mean,' Kine hastened, 'let's think. Calm down, Scrat, and think clearly, don't make too much ado, the brute may only be passing. Just passing by, like as not. The thing is, Scrat, to keep cool.'

'C-cool?' Scrat whimpered. 'We'll all be killed by the demon. Not even Kine can fight this.'

'I think we ought to stay mum.'

'Doom and woe!'

'Avoid panic. I'll keep it under review. We don't want general alarm. We won't say anything, midget.'

'J-just warn Clary.'

'*Nobody.*' Least of all, Kine mused, Clary. 'We don't want Clary to fret. Tell her, shrew, and you'll rue it.'

Already Clary was vexed. The truth would damn him completely. Confess the dragon was myth, the *real* terror still prowling – how could he face her with that? She would leave, her faith shattered. The valley creatures would scorn him.

He ought to kill the shrew now. Scrat was hopeless, a blabber, and yet Kine pitied the dwarf, his most constant admirer. Besides, he did pick up news. Scrat moved round overlooked; he saw things and heard talk.

'Listen, Scrat, you can scout. I'll give you leave to scout for me.'

'Scout?' Scrat blinked.

'You could do it.'

The dwarf looked up, his tail rising. 'S-scout for Kine?'

'You'd *be* someone.'

'I'd be a scout!' The mite strutted. 'I'd be a hero's assistant.
I'd bring reports . . .'

'To Kine, shrewmouse; to no one else.'

'They'd be secret.'

'Between the two of us,' Kine said.

On pigmy legs, the shrew paced. 'I'd be a hero myself.'

'If you kept quiet, earned my trust.'

'I'd k-keep mum.'

'You're appointed!'

A phantom early light glimmered, the land's shadows
stirring. The gloom was eerily silent. Woods stood out in grey
mist, advancing dimly in lines from the murk the marsh
harboured. 'Mum's the word,' hissed the weasel. 'A scout who
blabs is dead, shrewmouse. I'm going to sniff round the pump.'

'The p-pump . . .?'

'Keep in contact.'

The dyke was dark still, reed-shadowed, and Kine trod with
caution. He respected the marsh path. Down that track they
had charged, old-time heroes and martyrs, but they had
ventured by day – as of now, dawn was dragging. Until the
gloom quit the marsh even heroes stole lightly. '*Quack!*' A
duck sprang abruptly. It went straight up with a whirr and Kine
jumped, his heart throbbing.

The brick redoubt stood up darkly. He could smell the
mown grass and he paused. It was dewy. The river purled,
smooth and grey. No other sound reached his ears, and,
curious, he slipped forward until the wall stopped him. The
tunnel's entrance was close. It was as black as a crow and, if the
place had been used, the scent was cold. It was fusty.

Had Scrat imagined the terror? A lone frog croaked and was
quiet. The frogs might sing for the shrew but they had no
message for Kine. They had no liking of weasels. He sniffed
the hole and stepped in. It was a shrine, the old vault, a place of
weasel remembrance. He felt the spirits were with him.

But all the same he went slowly. At every twist of the
labyrinth he stopped, his nose probing. A whiff of carrion met
him, a smell that strengthened until, deep inside the foundations, he came on the rabbit. It was a large one, half-eaten.
He arched his spine. Scrat's buck rabbit!

'*Tchkkk*,' he spat, drawing back.

A surge of anger possessed him. There was, as well, a chill fear, a cold and crawling revulsion, but outrage was foremost. He felt the past was defiled, and he spat again in disgust as the Blood Fury gripped him.

He loathed the beast who had been there. No longer could he forget, for this was weaseldom mocked and *that* there was no forgetting. This was a weasel shrine sullied. Consumed by wrath, the sprite stomped. His fiery tantrum was brief but, for its space, so intense – a kind of feverish trance – Kine lost sense of all danger.

Outside, someone said, 'Right, then.'

Another cussed. 'The brute brute bit me.'

'Mag's keen.'

'Flaming stroppy.'

Kine listened. He knew them. 'Well, stick her in,' said the big youth, 'let's find out if they're down there. She'll shift them, will Mag.'

There was a sound at the hole.

'By heck, it's parky, this mist.' There was mumbling. 'I'd just as soon be in bed still.' There was a snuffling grunt and something moved in the labyrinth.

The weasel swore, easing back. It was pitch-dark in the vault, no escape save the tunnel. He felt his rump touch the side. It was of riveted steel. The sound of snuffling was louder. Above the reek of the corpse there was a fresh scent now. Ferret. The creature hissed.

'Who's there?' Mag said.

Compared with Kine, she was huge. He held still and said nothing. She had, he knew, reached the bunker; he sensed her snout, questing, vicious. She was of evil repute. While other ferrets were fair, pink of eye and lethargic, Mag was dusky, ill-tempered.

'Who's there?' She had stopped.

She had, Kine guessed, found the rabbit. If Mag was hungry she might be tempted to gorge. At least the thing would distract her. He braced and sprang in the dark. As he shot past, their fur brushed, then he was jinking away, weaseling through the tomb, racing on till dawn met him.

At the exit, he paused, the moist grass flecked with highlights. The youths were somewhere outside, perhaps with dogs or a gun. The choice was them or black Mag and Kine knew which was safer. Drawing breath, he rushed out.

It took three bounds to be clear, reach the tufts of the marsh, whereupon he was hidden. The waiting lads barely glimpsed him.

When Ploughman passed an hour later the youths were on their knees, cursing. 'We lost a ferret,' swore one. 'Flaming Mag won't come out.'

Ploughman joined them, lips pursing. 'She's no good, I told Poacher; she's wild that black devil.' He put his face to the hole, making small, squeaky noises. His colour rose. 'She'll be gorging. She's useless, that one, she kills 'em. Did any bolt?'

'Not a sign.' They scowled. 'She'd come for Poacher, the cow. We should've had a line on her. We put the other down after; that soon came back. Not the black 'un.'

'She'll gorge then sleep.' Ploughman straightened. He held his side, the pain sharp. 'She won't be out before evening. You'd best come back.' The man grimaced.

'You all right?'

'I'm all right.' He paused then said, 'If it suits her. I always said she'd go feral. I told him, "That one's no good. She'll be away one fine day."'

The big lad said, 'And small loss! I'm not returning this evening – I'll have my head down.'

'I'll find her.' The slighter youth had a conscience. 'She'd do some damage, run wild.'

'She'd only kill a few rabbits.'

'And the rest!'

'Aye,' growled Ploughman. 'I'll be along here tonight, there's hay to spin. I'll watch out. If she runs wild you'll not catch her. If she turns feral I'll shoot her.'

Climbing up from the marsh, Kine drew into the hedge. He felt drained, not by flight but by impotent outrage, his sense of horror and wrath; most of all, the frustration. No wonder Scrat was dismayed, since Hob alarmed even Kine. The shrinedefiler was death, invincible in their midst, alien beyond knowledge.

Kine the fox-taunter shuddered. There was no beast in the vale equipped to stop the berserker, obstruct its rampage. The only hope Kine could see was that the creature might leave, drawn by whim whence it came – for all he knew to the moon or some planet of darkness.

Meanwhile, Clary concerned him.

She must in fairness be warned but how much should he tell her? No need to go the whole way, confess that Hob killed the eel, that would be degrading. The so-called dragon was history.

The pond had been Clary's worry. No need to stir up *those* waters, for Hob was not a pond-dweller. He might kill eels and take geese, but many places had eels, not least the marsh, thought the sprite, while geese did not haunt the covert. Nowhere in nature was safe but Kine could claim the pond *safer*. There were more dangerous places.

At all events, Kine must not alarm Clary. He could not bear that she leave and, musing now in the hedge, resolved to break the news gently. So long as Scrat did not blab.

He found the shrew in the ditch. 'The rabbit's there, Scrat,' he growled. 'I penetrated the bunker.'

'Kine is fearless!'

'Listen. The ravager had gone out and we need to know where he goes. I want his movements reported. I'm posting you to the marsh.'

'The m-marsh?'

'Yes.' Kine nodded. A decent distance from Clary!

'But K-Kine . . .'

'Scout the levels, talk to frogs, stay there, Scrat. I'll make contact, don't worry.'

'Doom,' wailed Scrat. 'Not the marsh!'

'Scouting orders.'

'I'll perish.'

'Your first assignment,' snapped Kine. 'A chance to prove you're a scout. A chance to show you're a hero.'

'Woe,' moaned Scrat.

'A shrew legend!'

'A *legend*, Kine?'

'You can do it.'

* * *

'You're still here, Clary?'

'Of course.'

Kine sprang onto the Life Tree.

He said, 'I've been on the marsh. I went as far as the pump. There's something you should know, Clary.'

'Kine, I've something to show you.'

'Then show me first,' he replied, glad enough to be silenced. He feared the female's reaction.

She was at present serene, as undisturbed as the pool whose pacific brow twinkled. Leaves of lilies had surfaced and pond crowfoot was flowering. The little blooms raised bright eyes, gently twitched by small fishes. A swimming grass snake coiled by, yellow throat above water.

Clary stood by the den. 'Look inside, I've made changes.'

Her mate peered in. It smelled fresh. She had cleared out the old dross, let the floor take an airing. A cosy bed, clean and dry, had been made in the lair, thick with leaves and soft grasses. He said with awe, 'You've been busy. I haven't seen such a bed, not since Kia . . .' He held back.

'Go on, Kine, it's all right.'

'Not since Kia had her kitts.'

'Aren't you pleased?'

'It's fine, Clary, the finest nursery I've seen.'

Watchman scowled, perched above them. Kine was a fool – at *his* age! The rook squinted.

Kine looked out at the reeds. A moorhen's nest was complete, piled with twigs, the hen sitting. A crimson damsel-fly dived and dipped its tail in the water. Kine said, 'It slipped out, I'm sorry. I didn't mean to raise Kia.'

'Kine, I'm pleased, don't feel bad. I've come to terms with all that. I'll think of Kia as a friend and try to match what she gave you.'

'A nest of dandies,' he said.

'Sons for Kine,' said the female.

88

'Dancing daughters,' Kine added.

A brood of braggarts, thought Watchman, a clutch of uppity sprites. As if the world needed weasels!

'She'd be happy,' said Kine. 'If Kia could know, she'd be happy.'

'Perhaps she is,' pondered Clary.

He eyed her fondly. 'Perhaps.' And then he said, 'How long is it?'

'Not long now.'

'Bah,' growled Watchman.

'It's perfect weather,' said Kine. 'A weasel tribe by the pond, a pack of dandy hounds, Clary! They'll be the best.'

Watchman glowered.

'Fearless hunters,' dreamed Kine. 'They'll learn the signs and the seasons, the woods and coombes, weasel places. They'll learn the ways of the wild. Why, they'll inherit the valley!' He viewed the scene, his gaze proud. The grass was tall as a child – the cottage-child – dog rose opening; the song of skylarks incessant. The air was thick, sweet with hay, drenched with elder and thyme, harbingers of full summer.

He lazed a while, doubts forgotten. At length, they nagged and he brooded. 'There's something you should know, Clary.'

'So you said.'

'On the marsh.' He paused, reluctant to tell her. 'A stranger . . . roaming the marsh.'

Her glance was calm, mildly puzzled.

'A strange and crazed beast,' he ventured. 'They call him Hob, or the Night Lord. I have to warn you, he's dangerous.'

She seemed to take the news lightly.

'I'm glad you did, Kine. What species?'

He shook his head. 'I don't know. The brute's an alien breed. You'll take good care, won't you, Clary?'

'Of me *and* them,' she said, beaming.

'You won't go off on your own?'

She laughed. 'I'm *having* the kittens, I'm not a kitten myself, Kine.'

'I want to know that you're safe.'

'With Kine's protection I will be.'

It brought a sneer from the rook. Kine, the shrimp, the bold mouser! Kine the uppity fool!

The lissom female purred softly. 'What stranger's going to face *Kine*?'

'We must be careful, he's strong.'

'Strong?' she said with a laugh.

'And crazed, too.'

'So you say. I know one thing – he can't live up to my mate. This Hob, he's not slayed a dragon. I've got the perfect protector!'

Evening shadows. Voles burrowed. The blunt-nosed beasts mined the garden, digging under the lawn. The child pondered their holes. Ploughman called the beasts 'grass mice' and spoke of vole plagues as the 'mouse years'. It was a fact of the vale that voles abounded at times and were scarce during others.

That year there were many. It was bad news for the lawn but they diverted the child, who liked to watch the plump creatures. Some would sit by their holes, if he was quiet, and munch grass. Their cheeks bulged as they ate. Tonight he saw something else.

Squatting down on his heels, the boy saw Kine leave a hole, take a couple of bounds and dive into another. Then, like a Jack-in-the-box, the weasel popped from the third hole. This time only the neck came, a pointed head peering. Down it went, lost to sight, and the hole-watcher waited.

A moment passed, a fly buzzed, again the weasel's head surfaced. It had moved, now, to new ground and was nearer the toddler. He held his breath as it cranked, a small periscope turning, eyes keen, the throat snowy. '*Tchkkk*,' said Kine, who smelled vole. 'Tell me, plump one, where are you?'

He ducked once more underground. 'Stay and dance!' churred the goblin.

The vole was not without sense. As the hunter went down, it burst from yet one more hole and made with a quick, rolling gait for the hedge round the garden. Seconds later Kine followed. He had his head down, nose working.

'Ma!' the child cried, excited. He ran indoors. 'Ma, the weasel . . .'

90

'Child, it's late,' the girl said. 'Come and wash. It's your bedtime.'

When Kine had gorged he patrolled, vigilant at the woodside. The infant's protests had died, the day gradually closing. The time had come to keep watch, for now the night brigade stirred, its dusky prowlers afoot, and he was anxious for Clary. She had remained at the den. He toured the covert on guard, determined none would disturb her.

Athene bawled, her voice coarse. Smallest of the owl species, the little owl was a foul-mouthed marauder. She glared at Kine from her perch, a pole supporting a powerline. The cable ran by the copse to cross the marsh lower down, its destination the pumphouse.

'And how fares Kine?' screeched Athene. 'Our gallant goblin looks strained. Is she too much for you, sprite?' She blared a few obscene oaths. 'You're far too old to sire brats. I said a young mate would kill you.'

'That's more than *you'll* ever do.'

'Perhaps,' she yelled, 'but just wait. I'll snatch a kitt or two, Kine.'

'I'll see you dead first.'

She laughed. The sound was raucous, indecent. 'You're all tensed up, Kine. Relax. It's not *you* having the brats. I do believe the sprite's scared – I think he's scared of the demon.'

Kine moved on.

The bird swore. 'You're so stuck up but you're no one; you won't be when Hob finds you. If I were you, *I'd* be scared. He'd frighten anyone, Hob would. And, Kine, they say that Mag's prowling.'

'*Tchkkk!*' He swung through the wood.

Athene's hectoring vexed but taunts and oaths drew no blood; it was the stealthy who maimed. The danger signals were quiet: the phantom step of the fox, the white owl's whispering plunge. It was the rule of the wild that bluster captured few suppers.

Kine stopped, his head tilted. Not far away the brook chinked, a mere chuckling sigh, and the animal listened. Already night filled the copse. Within its canopied gloom, dusky columns closed ranks, the dim gloaming excluded.

Something glowed in the trees, a strange light, and Kine puzzled. It had a glimmering life, an oddly luminous soul like a lantern turned low or the night-light's frail wink from the cottage-child's bedroom. It was pale, a weird ghost.

When in a while it had not moved, Kine crept cautiously closer. The glow was raised from the ground, though not at any great height, shimmering near the brook where the garlic had blossomed. The flowers had died, the growth pungent. The weasel wrinkled his nose.

He paused again, in two minds, then stole forward. The light appeared to pulse slightly, an uncanny manifestation, not bright but persistent. At the rill, Kine took stock. There was an elm just ahead, blown askew, old and rotting. Its hollow trunk slanted dimly.

The pulse seemed part of the tree. Indeed, on looking again, he was convinced the elm glowed, the source of power at its heart, a kind of lustrous decay apparent outside the trunk where a large rift had opened. Now, espied from the brook, the luminosity throbbed, unnatural and awesome.

It was a sign, Kine believed, the signal of an event. And when the wood's ceiling drummed, rain descending abruptly, he turned and ran without doubt, for it had rained long ago when Kia's brood had been born and he had never forgotten. The new event was expected.

He reached the pond out of breath.

The deluge fizzed, bouncing on it. Aboard the Tree, he called Clary. 'It's me,' he shouted, 'it's Kine.' The hulk was black, the deck greasy. He stuck his head in the hole. He could just see the female.

'Rain?' she said. His nose dripped. 'Don't get cold, Kine.'

'How are you?'

'I'm fine, we *all* are. Don't wake us!'

Clary suckled four kittens. Blind and naked at first, they seemed unlikely young sprites, though fiercely prized by their dam who attended them closely. When the rooks came to drink, or duck and coot swam too close, she hissed and spat from the Tree. Even Watchman was cautioned.

Then when the kitts scampered out, their coats grown, she

watched strictly. Those who strayed, Clary scolded. Brought to heel by the scruff, they would mewl but soon learned. Lesson one: obey mother.

In time they romped by the pond, Clary never far off. Play brought out innate skills, their swift hops and reactions. With glee they chased after bees or would pounce on each other, or stalk big green-thighed grasshoppers. They took Kine back in his mind to his own bright beginnings.

Things had glittered in those days, the sky perpetually blue dabbed with clouds white as lilies. Every moment had thrilled, filled with vivid sensation: the earthy scent of the fields, hay in swaths and moon daisies, the pop of pods on the gorse, meadowsweet's drifting perfume.

He still remembered exploring, the smell of hot summer tracks, the dried-up ditches and rills, the gem-brilliance of bugs, cardinals, tiger beetles. Clary's kitts sharpened memories – his own small mother's quick tongue, pouting toadflax, cool clover, the flitting cinnabar moths, pink and brown with red patterns.

He had been innocent then, blind to peril and death. Giants had lazed in the shade, indolent and serene – dusty cattle round gates, Ploughman sprawled in a hedge, drowsing over his lunch – the only sound of a noon the sun-song of yellowhammers.

And now the vale shone again, time turned back by the brood, four small sprites and his mate, herself only a youngster. It put fresh spring in Kine's step, renewed pride; his cares vanished. He was, huffed Watchman, a bore, 'and twice as boastful as ever'.

'With five good reasons,' crowed Kine, 'and you have none, rook, not one.' He roamed the copse, his head high. 'Look and envy me, rook, Kine the hunter has issue!'

'Problems,' grunted the rook.

'Inheritors!'

'Mewling headaches.'

'Future heroes, bright dancers. Kine the legend is potent.'

'Watch your step, shrimp, you're old, an old fool with delusions.'

Clary stayed with the kitts. At times she played in the glade, tolerant of their pranks, letting one tug her tail or several climb on her back. They knew how far they could go and were nipped when too brash. At other times she would nap, half an eye on their games.

Once, alerted by screams, she jumped up, her heart racing. The kitts had cornered a shrew, making small growling noises through diminutive milk teeth. 'Stop molesting the beast.' She dispersed them. 'It's Scrat.'

The dwarf shrieked.

'Calm down, Scrat.'

'It's an ambush!'

'They're playing, shrew, it's all right. You were stupid to come here.'

'Stupid?' Scrat wailed. 'Where's Kine?' The kitts growled. 'Doom,' he whimpered.

Clary frowned. 'Let him be. Kine's away, Scrat. What's up?'

'He promised me he'd make contact.'

'Scrat, he's busy, we both are.'

'B-busy?' Scrat moaned. 'It's urgent!'

'You'd best come back.'

'My report . . .'

'What report?'

Mum's the word, Scrat remembered.

* * *

Ploughman's wicket gate creaked and he saw the girl enter, the child trotting with her.

'Here,' he called from the porch, 'come and listen to this. Hush,' he said, an ear cocked, and he tapped the wood lightly. Several rapid taps answered.

The farm man said, 'Deathwatch beetle, you know what that means? A death – someone's on the way out.' His brow dropped. 'Some poor wretch.'

'Poor old dad,' the girl drawled, an arm crooked through her basket. 'And only you in the household.'

'With my back,' he said, cringing.

'I've told you, dad, see the doctor.'

'Working dawn until dusk? When can *I* see a doctor? The quack did Poacher no good, he was dead in a twelvemonth.'

'Dad,' his daughter replied, 'Poacher's problem was different. Deathwatch beetle, indeed! Every summer it knocks; it's a love call, that's all.'

'It ought to have my back trouble.' He eyed the child, who looked thoughtful.

'Can a beetle knock, granpa?'

'Yes,' the girl answered for him. 'It bangs its head on the wood, like your granddad's needs banging. Old men are so stubborn! He needs some physio treatment – and a rest from that tractor. Dad, it's time you retired, you can't slog on forever.'

He glowered at her, his face set. 'I'd have nothing to live for.'

'Of course you would.' She glanced round. Things were looking neglected. Several wall tiles had gone, smashed to bits on the path, and the roses had wilted. He used to cosset his roses. 'You'd have the garden, the poultry.'

He turned and stumped to the huts. 'I can't dig, it's the pain. All I've got is a goose, one blamed friend, and she's threatened. There's something prowling at night.'

'Then take care,' the girl told him.

'I'll give it care if I catch it; I'll give it five-shot,' he mumbled.

'Did the youths find the ferret?'

'Those two lummocks? They'll not recapture that Mag. Bred from polecats, them dark ones.'

'What's a polecat?' the child asked.

Ploughman stopped. 'Not what *you* think.' He stoked his pipe and blew smoke. 'Not a pussy, my lad, a fierce beast, or it was. There's none left, not round here.'

'Were they killed?'

'Like wolves, laddie.'

The goose had joined them and honked.

The man said, 'Poacher went sudden . . .'

'But he was bad, dad, you're not. If you're so bad,' said the girl, 'how come you've managed to scythe?'

'I've not scythed.'

'You've been and scythed round mum's grave.'

'Oh, the grave.'

'I was there.'

'They don't look after the churchyard.'

'You might've trimmed round old Poacher.'

'He'd not've thanked me, the tramp. Besides, my back.'

'See the doctor. Do you want any shopping?'

The girl and child walked away, soon engulfed by the lane, its green walls high above them. 'Poacher's grave!' the man grumbled. He heard their voices trail off then it was quiet, the goose watchful. It understood him, the goose. 'More'n some do,' he muttered.

Flit and Farthing flew briskly. As they followed the hedge they met the engineer's van heading up past the copse, its two-way radio crackling. The driver's window was down, a tanned elbow protruding. Summer lightning flashed somewhere. Rain had passed, the fields moist, steaming gently in sunshine.

'That was needed,' chirped Flit.

Farthing swerved. 'The air's clearer. A nice clean day for a brawl.'

'Shall we go to the pump?'

'Mag was loose there, I heard.'

'Mag?' said Flit, changing heart. 'We could stop at the oak tree.'

'Right.' They shifted their course. At the marsh gate they wheeled, stubby wings set for landing. A stunted oak stood nearby and Flit picked out a branch. Farthing touched down beside him. There was a bees' nest below, in a nook at the base. Furry mites came and went, their soft humming incessant. 'This will do.'

The birds preened. Some way off, the pump roared, water slithered. 'Yes,' cheeped Farthing, 'it's shady. Not that I was afraid . . .'

'Of the pump? Nor I,' Flit said.

'*You* suggested the tree.'

'You agreed. I'm not frightened.'

'Nor am I, not of Mag. I'm not frightened of *Hob*.'

'You're a liar.'

'I'll fight you!'

They tumbled down to the path, tussling on the moist ground. Feathers flew and they squawked, rolling over together. Ignoring them, the bees droned. At length the birds drew apart, wings outstretched and plumes soiled, beak to beak as they tired.

'Want some more?'

'Do *you* want some?'

'Wait!' cried Flit.

They looked up.

A dark column had loomed as black as smuts from a fire, towering over the oak, a great host of rooks winging. Strident *caws* rang and echoed.

'It's the Dread,' observed Flit.

Farthing said, 'Best break off.'

They took flight, rising steeply. Back again on the branch the pair shook, aggravated. Heads cocked, they watched sourly. 'A decent scrap spoiled,' chirped Farthing. 'When I was winning.'

'When *I* was!'

'What's *that*?' The birds froze. 'Hush,' said Farthing.

Overhead the rooks bawled. The black army had spread, its rout spanning the marsh, splitting now into groups which flapped round, disconcerted. Flit and Farthing were tense. The sparrows peered at the grass in which something was struggling. A crippled wing beat the turf. A maimed rook threshed and lurched. It was the lookout's ex-spouse, she of rancorous temper. Mag the ferret had seized her.

They heard a crunch. Mag's grip tightened.

'One less rook.' Flit stared grimly.

'Is she dead?'

The wing twitched. It fascinated the sparrows.

'We could buzz down.'

'And mob *Mag*?'

'A quick swoop.'

'Wait,' said Farthing.

A dusky form passed their perch. Watchman pitched on the marsh gate. Bill agape, he cawed loudly. 'Mag,' he croaked, hopping forward, landing deep in the grasses. 'Watch your eye, Mag, watch Watchman.' His wings were splayed, his beak raked. 'An eye,' he wheezed, 'for an eye. Let her go, Mag, don't do it.'

'He'll be next,' muttered Flit. 'He'll be mangled, the dotard.'

'Scragged and plucked,' agreed Farthing. 'And for what? His spouse left him.'

Watchman flapped, hopping stiffly, a bleary eye on the ferret. The crippled wing had grown stiff, a black sail, its mast broken.

'It's too late now.' Flit was glum. 'A poor scrap. Ours was better.'

'Let's protest!'

'I'm for that.'

Farthing sprang. 'Keep together.'

They launched themselves from the tree and flew wing tip to wing tip. 'Ready, comrade?' They dived. At full power, they pulled out, clipping dandelion heads, passing Watchman at speed, making Mag duck and curse before climbing and turning. 'That was telling her,' Flit cried. 'It was Mag spoiled our dust-up.'

'And again?'

Flit's wings waggled.

They made a couple more swoops then gained height, cruising over. Mag had vanished from view. All they saw, peering down, were drag marks in the grass and a few scattered black feathers. Below them Watchman was airborne.

'We made a gesture,' said Flit.

Farthing chirped. 'I feel better.'

'So will Mag when's she gorged.'

Watchman climbed, oaring slowly.

'Nasty mess,' called the sparrows. They banked and flew alongside him. Flit said, 'Don't feel bad, Watchman, she's no loss. She was faithless.'

'A harridan,' observed Farthing. 'You took a risk for her, Watchman.'

'Did you see them?' the rook said. 'The others fled, her smart friends.' His wings creaked as he lumbered. 'Her smart young friends, did you see?' He nursed a bleak satisfaction. 'I hope she noticed, the harlot; I hope she watched them fly off, saw them scuttle in fright, put to shame by mere sparrows.'

'*Mere* sparrows?'

'Low brawlers.'

'Who's he calling low brawlers?' They broke formation, indignant. 'The senile fool,' spluttered Flit.

'The old ragbag,' flung Farthing.

Watchman's wings missed a beat. He fell through air then limped on, alone now, flapping feebly.

'Curse the bawd,' howled the rook, 'she had no right – not to die. She could've taken heed sooner. She had no right to be caught. She had a sheen like the moon, the moon on water,' he sobbed. 'Her eyes were gems, stars of lust. She was the spirit of life, she was peerless, unrivalled. She should've flown when I cawed. She should've listened . . .'

His voice broke.

'*Brek,*' the frogs called. '*Kroax-kroax.*' But to Kine, they said nothing. All he heard by the dykes was the plop as they dived, after which it was quiet. They distrusted the weasel.

You could not pinpoint a marsh frog, its ventriloquial voice baffled. It had a camouflaged skin hard to spot on the banks, harder still in the swill, the dykes spangled with duckweed. '*Brek,*' it croaked and was gone – somewhere, everywhere, nowhere.

Kine lay low by the pump, tired of seeking informers. From the covering reeds he could make out the wall, the dark hole to the labyrinth. Was Hob there? Had he gone? The weasel settled to watch. He could not rest for not knowing.

He thought of Clary, the kitts; he had to plan for their safety. The time would come when they roamed, left the Life Tree to hunt, to be taught by their mother. She must not lead them to peril; he had to know what was happening.

Nose alert, he stole forward. As he did the rooks panicked. The Dread was not to be scorned and, scuttling back to the reeds, Kine peered out, taut and watchful. There was a splash at his back. A fish had jumped in the dyke and he cursed, his nerves twitchy.

'*Pssst!*'

He turned, again startled.

'Pssst,' said Scrat, who was trembling. 'Over here, Kine, it's me.'

Kine's neck craned. 'Where've you been?'

'Where've *I* been? I searched for you. I thought you said you'd make contact.'

'I was delayed. I'm here now.'

'Doom,' piped Scrat, 'I'm not stopping, not *here*. It's the Dread . . .'

Weasel claws pinned his tail. 'A scout's bold, Scrat, be still.'

'You don't know what it's been like. I've spent nights on the marsh.'

'I'm proud of you,' Kine said.

'Making contact with frogs.' Scrat sat up, his chest rising. 'I met frogs in their haunts, where they hide. That's not easy.'

'Yes, yes. What's their news?'

'Would you say I'm a hero?'

'Almost, shrew. Your report?'

'Kine, it's bad, a bad story.'

'Well?'

'The f-frogs sing of doom.'

'Frogs exaggerate, Scrat.'

'A *bad* tale . . .'

'Tell me, shrewmouse.'

* * *

'A few nights back, at the pump, an act of devilry happened, a ceremony so base, so appalling in portent that the bats quit the marsh and the dykes themselves quivered. The sky was puce, rent by storms; prodigious fireballs descended. They made the pumphouse stand out, a citadel of dark power, spreading fear amid sedge, among rushes and bents, across clod, quag and rill until the snakes themselves fled and every merrow was spellbound. Not since Gru prowled the vale had the hour seemed so evil.'

So began the frogs' story. Nervously, Scrat continued.

'The frogs had jumped in the swill. They kept their heads out to watch, mesmerised by sheer dread so that all down the dykes, by the banks in the murk, pairs of amber eyes shone and throats gulped, pale and throbbing. Hob had towered by the pump. Every fearful orb stared. Hob the Night Lord loomed tall, a large frog in his mouth, its long legs splayed and limp. As the storm leaped and glared, so his crazed shadow danced until, suddenly still, the fiend lowered his head and stretched out his cold victim.

100

'Then, a foot on the corpse, he tore off its rear limbs. Hob the butcher ate neither. Instead, he left the three joints – the two legs and the rest – on the grass by the pump, each a little apart in what seemed to the frogs a strange, macabre device, a kind of gory triangle. It was, as they would perceive, a grim symbol of doom, signifying three terrors.'

The Unholy Alliance

'For barely had the bolts passed, flashing now round the hills where they twitched like white flame, than two creatures joined Hob hovering near the pumphouse. One was Mag, a squat shade, dim, voracious and sly, undismayed by Hob's presence. The other, perched on the pump, was familiar and feared, the sharp-taloned Athene.'

Scrat paused, rolling his eyes, then went on:

'They consumed the frog slowly. For quite a time they cracked bones and tore flesh, lost a while in the dark or, when the far lightning glared, cast in garish relief, a nightmarish triumvirate – a frenzied brute from the past, a cruel and fugitive ferret, the little witch of an owl with her loud, obscene screeches. Each ate a third of the frog, strong claws clasping its tissue, and each declaimed as it did so.'

Three Tirades

'Hob's tirade was the worst. Through greasy lips he exclaimed, "I am Hob of the Night and the vale is Hob's kingdom. My kind were here before Man, countless centuries before, and he has taken my rights, exterminated my kin, sought my death through the land. I have returned for revenge. It will be violent and crazed, a bitter blight on the vale, on all who flourished and bred while we, the rightful, were crushed. It will be merciless, savage."'

The frogs could not hear it all. There was a lot more besides, but by now Mag was ranting.

'She had suffered as well, bred and held in a cage, a mere serf, skills exploited. "It might suit some," ranted Mag, "the pink-eyed and the dim; Mag is not such a ferret. There's berserker blood in her, the blood of Hob, and she's vicious. Now she hunts for herself, kills in freedom, is fearsome." She sucked a bone and glared round. When lightning flashed, she looked up and her sharp eyes were wicked.

'Athene's rage was so gross, so unrepeatably coarse, that the frogs skipped the worst, a grudge held against nature. "Whee-yoo," she bawled, full of hate, "death and pain to the favoured, so cries stunted Athene, death to all blessed with graces." The small witch bounced in her rage, bobbing up and down, swearing. "Kill and kill!" she demanded.'

The Pledge

'Each frog gulped as it watched, each wide pair of eyes goggled. Then, the ritual meal done, Hob reared up by the pump which had churned as they ate, tossing spume, sloshing water. Its cavern seethed as it stopped, a sound that pleased the berserker. When it died, the fiend rasped, "The time has come for the pledge, the three vows of revenge." Whereon the brutes became quiet and each declared in its fashion:

" 'I forswear all compassion."

" 'I pledge violence and terror."

" 'By my oath, hate will reign until blood chokes the valley."

'Such were the vows of the crazed. There was a terrible pause. The frogs could hear the owl cackling. In the hills thunder tolled, its knell dim on the marsh where a mourning stream droned, its flow cold in black banks. Drooping reed pennons flinched. A hundred frogs, scared to blink, froze as if dead already.'

Here, Scrat's voice became hoarse.

'It's not a nice tale at all. I wish I'd never been told it.'

'Go on,' Kine rapped, 'go on.'

'The small owl . . .'

'Yes, don't stop!'

'The small owl gave a screech. "What's the plan, Hob?" she bawled. "Whee-yoo, where do we start?" Hob regarded her grimly. He must have had it worked out, for he told her at once. "On the marsh, on the frogs. First we plunder the marsh, then the slopes, the man's holding. Terrorise the man's poultry, kill his goose, the old fool. Bring the copse to subjection." That appealed to Athene. "Yes," she screeched, "seize the copse, deal with Kine, smash the weasel. Kill them all, all the weasels!" '

Here the tale stopped abruptly.

'Doom,' croaked Scrat, 'we're all doomed.'

Kine was quiet.

'*Tchkkk*,' he answered. 'If it's true,' he sneered lamely. 'If it isn't invention.' The doubt was false, a feigned hope – the frogs were not that inventive. The real untruth was his own, a lie adopted and used, a myth now coming to roost, red of claw, three times hateful: three times threatening his mate, their small and innocent offspring.

As Kine returned to the wood glossy buttercups shone, sky-blue chicory blossomed. On the track up the slope a pair of turtledoves sunned and small red-splashed birds paused, the first linnets of summer. Life seemed rosy and bright – a bright but maggoty apple.

Glancing back at the marsh he saw a young cuckoo pass, its foster parents in train. The pair of small birds were dwarfed, hypnotised by the giant, the deceiver they cherished. And was not Kine an imposter? He heard the little owl laugh, a chill shriek, and marched on, his step urgent.

Turning into the copse, Kine could hear the kitts squealing. He knew each small, joyful squeak, each excited inflection. The elves would be by the pond, pleased to see him as always. Often Kine watched them play, sometimes joined them in romping. Now each sound stabbed his heart, every happy sound numbing. With his burden of news, could he face Clary bravely?

For a moment he stopped, then moved on and they mobbed him. One, the boldest young sprite, grabbed his neck and hung on, full of mischievous growling. He shook it off, the act brusque, and heard Clary say firmly, 'Come here, Growler, be still. Show respect, Kine is weary.'

She turned her head, her eyes warm, her summer livery brilliant. She was a picture, he thought, more mature than before, with more grace since the kitts than the pert orchard female. 'Settle down, now, and play. Just let Kine rest a moment.'

The small quartet hunted bees then watched a butterfly pass, its wings buff, leopard-spotted. They chased it down to the pond then the fritillary lost them. Insects buzzed among foxgloves; flowers of bramble were out, white on dense, tangled growth, some as large as hedge roses. Kine felt Clary's shrewd gaze and tried to summon his courage.

A warbler sang, soft in cadence.

'Well?' she prompted at length.

He looked up. 'It's bad, Clary. Hob and Mag have joined forces.' He dragged it out. 'And Athene. An evil league to shed blood, sworn to mayhem and death, to despoil and cause havoc.' He hesitated. 'It's grim. I fear the covert's endangered.' He watched the kitts as they romped. 'You'll have to move them at once; they can't stay, it's too risky.'

The female frowned. 'Leave the Tree?'

'While you can; at once, Clary.'

'It *must* be bad,' she said calmly.

'It's critical – before dark.'

'Can't the Tree be defended?' Her tone was matter of fact. 'Can't we stand guard together? Kine, remember the snake: we soon dealt with that danger.'

'A snake's a snake, these are demons. You haven't heard the frogs' story. This is devilry, Clary.'

'I'm not afraid.'

'You've not seen them. Hob's a fiend, a crazed fiend. Mag's as strong as three weasels and the little witch adds her spells. It's a deadly alliance.' Every hero of old would have blanched at such force, even Kine in his prime. It was more baneful than Gru, more envenomed than Rattun.*

'The dragonslayer will save us.'

'Don't keep saying that, Clary.'

'It's true,' she said.

Her mate groaned. 'It isn't true, it is *not*. Never was, never, never . . .' It seemed to rise from his gut. 'I never slew any dragon, never fought one or slew one. There never was a pond dragon. There was an eel and Hob killed it. I watched them fight. It was Hob.' He felt smaller but purged.

'You lied?' Clary said quietly.

'I never lied,' Kine replied. 'I never *said* it was me. The others might've, I didn't. They jumped to hasty conclusions.'

*The Rat King, see Witchwood (Arrow Books, 1990)

'You let me *think* it was you.'

'To keep you here, I admit. I was betwitched by you, Clary.'

'And now you want me to go.' She contemplated the Life Tree. Its weathered wood caught the sun, old and firm, the trunk thick, snug inside and well lined. She had liked it at once and now loved it as Kine did. 'Leave the pond and the covert.'

'As if I *want* you to leave!'

'Nowhere's safe – you said that, Kine.'

'The kitts come first – *you* said that.'

Clary's nod was reluctant. 'Then we'll all go,' she sighed. 'If we must, we'll all quit. Come here, Growler,' she called, 'all come here and be still.' She viewed Kine with resolve. 'We'll have to go to the orchard. We'll take them now, before dark.' She gave the Tree a long glance. 'The copse can go to the devils.'

A blackbird sang on its fringe. Kine sensed Clary's emotion; tried to keep his own hidden. The pond was misty with gnats, skimmed by brisk water-skaters. Little flowers laced the reeds where bright skullcap had opened. It was his birthright, his trust, a weasel place in the wood filled with ghosts of the past, his far youth and Kia's kittens, good and bad times, all poignant. He could not speak for a while. At last the blackbird's song closed, a slow, rambling ode, and his own memories faded.

'I have to stay,' he asserted.

'Why?' she asked, though she knew.

'It's my land.'

'They're your kitts.'

'Yours,' he said, 'teach them wisely. It's my duty to stay.'

'And be killed?'

'With luck, quickly, before the truth goes much further. The dragonslayer!' he spat. 'I'll be the joke of the vale, Kine the bold an imposter! I couldn't live it down, Clary.'

She said with scorn, 'Bah, what's pride?'

'Everything.'

'A conceit.'

'Without pride, Kine is nothing.'

'That's because you're a braggart.'

'*You* think that?' Kine was shocked. 'Yet you joined me,' he puzzled.

'For what you are, for yourself.'

'I am what I believe.'

'What you *do*,' she corrected. 'You've done many brave things, earned your place as a legend. But Kine you're not perfect. Even Scrat would doubt that. One deceit doesn't damn you, nor will moving to safety.'

'Take the kitts, I must stay.'

'We'd make home in the orchard.'

'I'd make home with my shame, a deceiver and quitter.'

'*Alive*, Kine.'

'Just take them!'

He watched them go, scarcely able to bear it, then tore the grass in his anguish. A frightful silence was around him, a still and terrible calm from which the sun slid at last and the long shadows slithered. A rook descended and scratched. Watchman sat on the Tree looking into the water. He preened, pecking his wings, then eyed Kine in the gloaming. Neither uttered a sound. Slowly, dusk closed about them.

* * *

When the girl reached the church the sun had gone, the graves darkening. She had been slow with her ironing then dawdled picking the flowers, a trug of pinks from the garden with fern and some roses, most of them for her mum but a few plucked for Poacher.

Not that they would last long, a week at the most on the graves. But it was something to see, a splash of summery colour, and the scent would be welcome.

Perhaps, she thought, looking round, they would chat when she left, the quiet souls of the tombs, compare views on the flowers, deprecate her attire (shirt and jeans), exchange gossip. They had enough to chew over: generations of scandal, old loves, bygone crises.

All village history was here: the pompous with their big stones; the poor with small, slaty slabs; the grey blocks of the dour and at least two white cherubs. You could, by noting the graves, follow family fortunes, one clan growing in wealth, sprouting costlier headstones; another's slabs shrinking.

She had brought pots for the flowers and there was a standpipe for water. Jackdaws clacked round the church, their roosts high in its tower. Her interest lingered on dates, couples rejoined in death, sometimes after decades; folk Napoleon frightened; the tiny tomb of a babe beside an elderly lady, the pair of them sisters.

Time was mocked by the grave, her mother young when she died, Poacher old and rheumatic. Yet they had walked out together, a paltry difference in age, before the war changed his life and she had married the Ploughman. Perhaps they talked of that sometimes across the slabs set between them.

Ploughman still became jealous and spoke of Poacher the heathen. A reprobate, she allowed, but she had not seen him that way for he had opened her eyes, a child's eyes, to creation – the rainbow kingfisher's plunge, the fanning fin of a trout, a hawk moth struggling from pupa.

The tramp had known the wild creatures and taught a small girl their secrets. 'Immortal knowledge, they have, eternal memories, the varmints!' The bird that built its first nest, an instant master of crafts, or crossed the world with sure instinct. ''Tis like a deathless soul in 'em.' Had people lost nature's soul, their immemorial talents? Perhaps some had, some had not. The man had thought like a stoat, had the mind of a weasel. He knew each trick of the rabbit.

She made her mother's flowers nice and took a small bunch for Poacher. His grave was tangled and rough – the way, maybe, he would like it.

The dusk was thick now and cool. A droning insect annoyed her. At the gate, by the yews, the pools of shadow were black, the gnarled trunks hidden in them. The bats had left the church porch. Round the tower, the 'daws settled.

Something pale crossed a grave, pausing now by another. Smooth and ghostly it moved, visiting a third slab, quiet as night, glowing faintly. It made the girl hold her breath. Luminous, it stole on, haunting this tomb and that, whispering, she imagined. As it turned, she grew stiff, watched it sway, glide towards her.

She did not move. A gnat whined; a wisp of hair stroked her forehead. She had not reckoned for this. To *sense* the spirits,

107

perhaps . . . And then the wings as it passed, and she tossed back the hair. She might have known – the white owl. There were voles in the churchyard.

Still, its eerie glow puzzled.

The elm, she thought, in the wood! There was a gash in its trunk where she had found honey fungus; it made the rot phosphorescent. The owl must rest in the hole. Particles would cling on, make the bird's plumage glimmer.

She chuckled, hurrying home to tell her husband the story. The parlour light shone on toys. 'And *you*, child, it's past bedtime!'

'Tell her, dad.'

The man grinned. He said, 'We went to the pump. We saw something, as well.'

'We saw *two* things,' the boy said.

'Let me guess.'

'No, you won't.'

'One was Mag,' she conjectured.

The toddler frowned. 'One,' he mumbled.

'Now she's beat,' said his father.

'Yes, she's beat – tell her, tell her.'

The young man laughed. 'It was luck. We took a look at the valve and stood a while by the reeds. There was a sound by and by and there was Mag, bold as brass. She ran away up the path and out came this larger brute.'

'F'rocious, mum. Tell her, dad.'

'It had a devilish eye. I didn't think it belonged, not round here, but you'd know. We kept quiet and it glared then went off with the other. We got your book of wild creatures.' He tapped a page. 'That's the beggar.'

The girl bent forward. 'A *polecat*?'

'That's the brute.'

'Yes!' the child said.

'Well go on,' said Kine, 'say it.'

'What?' said Watchman.

'Kine's finished.'

'Hmm,' the rook said and shrugged. He scanned the twilight. 'It's quiet.' A dead branch clawed the gloom.

Watchman sat where it crooked, Kine below on the deck. Neither said very much, their pond images brooding. 'Strangely quiet,' sniffed the rook. 'I'd got used to them, your lot.'

'At least *they're* safe.'

Watchman scratched.

'They don't need me, not with Clary.'

'Ah,' the rook said and grunted.

'She's at home in the orchard.' There was a pause. 'My time's up, let *them* live, take their turn.'

'You could run.'

'Did I ever?' They mused and Kine said, 'Not ever. I held my ground without fear.' He thought of Clary and asked, 'Would you say I've been boastful?'

'Huh!' said Watchman succinctly.

'I had my pride.'

'You had *that*.'

'Weasel pride,' Kine reflected. 'A hunter needs to be proud.' Especially when he was small. He had not won himself fame by being small and retiring; he would have perished unknown had he been self-effacing. Modesty was for sheep, ruminants, meadow-nibblers. In any case it was too late, it hardly mattered at this stage. 'I'll die unbowed,' he determined.

The rook's beak ruffled his breast, dark as dusk, his eye sombre. 'Die?' he said.

'With my head up.'

'Huh,' the rook said again.

'I'm prepared. Hob can have me – or Mag. In the end, someone has to.' He viewed the pond, casting back, recalling Hob in his wrath, the great eel's final torment. Kine might have vaunted his skills, he had not doubted death's passion for he had danced with her often. There was a limit to flirting. Either you quit while you lived or the last dance was earnest.

He said, 'I'll go like a weasel. There'll be no cowering, no waiting. A weasel dies on the attack.' He felt a tremor of passion. 'Attacking fiercely,' he added.

'You'd better run.'

An owl screamed.

'They could be coming,' said Watchman. 'They could be close in the shadows. You'd better bolt while you can, for it's the hour of the devils.'

'I can't surrender the copse. I can't betray the trust, Watchman.'

'Bah,' said Watchman, 'clear out. I've seen their work, it's not neat.'

'The old hen?'

'We were partners.' The corvid ruffled and sighed. 'Then I was somebody, Kine, an elder voice in the council, a star debater, still handsome. She used to listen and yearn. Oh, I was somebody then, widely heard and admired, a trenchant voice in the senate.'

'And now a lookout.'

'The fools! The world is full of fools, weasel. They flock as one against wisdom. The wise are seldom in fashion.'

'Then spread some wisdom now, Watchman – confound the Evil Alliance.'

'It's getting late.'

'*Tchkkk*!'

'Tomorrow . . .'

'The time for courage is now.'

'Oh, well,' huffed Watchman, 'be off – go and die, shrimp, I'm weary.'

He watched the other get up and spring down from the Life Tree. The weasel paused on the bank then moved forward. At the gloom-swaddled path he glanced back at the pool, the grey hulk, Watchman's outline. He felt empty inside, an aching vacuum of sadness, and then inexorable anger, a burgeoning fury.

'*Tchkkk*,' he snarled on the marsh track.

'It's Kine,' a voice said. 'Hold up.'

Another said, 'Flit, it's late. It's time we roosted.'

'No, wait. There's something on.'

Kine marched grimly. 'You're right,' he blazed, 'a death battle.'

The sparrows wheeled. 'Where?' they twittered. 'A fight, Kine? Who's fighting?'

'You'll see. Just take me to Hob and you'll see a death dance, I promise.'

'But you'll die!'

'Like a hero. You want a dust-up, you'll see one.'

'The sprite's last fight?' They were awed. 'He'll go down tussling,' thrilled Flit, 'go in glory, jaws leeching. We want to see it, to cheer him!'

'A hen and horse fight,' cried Farthing, 'hopeless odds. That's a battle!'

'We'll be there rooting,' breathed Flit.

'We'll shed a tear.'

'Several,' Flit said.

They went as far as the gate. A three-quarters moon shone, its glare pale on the marsh, the low counterscarps silvered. The scene was haunting and vast, the chill emptiness sombre. The vale wore a death mask.

'We should be roosting,' said Flit.

Farthing stared, feeling twitchy. 'Are you afraid?'

'Me?' gulped Flit.

'Then let's search, the night's bright.'

'The right night for a scrap.'

'Let's find Hob. The champ's waiting.'

They flew off over the dykes and Kine watched, his gaze distant. He was prepared, his veins primed, the night's aspect inspiring. He would go with a flourish. The clustered stars would approve, gathering in their groups. The moon's palace was packed, filled with shimmering heroes.

He sensed the welcoming tribes, the bright halls open to him. Old comrades would be there: Kia and Ford, Chukra, One-eye. They would remember old times, old campaigns, the Mink Battles, Rattun's wrath and the Witchwood. They would recall bygone summers, old-time scents, vivid sounds – the great hum of bees swarming, the honking of marsh geese.

Kine cast round. The vale glittered. It was a ghostly arena, no sign of the sparrows. Ahead the pumphouse rose dimly while, far behind, up the track, the wood's carapace sprawled, half ice-grey, half in shadow. Where the small cottage crouched, a light shone in a window.

There was a chirp. The birds circled.

'Kine,' said Farthing, alighting, 'we've searched as far as the pump, every dyke, the low meadows. We can't see Hob or black Mag. Nothing moves, the night's eerie.'

'The frogs,' breathed Flit, 'have submerged, dived in panic. All we heard was one plaint, an old croaker's lament.' He looked glum.

Farthing ruffled. He said, 'It's jinxed, the fight's jinxed. Not a mention of Hob, just a dirge of Athene, a dreary song of her antics, how she haunts the ridge gloating.'

'The ridge?' said Kine.

'Spreading terror.'

'The ridgeway leads to the orchards . . .' The weasel turned, his voice low, as if it came from far off, homed from some unknown region. It seemed to break a long trance. He swung round, his bark urgent. 'Move,' he snapped, shot with life, 'across the cornfield, be quick. They'd go by the ridge to the orchard. Move quickly!'

He drew his head back and sprang, wildly butting the hedge, breaking through to the wheat, racing on between drills. The dark alley led upwards. Blindly, Kine charged the corn. Towering stalks chaffed his flanks, the rough stems leaning inwards. Temples skinned, the sprite surged, bounding fiercely, his mind on the summit.

All else was forgotten. He had to get to the ridge. It was no longer a death wish but care for Clary that drove him, care for her and the kitts. A screech skirled and he stopped. He knew the voice of Athene – harsh, obscene – and barged on. Somewhere close he heard sparrows.

'I don't much care for it, Flit.'

'Nor I, Farthing, it's late.'

'Time we roosted.'

Kine burst out of the corn. The sudden moonshine was dazzling. Before him stretched the cropped ridge, a black tree and Athene. He must have startled the witch for she rose, prey forsaken. 'Curse you, Kine, the thing's yours. A poor catch – you can keep it!' He eyed a small, claw-whipped corpse.

It was Growler, the kitten.

Part Three

THE WAR WEASELS

The man strolled round to the yard. His wife had settled to read, the child in bed, evening peaceful. A bulb was shining ahead and he found Ploughman working, a halo spread on his back, the lamp clamped to the tractor.

'Need a hand?' It was eager. The younger man viewed the scene with eyes that revelled in bolts, gleaming spanners, all engines.

'Blamed oil filter to change. Overdue. Summer's hectic.' The other drew on his pipe. In its glow he looked tired, stiff and old as they talked, his hands fiddling. A spanner slipped and he cursed. At length, he said, 'You saw *what*?'

'With the kid, we both saw it.'

'You mean a fitchet, a polecat? You mean the brute's a *foul-marten*? It's hard to credit, is that; that's going back to the Ark, before the Kaiser's war, that is.'

'Still a few in wild parts.' The other aired his new knowledge. 'At any rate, the book says so.'

'Books aren't gospel, not some. How'd it get to the valley?'

'From the hills.' Or so the girl had proposed. Her husband did not much care; the tractor offered more interest, its engine seductive. 'She says it fits what we know – the dead eel, your dead gander.'

'Oh, *she* says so? That's gospel!'

'I wouldn't know, I'm the dunce. I never heard of a polecat, a what-you-call-it, foul-marten.'

'A bloody fitchet, my lad. And nor you'd wish to, by God. My old man talked of fitchets; he called them crazed, plumb berserk. They'd clear a hen run, he said; you dare not blink, they'd have cleared it.'

'Your daughter says they're nocturnal.'

'We'll have to reckon that's gospel.'

'I think she heard it from Poacher.'

Her father scowled. 'That old thief!' He gave the lamp a rough jerk, making dusky shapes leap, the giant shadows of posts, farm machinery, sheds. 'Flaming tractor,' he grunted.

The startled gloom was bizarre, alive with mind-boggling forms like grotesques from her stories, the engineer mused, the tales his wife told the toddler. He eyed the cottage and smiled. An engine made better sense but that would strike the boy later.

Ploughman swore. 'I can't see.'

'Let me try.'

'No I can manage, A flaming polecat!' he rasped. 'I'll blast it back where it came from.' He fumbled, groping for nuts, the other watching, frustrated. 'Let me glimpse it, I'll blast it!'

The younger man's fingers itched. 'Don't say you'd shoot it,' he counselled, 'she'd not approve its destruction.' Not that Ploughman's aim threatened; the man could not aim a spanner. 'Here, for Pete's sake . . .'

'Bah, take it!' The tool changed hands. There was silence. The farm man gave a low snort. 'Not approve?' he said slowly. 'There's plenty she'd not approve. I don't honey the creature, don't placate her like you do.'

'Would you say so?'

'She *runs* you.'

The young man grinned, working deftly.

'She can approve or not, mister. If she kept fowls she'd approve, she'd soon want it got rid of. And that Mag,' Ploughman brooded. 'You know the next thing?' he huffed after a long pause for effect, like the lull before thunder. 'They'll bloody breed, that's the next thing – if that damned polecat's a hob. That'll breed with a ferret. We'll have a brood on our hands.' He spat the juice from his pipe. 'A flaming fitchet nest, mister.'

'You'll have to look to your fence.' The other straightened. 'Make that old hen run safer.'

'I've got no time to be fencing. It's working all hours this season.'

'Well, that's the oil filter fixed – one job less. Coming in?'

Ploughman coiled the lamp's cable. The moon picked out his flat cap. It was greasy with handling. He eyed the night, his head shaking. 'Much chance of that,' he replied. 'Standing guard, son, more likely.'

The next day dawned like a torch, as if heralding marvels. It made the shrew rub his eyes. It was brassy, a blinder. In the heat the ridge gleamed, its dry grass thin and sear, each lean summer blade burnished. Poppies flamed. The marsh steamed. Near the copse the shrew dithered.

116

There was life on the hillbrow. It started down the slope briskly, at first a series of specks, growing as they advanced, then in smart chestnut coats bounding forward in line like small, cantering troopers. They were three, the sun on them; three in line, prancing boldly. Scrat blinked twice, his eyes straining.

Flank to flank the three pounded.

'Kine . . .' The shrew turned and fled. At the wood he paused, breathless. 'Kine, they're coming, they're coming.' He turned to stare. 'Three!' he blurted.

'Then this is it, the last stand.'

'Not the demons, Kine, weasels.'

'Three?' said Kine, disbelieving. He joined the shrew, his gaze sharp. Wispy clouds hung in space. They were high, like bleached bones. Lakes of corn had turned pale, not yet ripe, their crests steely. Now and then they seethed quietly. Kine was stunned by the brilliance.

And then, as if from the sun, as if cast in its furnace, the creatures loomed from its glare and stood squarely before him. The shrew had dived under cover. Still dazzled, Kine squinted.

'We meet again, Kine,' cried Brat.

'We come as comrades,' hailed Scoter.

Bald-ear beamed. 'Reinforcements.'

In the silence Brat laughed. 'Kine the legend is speechless, he can't believe it, eh Scoter? It's simple, Kine, Clary sent us; she said you needed our help. That's good enough, Kine, it's yours. You're her mate, we respect you. Clary's foes are our opponents.'

'Our problem,' rasped Scoter.

'Where are they?' growled Bald-ear.

Brat said, smiling, 'Well, comrade?'

'Is she safe?'

'She's unharmed.' The smile died. 'They got Growler.'

'Yes, I found him,' Kine answered.

They paused in anger and sorrow. 'You're not alone, Kine,' said Brat, 'we're four now against Hob, four against the destroyers. Each one here is a fighter.'

'I know that, Brat.' Kine reviewed them: the powerful

youngster and Scoter, quick and sly as a snake, and his friend of the blemish, bull-hearted and dogged. Kine was moved. 'Brat, I'm grateful . . .'

'Kine, we're ready,' snapped Scoter, 'don't waste time. We need war plans.'

Scrat bobbed up. 'A war c-council!'

'Who's *that*?'

'Scrat's my scout.'

Bald-ear grinned.

'He knows the dangers,' Kine said. 'He knows the evils against us. I have to warn you, they're grim.' He led the way to the pond. 'To be quite blunt,' he confessed, 'the odds are still suicidal.'

'Weren't they always?' said Brat. 'Weren't they so in the Mink Wars?'

'That's the legend,' sneered Scoter.

'The *truth*,' said Kine. 'We fought monsters. The old heroes feared nothing. They were giants, hearts of oak.'

'We've got Bald-ear,' said Brat. 'His head's oak – wooden-headed!'

Bald-ear beamed.

Scoter frowned. 'We need briefing. Convene a council, let's talk.'

'Kine's the leader,' said Brat.

'Why?' said Scoter. 'He's old.'

'Kine's fought wars.'

They disputed. The glade was peaceful and bright. Sun-drenched mallow was there, thick with crinkly pink flowers; viper's bugloss raised spires, minarets of such a blue the eye reeled. Blossom charmed, spread its scent. It hardly seemed a war setting.

'*Caw!*' a voice cried above and Scrat bolted for cover. Kine peered up at the trees.

'Caw,' rasped Watchman, 'it's Mag!'

'Where?' bawled Kine.

'On the track.'

'Coming this way?'

'Approaching.'

Kine surveyed his companions. 'You want war, the war's started.' His voice was calm, the tone forceful.

'Follow me and keep close. Do as I do, no noise. Don't ask questions, *obey* me.'

Scoter glared.

Kine ignored him. He led them out down the path, stopping where the copse ended. There he told them to wait. Across the track beans were growing, a field of bushy plants in long rows. They formed one side of the lane, a thick hedgerow the other.

Alone, he wormed his way forward. Rabbit runs scored the verge, brambles snaked from the hedge. Kine held still, his eyes sharp. He could see Mag coming on, swaggering and malign. She cast round as she came, sometimes sniffing the beans, a dark and menacing brute full of arrogant boldness. For a moment he watched, then slipped back.

'We'll lay an ambush,' he breathed. 'I'll take Brat through the beans; you two cut through the hedge. There's a small ash tree in it. Wait for Mag at the tree. When she's level, we'll pounce, two from either side of her.'

Scoter shot him a glance. It held grudging approval.

'Right,' snapped Kine, 'let's be quick.'

He nudged Brat and they moved, swiftly crossing the track. It was cool in the beans, the dense leaves forming tunnels from which they bobbed now and then, keeping line with the ash tree. 'Almost there, Brat, come on.'

'There she is!'

A dark flank moved ahead. As they drew near the path small green beans hung in clumps, dangling in thick fringes. Kine brushed through without pause.

'Straight in, comrade, no flinching.'

As they sprang, Mag turned on them, She had an indolent grace, scything round, her arms wide, hurling Brat to the gravel. A great clawed hand met Kine's head. Thrown with force to the ground, he lay stunned, blinking up.

'How very rash.' Mag observed. Her thin lip was contemptuous. 'I see Athene was right, you need teaching a lesson.'

'This is Kine's land.' Kine rose.

Black Mag laughed. 'A quaint notion. Kine, you live in the past, it's all changed, the regime. The New Order has come, an alliance of hate.'

'Evil,' Kine said.

'You're dead!'

Brat and Kine got up slowly. 'And your friend, shrimp, both finished.' Mag came at them, still laughing, and as she did the hedge shook, disgorged Scoter mid-leap and then Bald-ear. Suddenly they were dancing, four sprites in a ring, darting round her, snouts stabbing.

'Not finished yet Mag!'

'We'll see. Hop!' she taunted them, swatting.

Lashing out, Mag traversed, catching Bald-ear and Brat. They went down, rolling over. Kine was next, hurled aside and she turned, seeking Scoter. He had attacked from behind. 'You're the sly one,' she rasped, lunging at him, 'a smart one.'

Scoter ducked.

'Dance!' Mag told him.

'Turn her,' Kine cried, 'keep moving!'

Again, the weasels formed a circle, raising dust, their necks swaying. They waltzed like wasps round a pear, teasing, hovering, spinning. They seemed to fly as they pranced, lightly land then bound higher. They were heady with fight and Kine felt his old self. She might not be a pond dragon but Mag was feared through the vale and they were holding their own. He had his pride back, his bounce.

'Faster, comrades, dance faster!'

Mag glared. They confused her. At intervals she dashed at them in bursts of rage, squalls of fury, but they were will-o'-the-wisps and eluded her, spitting. 'Stop,' she snarled, 'stand and tussle.' Each was bruised, lacerated. 'You're dead,' she howled, 'every *one*.' Still they whirled, made her giddy.

Kine, an eye partly closed, could see Scoter's neck bleeding. 'Stick it, Scoter, she's flustered. Brat, Bald-ear, keep going!'

'She's drawing back,' Brat declared. 'Keep it up, she's retreating.'

'She's had enough,' Scoter whooped.

Kine took stock. They were dazed, eyes were popping. They stood and watched, mouths agape.

'Let her go,' he enjoined. 'Don't be fooled, she's still strong. She's surprised but not beaten.'

'We could harry her, Kine.'

120

'If she turned, we'd be sorry.'

Bald-ear rumbled, 'I'll thump her!'

'No . . .'

The cry was too late, the battered Bald-ear had gone, lumbering in pursuit. He was too weary to spring. 'Bald-ear, stop!' He did not. He struck Mag on the rump and they watched as she turned, rearing up, falling on him. A cloud of dust marked the blow then Mag's journey continued. At the marsh gate she paused, glanced back grimly and vanished.

Appalled, the weasels lurched forward. The dust was settling down, shrouding Bald-ear's bruised body.

'The numskull, the fool . . .' Scoter sighed and Kine shrugged.

Bald-ear's snout twitched. He beamed.

'A head of wood!' Brat said, grinning.

* * *

Scrat watched the bee work the flowers. It toiled from one to the next, diligent in its task, a brief moment in each, then was suddenly still. Seconds passed and it stayed put, making no move from the bloom and the shrew's interest quickened.

He was an expert on insects. They were his diet, his passion: red bugs, shield bugs, froghoppers, beetles, chafers and flies – sawflies, robber flies, gadflies. Scrat was wise to their habits. He knew, as well, about spiders and, hence, what had happened.

There was a clan of crab spiders – they could run backwards and sideways – which, scorning webs, lurked in plants, snatching unwary insects. One clan member killed bees. Scrat had seen her, a yellow female with spots, shinning up to the petals. She would have waited inside, her fangs lethal and ready. The bee had flown its last mission.

Scrat gazed up at the bloom. Could he climb the plant's stem and claim two meals at a stroke? He was about to decide when Watchman swooped to the Life Tree. Startled, Scrat lost his nerve.

'That you, dwarf?' Watchman scowled. 'Mag escaped – a fine ambush! A fancy frolic,' he huffed. 'All the fools did was prance, let her walk off unhindered – Mag, who killed my old mate.'

'*Tchkkk,*' cried Kine, reappearing.

He led his battered band proudly. They made their way to the pond, found a creek and trooped down, dipping into the water. As the sprites washed their wounds, Watchman sniffed, glaring at them.

'Walked away,' the rook sneered. 'A fine ambush!'

'Pluck him!' Bald-ear exclaimed.

'Drown him,' Brat said. 'Who *is* he?'

'He gave the warning,' soothed Kine. He was accustomed to Watchman and cooled down in the pond, diplomatically adding, 'The rook's an elder and sage, an eminence of the copse.'

Watchman preened. 'Much revered! An oracle of some note. Mind,' he judged, better pleased, 'it was a start, a fair skirmish. You had the *moral* advantage.'

'We had her rattled,' growled Brat.

'Took her measure,' said Scoter.

Kine shook, spraying spume, his assessment objective. 'We broke the spell,' he allowed. 'We've faced Mag and survived. We'll fight on, it's not hopeless.'

'You're heroes,' Scrat cheered, 'four heroes!'

But Kine was grave. 'Mag's only part of the evil. We face a demon alliance, the base Athene and Hob – Hob the arch-foe, the night fiend. Compared to Hob, Mag is nothing.'

'*Doom,*' quailed Scrat.

Kine said, 'Courage! We have good friends in the rook, Watchman here, and the sparrows; a flying force, that's important. If we could find more foot fighters . . .' He stretched to dry on the strand. The sun was fierce. He thought, Wonder . . .

One tiny kitt had escaped when Kia had died with her brood. That it had lived was a wonder, and so was she, a bright Wonder. The sprite had fought like a spitfire, fought mink with the heroes. He thought aloud, 'Heath and Wonder – she took young Heath as her mate. They crossed the hills and reared young. Heath and Wonder . . .'

'Fighters?' Brat asked.

'The best. If they're alive, Brat, they'll join us. That's if we can make contact.'

'Send Watchman.'

'We need him.'

'Indeed you do,' puffed the rook. 'And I'm not here to run errands. Send the sparrows, the riffraff. Let them work off some bounce since they've got more than their share. Let the hooligans labour.'

'It's worth a try,' Kine said, nodding.

'We've still no plan,' Scoter told him. He licked his rinsed coat and frowned. In the heat the pond stewed, a thin organic film spreading. It shone in parts, rainbow-coloured. They sought the shade, Scoter adding, 'We've got no plan of defence. At dusk, the rook goes to roost; they could break in unnoticed.'

'You're right,' said Kine, 'so how's this: there are four sides to the copse, one apiece. Each patrols his own side and keeps in touch with his neighbours. If peril threatens, we muster. Apart from which, there's a scout.'

'Woe,' moaned Scrat.

'He'll keep watch. We'll place him just down the track, the way they're likely to come.'

The dwarf wailed.

'He'll give warning.'

'No!' gulped Scrat.

'Any questions?'

'Must not run, must not run.' The shrew whimpered it quickly. 'I must not run, must stay put. Doom, it's dark. Must be brave. Woe, it's lonely and dark. Must stay p-put at my post.'

The night had scarcely begun. Big fat beans hung beside him; countless leaves hid the stars. Through a myriad stems, a Cimmerian grotto, the track glimmered dimly. 'Must p-put my p-post.'

A mighty slug slithered past him, twice his size, and jet black. Others slid through the growth, the cool dew to their taste. They were muscular, loathsome. 'Must p-post put,' he stammered. Something, somewhere, was shrieking. He could hear foul imprecations. The small witch, Athene!

What was that? Beasts were moving.

Only grey, long-backed rabbits sloppeting on the path, sitting up, munching beans – the last chance they would get, for the harvest had started. All day long in the distance the bean machine had crawled on, belching derv fumes and dust, tossing out the green debris. The rumbling giant threshed the crop and leaves and stalks were ejected.

Now it toiled in the dark, its lamp flaring. Across the yet unplucked field its slow heartbeat was faint and shrew and rabbits ignored it. Searchlight eyes probed the drills, blinked and rocked, struck the cottage. With a start, the child roused, his small nursery shining.

Slipping out of his bed, the boy crouched at the window. The headlamps slewed, lit a hedge and then were small, winking at him. The great machine stomped the headland. Against the sweep of the marsh, its advance was ungainly, a jerking, lurching assault, as ponderous in the gloom as some ancient war engine. Above the cab, in dim plumes, jets of mangled leaf fountained.

The toddler looked at the stars. He eyed the ribbon of track and it beckoned, called him out to the lamps, to the enchanted bean-stripper and its magician, his grandad.

In dressing gown and sneakers, he tiptoed down to the door and eased it open. The air was warm and he ran, slowing down in the lane, listening to the night's sounds. The engine's thrum filled the vale. In the hedge roosting starlings, startled by his excursion, made throaty noises and scuffled.

He reached the barn and looked up. Its sagging roof nudged the stars and, in a canopied maw, once the refuge of wagons, he glimpsed the ghosts of old timbers. A fusty straw odour rose, as thick and sharp as sour milk. Every smell was intense, emphasised by the evening.

Silently a hare loped, crossed the yard in slow motion. Oblivious of the child, who had stiffened, enthralled, it advanced on stilt legs then, as hares will, sat dreaming. Perhaps the far lamps bemused it. They made small lights in soft eyes, almost in the boy's reach, and he stretched trembling fingers.

'Stay,' he breathed, 'we'll be friends.'

Annoyed, he snatched back his hand. The hare had fled, a

wild shade, a lean emblem of fright streaking into the murk, the beast's panic insulting. 'Oh, then go – I'm not bothered!'

He hitched up his pyjamas and left the starlight behind, shuffling into the dark, a reef of leafy-edged gloom, the track black by the covert. He groped a few steps then stopped. The woodside cast its odd spell, a moist breath at his neck, eerie draughts at bare ankles.

He liked the copse in the day, when it was bright by the pond; he liked the Tree and the weasel. When he grew up and was strong, an engineer with a van, he meant to build a great bridge, span the pool bank to bank so the weasel could cross it. A weasel bridge with an arch! And, he thought, a large lamp, because the darkness was scary.

Something moved in the wood. He could not see what it was but it crackled dead leaves. He did not like the deep shadows; he did not like their dank breath, the leaves crackling. He looked away at the beans, their tops magically lit, and did much as the hare had – ran hotfoot towards them.

Suddenly the lights glared. The churning bean-stripper roared, sweeping up the night's wall, blotting stars, constellations. There was a jolt and it stopped. Dim and monstrous it towered, snorting dust, its heart throbbing, a thing from somewhere in space and his grandad climbed from it.

Squinting, Ploughman bent forward. He straightened, weary and aching. The monster jettisoned debris. As the rubbish subsided, festooning wheels and hydraulics, he said with phlegm, 'I'll be damned.'

'Come to see you,' the boy said.

'I need that.' The man spat. His face was pained in the lights, grease and dust in its lines, sweaty under the cap. 'She's clogged rotten with weed.' He eyed clumps of bistort, skeins of rambling knotgrass. 'She's barely shifting and me done for, a cripple. Worked since dawn. Spent, lad, knackered. It's all I need that, a visit.'

'Want some help?'

'Huh – look here . . .' The man tugged at the growth. 'It's like twine,' he growled fiercely, so consumed with disgust that the child in the lights, gnomelike, got up for bed, might have

125

been one more plant. 'The stuff's spread through the field, flaming acre on acre. There's more weed here than beans.'

'I could pull some.'

'Damned acres . . .'

The infant frowned. 'But I'm clean. I've come out in pyjamas.'

'I noticed, boy,' Ploughman glowered. 'She'll go spare, will your mam. Here, get up in the cab,' he said, wiping his hands. 'We'll flaming call it a day and take you home in style, shall we?' He revved the giant and it shook. 'Tight, now, mind; hold on tightly.'

'Bright lights!'

'Aye,' said Ploughman. 'Just as well, too, I reckon.' The headlamps floodlit the copse; rabbits flitted like spectres. A tiny beast crossed the track, vanishing in the hedge. 'Shrew,' the man said. 'Did you see it?'

'I heard a noise in the wood. When I passed leaves were moving.'

Ploughman grunted.

'I think the polecat was prowling.'

'Sit tight, youngster, it's lumpy.'

'We saw the polecat, it's *wild*.'

'That's my problem, not yours. You watch out for your own.' The giant lurched. The man sighed then he smiled grimly, head shaking. 'Heck, you're worse than a pup, a blamed pup – straying off. You watch out for your mam, *she'll* be wild, son, I warn you.'

'The outpost's gone!' Scrat ran squealing, scrambling into the hedge, floundering at its bottom. The beans had gone near the track, plucked from over his head. Piercing lights and a roar – the lot gone in a trice! 'The post's gone!' He ran blindly.

He struck a lump of dry earth and drew back. Dazed, he blinked and sped on, stumbling into small pits, tripping up on dead twigs, all his valour at nought as his mini-legs beetled. No more scouting for Scrat, a shrew's life was too short; that was *it*. He fell over.

Athene screeched and he froze. Peeping up through the

growth, he saw a limb of the ash, a round moon clear behind it. On the bough sat the owl, squat and fierce, silhouetted.

'All clear now,' hissed Athene. 'The engine's gone, it's moved on.'

Scrat knew that much. He quailed.

A second voice said, 'The man?'

'The old man's in the engine.'

A brutish shape passed ahead, vague to Scrat but forbidding. 'Old fool.' It was violent. It had a blade edge of hate, a crazed rasp, and he gulped.

The owl cursed. 'Old like Kine!'

'Kine needs killing.' Dimly Scrat saw Hob's back, long and raffish, hairs bristling. 'All the weasels need killing. They pestered Mag,' snarled the fitchet.

'Let's kill them now, clear the covert.' Athene bobbed on her perch. 'Kill them, kill them!' she hooted.

'No, they'll keep, let them wait.' The powerful animal stirred. 'Tonight, Hob feasts, the man's working – working late, not been home.'

'Ah!' the little owl cried.

'Not been home to shut up. Tonight's the night that Hob feasts; a night of hate, owl, of havoc. A banquet fit for Lord Hob; an open poultry house waiting. Tonight I'll show the fools carnage.'

'Blood and hate,' screamed the owl.

'A berserker in action.'

They roused themselves from the hedge and set off, the shrew peering. The moon was cold on the field, on straggling drills of stripped beans, the skeleton of a crop, and dark tangles of dross sprawled like battleground victims. 'Death and havoc,' moaned Scrat. 'Kine . . .'

The sound shrivelled.

* * *

Kine said, 'Well, you've heard Scrat. That's where Hob's gone tonight.' The weasels glared from the copse. Across the moon-silvered fields Ploughman's dwelling was dark like some old badger's retreat, evening black in its windows. 'That's the scout's information.'

'Let's go fight him,' said Bald-ear.

Scoter sneered. 'And get skinned? We're not ready for Hob.'

'*I* am, Scoter.'

'You're thick!'

Brat put in, 'A bold stroke – it's the weasel way, Scoter.'

The goblins pondered the stars. 'The weasel,' Scoter said, '*thinks*. That's the way of the weasel.'

Sighing, Kine pined for Clary. Both were right, Brat *and* Scoter. The weasel's boldness was famed but a weasel was cunning. If only Hob could be slain: it would demoralise Mag, crush the bounce of Athene, confound their ambitions. One bold stroke, blessed with luck! It would absolve him of guilt, the dark stain of deceit, and restore his old glory. And yet, Hob . . . The thought daunted.

He said, 'We dare or we wait. We can be patient and wait – help might come or might not. We can face Hob at dire risk or we could wait and face worse, all three fiends coming for us.'

Scoter said, 'Then we'd fight, we'd defend what we value. A weasel fights for his land, hallowed ground, not for chickens.'

Bald-ear flexed. 'I'm for going.'

'And leave the copse undefended?' Scoter's eye fell on Brat. 'Use your head, Brat, you're smarter.'

'It's a chance. I say go.'

'Then,' said Kine, 'I go too.' And turning slowly to Scoter, 'It's up to you, friend. Either you come or stand guard. If you're prepared to hold fort . . .'

'Someone has to.'

'That's good.'

'No, Kine, bad,' Scoter fumed. 'It's a bungled decision. You've grown too old to make plans, to decide on our actions. You're too easily swayed, too impulsive. Now you're hot, now you're cold, there's not constancy in you. You've no head for command, you're too old to be leader.'

'Come on,' Brat said, 'ignore him.'

Kine looked back as they left. The three crossed the track and he glimpsed Scoter's disgust, the lone sentinel's anger. He was defiant, rebellious. Brat said 'Hurry, lead on. Don't mind Scoter, he'll sulk.'

'He'll come round,' Bald-ear said.

'Right,' said Kine, 'let's keep course. Not too fast, it's some distance.' He loped, undulating. They passed the dregs of the beans, leaf and stem on hard ground, the parched earth deeply cracked. Scarlet pimpernel slept, the knotgrass was entangled. Almost white in the moon, drills of bean stubble marched, countless rank upon rank like small waves at low tide when the sea barely ripples. Rhythmically the sprites hurdled.

A hedge of gorse spread dark shadow. Within its gloom lay a ditch, steeply cut, the floor arid. Scrambling down, Kine exclaimed, 'One more field then the garden. The huts are placed at the end. Keep close, Bald-ear, no straying.'

'Lead on,' Brat said, 'we're with you.'

Clambering from the gorse, they paused, eyeing the dwelling. It had grown larger, forbidding. A light had risen downstairs as though the man was just home, its glow dim and confined. Ploughman's plot was still black, the huts gloomily brooding.

Silently the sprites forayed, light-footed. Their heads were low, their steps swift. They were not easy to spot, shades that slipped clod to clod as a zephyr whisks leaves or as night shadows flutter. Once or twice they held still, counterfeits of the turf, taking stock, then dashed on.

'Ploughman's hedge,' Kine said tersely.

Slower now, they advanced, their snouts sharp, apprehensive. The straggling scrub pushed up poles and Kine threaded them tensely. Then there was wire, broken mesh, a dark coop, its door open. The shapes were dim; nothing moved. There was no babble of fowls, no disclosure of panic. The very calmness disturbed and he cocked his head, listening.

At his flank, Brat was taut. Bald-ear peered, his teeth gnashing. The place was spookily quiet, not an untoward sound, the still shadows moon-marbled. 'Psst,' said Bald-ear, 'up *there*!'

Kine's gaze slewed to the shed. On its roof crouched a hen, a leghorn, its eyes fixed on the ground – eyes that glittered with fright, spellbound by a grey bundle. Kine could make out a beak. It lay flat, oozing blood, while two legs, widely splayed, seemed arrested in rout.

'Look,' gulped Brat, his voice thin.

A second bundle lay near, a red hen, wings spreadeagled. Not far away, more bizarre, a third was lacking its head, a large, fiercely mauled cockerel. 'And there,' Brat croaked, 'and there, too . . .'

Everywhere they saw heaps, feathered hummocks of gore, this one torn on the back, that one ripped underneath, yet another grotesque, its neck twisted absurdly. Some were dead in the hut, more outside in the dust; some obscenely dismembered, some with scarcely a lesion. One small hen, stretched in death, might have dropped from sheer terror.

Shocked, the weasels drew close.

Brat said, 'But it's unnatural . . .'

'The berserker,' growled Bald-ear.

Jumpily, their heads cranked, darting glances to nooks, scanning ominous shadows. Kine stared hard at the shed. '*Tchkkk*,' he snarled, inching forward.

'Kine, you're late,' a voice told him.

'Who's that?'

'The fiend's gone,' hissed the goose. It was husky, wild-visaged. 'Hob's replete, Kine, gorged full. He came for *me* when he'd done but I faced the brute down. He was too laden to care.'

'Where's the man?'

'The man wept.'

'Where's he gone?' Brat said, puzzled.

'Where d'you think?' the goose honked. 'For his gun, sprite, his gun.'

Kine swung round. 'We must go.'

'Bah,' said Bald-ear. 'Where's Hob?'

Brat swept past him. '*Run*, thickhead!' They reached the scrub and stopped to listen. BANG! The weasels raced on. They could hear pellets whistling. The shot struck trees, ricocheting. The man was semi-demented. *BANG!* The weasels ran faster. Down the field's edge they chased, hit the ditch and lay panting.

A torch flashed. *'Damn you, fitchet!'* The voice was strained; boots were clomping.

'Quickly,' Kine cried, 'come on!'

He jumped up, again sprinting. Head to tail they careered, following the ditch bottom, retreating down its dry course like some aberrant serpent, their lean bodies twisting. A falling star streaked above. *Bang!* The gun was more distant. They were, thought Kine, out of range. He watched the star flare and die and then thought briefly of Scoter.

They should, indeed, have stayed put; events had proved Scoter right. They might, all three, have been shot. Or met the fate of the chickens.

For a time, no one spoke. Their mood was grim and the sky, as if in sympathy, glowered, a grid of drab cloud descending. There were a few stormy rumbles. Now and then Bald-ear muttered. At last, approaching the copse, he said, 'We should've done more; we should've hunted the ogre.'

'At night?' groaned Brat as if pained. 'How would we find Hob at night? The night's his kingdom, you ass.'

'We *might've* found him.'

'You dunce!'

'At least,' said Kine, 'we're alive,' He viewed the wood with relief. 'There was no loss, if no gain.'

'There was, there was!' They met Scrat, who ran to welcome them, wailing, 'D-doom, d-doom and death. Kine, don't dawdle.'

'The dwarf's hysterical,' Brat said.

'Scrat, stop raving!' Kine shook him. 'Calm down, shrew, we're all back.'

'M-Mag . . .' the shrew gulped.

'What of her?'

The midget blinked. 'Mag was *here*.'

'In the copse'

'The T-Tree – at the Tree, Kine, the pond . . .'

Kine released him. 'Where's Scoter?'

Scrat moaned.

'Where *is* Scoter?'

They sprinted through the dark oaks, reached the glade and

stared dumbly. Scoter lay on the bank near the roots of the Life Tree. His broken body was scored, striped with wounds, his teeth clamped, Mag's black hairs still between them.

'He fought t-tooth and claw,' Scrat sobbed. 'He could've run but he battled. Now, the c-crows will attend him.'

Their heads dropped.

'And the ants.'

'He defended the Life Tree.' There was a lump in Kine's throat. 'He was alone but he fought.'

'To the end,' Brat said hoarsely.

'He was a fighter,' said Bald-ear.

'A brave fighter,' Kine added.

They stood saluting the corpse, the small, scarred thing on the bank that had refused to seek safety. Kine was deeply affected. It seemed unreal, incomplete, as spiritless as the hens, the mere husk of a weasel. The scowling Scoter had gone, the bold and critical Scoter – rightly critical, Kine thought.

'He was quite right,' he confessed, 'I was wrong and it killed him. We should've stayed in the copse. It was a bungled decision. He spoke the truth. I'm too old.' Kine felt numb. 'I am too old,' he intoned. 'Why don't you leave me, my friends, go back home to the orchard?'

Perhaps the valley *was* doomed. He thought of Hob at the pump, the threat the marsh frogs had echoed: '*I have returned for revenge. It will be violent and crazed . . . it will be merciless, savage.*' He thought of Hob with black Mag, lord and spouse, the owl gloating. Once he might have felt strong – in his heyday, long past.

'No one's quitting,' snarled Brat. 'They'll pay for Growler and Scoter.'

'I'll take Mag,' Bald-ear grunted.

'We'll fight together,' cried Brat, 'until the evil's destroyed. Either that or we perish. It doesn't stop at the wood – give them that and they'll move on. Hob will be in the orchard. Here we stand, Kine, as comrades.'

Slowly, Kine raised his head.

'Each for all?' Brat inquired.

'Each for all!'

'And for Scoter . . .'

Solemnly, the sprites stomped. Beside the pond they danced fiercely, their steps the steps of the fight, honouring their friend. At the end Kine spoke gravely. 'I'm standing down from command. Brat, you'll be the new leader. Kine is weary of leading.'

'Weary?' Brat scoffed. 'You lie. Kine, the greatest of fighters? Kine the captain of heroes? Say you lie, Kine, we need you – your skills, your flair, inspiration. The valley needs your resolve. Only Kine has fought demons, vanquished Gru, toppled Rattun. You'll lead us, Kine, tell the truth.'

A slight shrug condescended. He told the truth: 'I felt old.' He stood tall, the bold general. Kine the brash had felt old – for one preposterous moment.

At the side of the sink tiny silverfish glimmered. They caught the day's early gleam while the girl, getting breakfast, paused to yawn then regard them. A slap and they would be dust, but when she lifted her hand they fled like little toboggans and the girl filled the teapot.

Her husband joined her, fists clenched. He forced them upwards like weights, dropped them limply and scratched. 'I see our son's still sleeping. His adventure was tiring.'

'I'll give the monkey adventure! Here's the bread for the toaster. I'll scalp him next time, young scamp – just let him slip off again.'

'It was the beaner that lured him.'

'Oh, never mind what it was. Pour the tea out, it's made.'

'He's like your dad, he works late.' The young man grinned, his eyes drowsy. 'An outdoors child; you're the same. Show you fields and the woods and iron chains can't restrain you.'

'No? Then who keeps the home? Who cooks, shops, does the washing? I'll restrain him, the rogue. You, you're soft, you give in. What he needs is firm handling.'

'Like his mum!'

'Watch the toast.'

He watched *her*, his gaze sleepy. The fair hair bobbed when she turned, tousled still from the night. 'By the way,' he said changing tack, 'there were shots later on. Did you hear them?'

'Dad,' she said, 'he gets dafter.'

The silverfish had come back and in her mind she reprieved them. They did no harm, she supposed, primitives from the past, from life's furthermost ages. They were part of the cottage, like the wainscot-wise mice and her murmuring friends, the dead folk of the vale *he* dismissed as winds droning. They did not speak to incomers, for they were suspicious.

'Poor old dad. His sight's bad in the day, let alone when it's dark. He could've run down that infant.'

They sat and ate, the man quiet. He spoke when she had relaxed. 'The little fellow's not scared, he's not frightened, your dream child.'

'I'm glad he's not – to a point.' But it was all very well. 'I'm the one who gets scared and I don't want it happening.'

'I'll tell him firmly. We'll talk.'

'And let him see that you're *cross*; he'll take no notice unless. He'll only do it again. And next time . . .'

'Yes, don't fret.'

'He could've gone to the pond.' The girl felt sick at the thought. 'Gone to the pond in the night. He wouldn't be with us now. My God, if that ever happened . . .'

She looked out of the window, her mind demanding distraction. A pair of sparrows flew past. She rose and charted their flight, watching as they winged briskly. They had a purposeful style, reaching far down the vale until, silverfish small, they were lost in the hill haze.

* * *

Flit watched Farthing ahead. He rose and fell as he flew, bearing south, striking crisply. The morning's haze, burning off, hung in nebulous strips into which he would plunge and emerge as abruptly. Below them, dwarfed by the marsh, a tractor crawled back and forth. It was moving the flood bank, felling tall, flowering nettles.

Steers lay out by the dykes, clouds of insects above them. A single willow stood up, its cool curtains inviting. Farthing waggled his wings. 'That'll do,' he called back. 'We'll take a break in the shade before we tackle the hills.'

'Our last chance.' Flit caught up. 'No one stops in the Hawk Hills.'

'I'm not afraid of the heights.'

'Nor am I, never have been.'

'Oh no?'

'No,' snapped Flit. 'Want to make something of it?'

Farthing planed. 'It's too hot.'

'It's going to get a lot hotter. We must be daft,' complained Flit, 'travelling in this weather.'

'Kine needs help.'

'That's for sure. Sooner watch a good scrap, though.'

'We will, partner, we will.' They fluttered as they lost height. 'First we've got to find Wonder.'

The willow loomed, its leaves rustling. 'If she's alive,' shouted Flit. 'As like as not, she'll be dead. She'd not be young, nor would Heath.'

'We'll find out.'

'In the end. A nice trip if it's wasted.'

They bustled into the tree. Deep green shadow enclosed them.

'What trip's that?' a voice challenged. Athene sat in the shade. 'Trip?' she rasped. 'A *nice* trip?' Her speckled brow was drawn down, her broad throat darkly necklaced. As the visitors blinked, sulphurous eyes searched them closely.

'A little jaunt,' blurted Flit.

'A short break,' Farthing croaked.

The witch glared, bobbing slowly. 'It's not like sparrows to travel – idle dregs, good for nothing. Don't I know you from somewhere? Aren't you friends of the weasel?'

'Weasel?' Flit cheeped.

They swallowed.

Farthing twittered, 'What weasel?'

The bobbing grew faster. 'Don't rile me, riffraff, it's hot. The day's too hot for exertion.'

'Perhaps we'd better move on.'

'You're going nowhere, stay put. I'd snuff you both in a pounce. No one comes or goes now, the Night Lord forbids travel. All frontiers are closed; the vale's sealed for the sport. We can't kill beasts who've escaped. Hob does not like escapers. Travellers raise our suspicions, especially rubbishy sparrows: especially riffraff like you, who might be acting for weasels. Try to leave and you'll find out. Your little jaunt won't be pleasant.'

'Yes, well, we could turn back.'

The trapped pair exchanged glances.

'If that's the law,' simpered Flit.

The witch scowled. 'It's Hob's orders.'

'We're law-abiding.'

'Get home!' They moved to leave and she purred, 'We'll send for you when *your* time comes.'

Bursting out of the tree, they fled back on their tracks. For a while they winged quickly then, '*Pssst*,' said Farthing, 'the reeds!' and the sparrows had vanished. In the reed bed they paused. Through the dense screen of growth, a dyke stretched to the pump, running well past the willow.

'Right?' said Flit.

Farthing leered. They set off, skimming water.

The narrow aisle was quite still, paved with duckweed on which little snails had emerged, surface-browsing in hundreds. Past the tree flew the birds, now concealed by the reeds, past the pump to the river. Here their cover ran out and they stopped, glancing back.

'She's not seen us,' said Farthing.

'I doubt,' said Flit, 'she could now.'

'Then, full speed!' cried his comrade.

Wing to wing, the pair batted, almost touching the stream, clipping bullmace and sedge, daisy-hopping a glebe before easing their efforts. Behind, the tractor had shrunk, its hum faint in the heat, the flow's curve a mere sickle. Sheep began to appear. Grey on sun-faded green, they flecked a shallow ravine, browsing widely ahead, their trails scoring the hillside.

'We're safe, Farthing.'

'From Athene. We're under hawk skies, be watchful.'

A swallow circled them, gleaming. It made superior sounds, showing off its fine graces. 'A pair of mutts! You'll be caught.' Speeding close, it surveyed them: urchin faces, dull caps, their inelegant progress. 'You'll stand no chance on the hill, you need *performance* up there.'

136

The glossy bird raised its beak. Soaring high, it hung still then glissaded, streamed sunfire. 'You need *class* on the hills, you can't hide from the hawks. There's no shelter to save you.'

'You want a dust-up?' huffed Flit.

'A good drubbing?' offered Farthing.

The swallow banked. 'Gutter-hoppers!'

Derisively, it made off, and they envied its sleekness.

'That's speed, Farthing, that's *fast*.'

'Fast to leave, I should say, when we mentioned a barney.'

Flit's gaze ranged. 'But it's right, the brow's bare. Not a bush, not a clump – and hawk country.'

'I'm not frightened of hawks.'

'Just as well.'

'Why, are you?'

'No,' said Flit, 'but look there!'

Broad round wings sailed ahead, wheeling high on a thermal. They were distant as yet but if the sparrows had doubts a small, fierce head soon dispelled them. 'Hawk,' breathed Flit. 'He's not seen us.'

'He soon will!'

'What's our dodge?'

'*Think*,' urged Farthing.

'I'm thinking'

The lofty predator turned, eyes cast down for small victims.

'The 'daws!'

Noisy jackdaws soared slowly. Straggling up from the marsh they overtook the two sparrows, intent on crossing the hills. They disregarded the hawk, their powerful squadron secure, floating low on the slopes, silver-helmeted, bugling. Farthing whooped. 'There's our cover!'

'You're right,' cried Flit, 'let's be moving.'

Winging down, gaining speed, they vectored on the armada. Its lazy wing strokes deceived – now above, it surged swiftly.

'Faster, Flit, climb beneath them!'

The sparrows rose, toiling hard. Flit's wings ached as he climbed and, picking out a black hull, he at last berthed in its shadow. The jackdaw flung him a glance. Icy eyed, it ignored him.

'Can you stand the pace, partner?'

'I can stand anything *you* can.'

Watchman scanned the hot valley. The tawny distances glared, sultry, ominous almost. They lay like smooth wheaten seas, their sheen fierce, the corn ripening. Even pastures and marsh had a scorched, tetchy aspect. The world the lookout perceived was of sweltering sameness, relieved by one distant movement.

And that, the crawl of the tractor, was hardly enlivening. Back and forward it went, its very dust near-inert as it tidied the flood bank, attacking the nettles. Drowsily the rook watched it.

Below his perch, by the pond, a moorhen's addled egg burst, its effluvium rising. The sudden pop made him start but Watchman's gaze held the bank for as the tractor turned something ran from its path down the slope, seeking cover. Mag, he thought, his eye hostile.

'Kine,' the rook cawed, descending, 'show some life, look smart, weasel.'

'Huh?' said Kine. 'What's that, Watchman?' He had been dreaming of Clary. Brat and Bald-ear snoozed near him.

Watchman dropped to the Life Tree. 'Mag,' he rapped with disgust. 'Rouse, you sluggard, I've found her.'

'Where?'

'She's under the flood bank. I can take you right to her.'

'Leave your post?'

'And why not? What have that lot done for me?' The rook considered his kind and answered his own question. 'Overlooked me, that's what; neglected Watchman the sage, let a presbyter languish. Let them stew, this is work. Mag the vile killed my consort. Stir your warriors, weasel!'

'Three of us and a rook?'

Brat and Bald-ear eyed Watchman. He was a ragbag, a sketch. He had a permanent moult, joints that creaked and a stoop. He was a flying antique. 'Don't stand gaping,' he wheezed. 'Forward, shrimps, trust the war bird!'

'Hold on,' Kine said, 'let's think. We've made one ill-fated foray. It cost us a comrade.'

138

'Think?' the rook fumed. 'What with? A word, you shrimps, from the wise, for you have no brains to speak of. Mag's been forced from the bank, lost the cover she favours. There's no danger from Hob. Hob is passive by day and won't stir until dusk. Don't you see? Now's the time. Forward boldly!'

Kine said, 'Help is expected. Flit and Farthing are travelling.'

'Sparrows!' Watchman despaired. 'What's the use of a sparrow?'

Kine consulted the pond. Brave white lilies were floating, as they had in the mink days – days when fear was unknown and no weasel had dithered. Age had taught him to doubt; doubt had shackled decision.

'Are you coming or not? Does an old rook fight solo?'

'*Tchkkk*, we'll come. Lead on, Watchman.'

The weasels filed from the copse, the sun suddenly brilliant. The track was hot under their feet, the earth parched, its grit fiery. It had a whiff of dry herbs, that special scent of the land when high summer is acrid. It smelled to Kine of old battles.

Rolling corn filled their view, the sky's gloss on its brow so it shone like waxed deal. Where birds and squirrels had fed, pulling down the crisp heads, grains lay loose in the dust, amber drips, hard and nutty. Now and then the corn rustled and as the animals ran wiry grasses raised plumes, glistening fountains of seed or small, ragged-edged pennons.

Watchman lumbered ahead. As he flapped down the track, the three weasels kept pace, glad to move by the hedge for its margin was sunless. Little trees cast more shade. In one spot, red as blood, small wild plums made a carpet.

Then the marsh had begun and they marched by its channels. The rook dropped back, his voice hoarse. 'We'll go straight to the bank. Follow downstream at first and I'll mark the position. She's just below the wall's face, almost under the tractor.'

The engine's blare rose and fell. Kine could make out the pump, a van parked alongside: the engineer would be working. They reached the flood bank and stopped. They could hear chatter, a splash. The sounds denoted youths fishing, hidden by the high ridge, the broad, tractor-mown plateau.

Kine turned to the others. 'They won't be leaving the stream. They can't see us, they're harmless.'

'Wait,' hissed Brat.

Kine looked round. His gaze swerved to the willow. Its long green drapes fluttered slightly. There was a howl at their backs and, twirling, Kine glimpsed the witch, her claws levelled, approaching.

'Flat!' he shouted. 'Drop down flat!'

He felt the draught on his hackles. Then, with a hideous oath, the small owl overshot and banked steeply. 'She's turning,' Kine warned, 'look out.'

Bald-ear blinked. 'So's the sage – so's the ragbag,' he spluttered.

The tattered corvid stroked grimly. His fingered wings hammered air, shedding great dusky feathers. They spiralled down, dry, autumnal. His hoary beak was a spear; bleary eyes sighted fiercely. Like some decrepit black knight, the rook lurched into action.

'He's charging headlong,' whispered Brat.

'Beak to beak,' marvelled Bald-ear.

Kine sprang up. 'The old fool. Break off, Watchman, you'll perish!'

'No,' cried Brat, 'the *owl's* turning.'

'Lost her nerve . . .'

They watched, breathless.

'Curse you, rook,' screamed Athene. She seemed inclined to hold course, then, at the very last moment, clawed clear, veering sharply. Watchman's beak stabbed her tail. 'Aaoueeh!' howled the witch. Goosed again, she shrieked wildly. Watchman rattled with triumph, flailing obsolete pinions.

'He'll fall apart,' anguished Kine. 'That's enough, rook, come back.'

Watchman turned and landed, joints creaking.

'Amazing,' Brat cried. 'Well done!'

'Bah,' gasped Watchman 'Old skills . . . used to outfly the best. Flinty nerves, that's the trick. Haven't lost it, not yet.' He gulped deeply, exhausted. 'Mag's still there, I caught sight.'

'Right,' said Kine. 'When you've rested . . .'

'Don't need rest, it's not far.'

'Then take care, no risks, Watchman, leave the business to us. Steady, Bald-ear, don't rush. Let the rook spot the target.'

They moved below the escarpment, threading spiky marsh-grasses. Atop the bank, overhead, the earth shook, dust erupting. A rumbling roar marked the tractor. At times it came near the edge and soil avalanched on them. Kine glanced up and Brat shrugged. At least Mag would not hear them.

On the bank the noise mounted. It disconcerted the trio, almost deafening in pitch. Now the tumbling earth drubbed, mixed with clumps of mown nettle. A massive tyre crushed the ledge, its treads visible to them, half in space as it churned. All three weasels looked up. The roar had soared to a scream and a huge wheel was spinning.

'Run,' yelled Kine, 'get away! Run, the tractor is toppling!'

* * *

The child cried, 'More, don't stop yet. Tell the rest of the story.'

'Later,' said the girl, laughing. 'We'll have to see if you're good.'

'About the sparrows, the sparrows! About the *polecat*,' her son said.

'If you're good, more at bedtime.' She stretched herself on the lawn, part in sun, part in shade. It was a time of wellbeing. She loved the weeks around Lammas, the crops and garden full-blown, apples bending the boughs, a misty bloom on the damsons.

Warm nooks smelled of tomatoes, mighty leaves hid her marrows. The largest, green as the sea and watered nightly, was huge, her harvest festival marrow. Thirsty songbirds hopped round, blotched with red by mulberries. Bees hummed over her head in the sycamore's cavern.

The toddler played with his trike. He wore a floppy white hat. In a while, growing bored, he splashed about in his pool, a little plastic contraption, floating plantain heads in it.

'Why can't we go to the pond?'

'Not now, darling, you paddle.'

'I could *swim* in the pond.'

'You can't swim and it's deep.'

'We could look for the weasel.'

She smiled. 'Be good, like I said. You want that story,' she bargained. He nodded, growing content, and the girl lay back dreaming. She watched the butterflies drift: golden commas, wings crimped, and small powdery blues which a languid sky swallowed.

Secretive in the hedge, slim convolvulus prowled, throwing magical blooms, short-lived trumpets of white, mirages in the sunlight. A gleaming dragonfly swooped, hovering by the playpool. Amber fuselage poised, it took stock then swept forward. Gleefully, the child chased it.

The girl looked up at the cottage. Her drowsy gaze searched the eaves, little shadowy windows. Were *they* there, out of sight, peering into the brilliance? Were the silent ones watching, marvelling at her luck? Were they truly amazed, poor impoverished souls, by her life in their dwelling?

They had slogged to subsist, slaved in fields for a pittance. Did her welfare astonish – her happy child, handsome husband, her easy love, summer leisure?

It made her slightly afraid, as if her blessings were sinful. Counting them aroused guilt, like greedy moments when young, gloating over the jam, spreading honey too thickly. It did not do to be smug for all spells could be broken.

She heard a step in the lane and jumped, her thoughts interrupted. A chill presentiment gripped her. The girl possessed a sixth sense, the wild awareness of marsh life. A gate clicked and opened.

'Someone there?' called the youth. It was the scrawny one, panting.

She rose abruptly. 'What's up?'

'There's been an accident, missus. Ploughman's toppled the tractor.'

'Dad?' she said, her face taut.

'I don't think anything's broke. They're bringing him in the van. He was queer, kind of mumbling.'

'Then he's hurt . . .'

'He's shook up.'

'Watch the child, I'll run down.' She took a stride to the gate, stopping short, the van looming. As it braked she peered in. Ploughman looked in one piece, more bemused than in pain. 'Dad?' The window was down. He stared forward, unmoving. 'Dad? You safe, dad?' she blurted.

'Be all right,' he said slowly. 'Mind the goose . . . the old goose . . .'

The girl glanced at her husband. He gripped the wheel, his face anxious. 'Still in shock,' he surmised. 'Got a touch of concussion.'

In the back, on the tools, the big youth goggled dumbly.

'Gun,' said Ploughman, 'the goose.'

'God,' the girl sighed, 'the fool! *You're* the goose, you old fool – on that bank in a tractor. With eyes like yours. Dad, you're mad!'

'Wiser now,' soothed her husband.

'*Babbling* now!'

'Could be worse.'

'Needs sweet tea, a lie down.'

'Call the doc, girl, we'll help him.'

Mag's snout rose; she smelled derv. The tractor lay on its side, the men gone, and she snarled. The monstrous engine was still, as impotent as a corpse. It had flattened her lair, driven her down the bank, almost crushed her in falling.

Two wheels hung in space; a cab window was broken. With its belly exposed the great engine seeped oil, its clogged mower on end, the hydraulic gear twisted. It was a danger no more and Mag sniffed her contempt, rearing up on her haunches.

'I hope,' came a voice from the willow, 'they were caught, smashed to pulp.'

'Who?' snapped Mag. 'I saw no one.'

'The weasel vermin, the rook.' Athene nursed a sore tail. 'They stalked you under the bank. If you were smart you'd have known.'

'And what did *you* do, small owl?'

'I'm a night fiend, like Hob. I scorn vermin by day.'

'You're a liar,' sneered Mag, 'a loud, pustule-tailed liar.'

The tree resounded with oaths. 'The rook surprised me, that's all.'

143

'We'll tell Hob, he'll be pleased.' Mag's sarcasm was fierce. 'He'll be proud of you, witch, you're a real terror.'

'You wouldn't tell him!'

Mag glowered. 'Shut you beak, it'll keep. Weasels stalked me, you say? And the rook from the copse?' She ventured nearer the tractor. 'No one tweaks *Mag's* tail, witch owl.'

She caught a scent on the air and approached the farm engine. '*Something's* trapped,' she opined. 'The machine's injured someone.' The cab claimed her interest. It was a vast, upturned hutch, a strange wreck of a prison.

Mag sniffed the smashed window. It reeked of prey and she drooled. Pushing forward her head, she examined the contents.

On what was now the cab's floor – in fact, its righthand side door – lay Ploughman's lunch pack and thermos, a coil of rope and a spanner. Flung loose in the crash, they sprawled now amid dust, scrapes of clay and an old sack. The predator eyed a rag, its folds pungent with oil. Her gaze flicked to the pedals, tipped in vertical line, then homed into a corner. At last her chilly orbs gleamed.

Watchman crouched in the dust. One wing stiffly out-stretched, he drew back in the crevice.

'So!' Mag crowed through her fangs, 'what an apposite pleasure – first his spouse, now the sage.' She curled in through the gap. 'There's *some* use in a tractor.'

'Don't come near,' wheezed the corvid. 'I don't advise it.'

'Words of wisdom?' she sneered. 'Still the sage of the covert?'

'It broke my wing, Mag . . .'

'Then greet me! A broken wing – a harsh death. Let me spare you the anguish. Why wait, Watchman, for death?'

She took a step, her teeth bright, the maw pink as it opened. The rook allowed her a pace then rose, suddenly fit, perching high in the ceiling. Here a second door gaped, used in Ploughman's escape, and the bird settled on it. 'Caw,' he croaked, peering down, 'I did warn you to stop. Now you're here, Mag, enclosed.'

'You're not hurt?'

'Ah, my wing – the deception. The oldest ruse on the marsh. Mag, you're cruel but not clever.'

'Ruse?' she hissed. She spun round. The broken pane had been blocked, the gap filled by two weasels. Brat and Bald-ear stood in it. Again the ferret turned quickly. Kine had popped from the seat, squirming out from the springs. With a dazzling leap, he transferred to the helm, at the steering wheel's centre. 'Mag,' he churred, 'You can't run, not this time. You're imprisoned. Like you used to be, ferret. Watchman's notion, of course – as you said, still the savant.'

'Kine, I'll tear you apart.' Mag felt cramped, claustrophobic. 'In the *open*,' she grated.

'Oh no, Mag, in the cab; in four walls, like your bad days.'

'Walls . . .' She stared at the windows. 'Stand aside from that gap.' Brat and Bald-ear did not move. 'Clear the way,' cried the giant. 'I'll break out, you'll be smashed.'

'No, Mag,' Kine hissed, 'You'll stay here.' From the wheel he curved down, landing pick-a-back on her, teeth in fur, his claws bedding. Mag stood perfectly still. She seemed stunned then reared up, whirling round as Brat struck, Bald-ear with him.

Kine was close to her ear. 'Like a hutch, Mag,' he whispered.

'Back in prison,' put in Watchman.

Mag's hands slashed and Brat fell. He struck the hand brake and slumped. With a roar the giant shook, flinging Bald-ear aside so he drubbed the gear levers – low range, half gears and main gears. As he slid to the floor, rapping earth-choked foot pedals, a grim smile escaped him.

Kine was hurled from his seat.

'Dance,' he rallied the sprites. 'Dance within the glass palace!' He twirled away, leaping high, bouncing off the rear window. Zooming to the cab's roof (now a vertical plane), he kicked hard into space, bounced again off the windscreen. From wall to wall the sprites whisked, pane to panel, teeth snapping. They flew like small trapeze artists, soared like trampoline experts.

As Mag swatted and cursed, they multiplied in her sight, framed in cracked driving mirrors. Dizzily the brute clawed.

Kine paused on the clutch pedal. With another swift plunge, he struck out with his feet, raked Mag's flank then was gone, screened by levers and knobs, the cab's hydraulic controls, the independent power take-off.

Bald-ear charged, his head levelled. He caught the enemy's ribs, twitched a bruised snout and ducked. Mag clawed air, her oaths violent. 'Just stand still – I'll destroy you!'

'Mag,' purred Kine, 'your head's swimming.'

'The walls are close,' droned the rook, 'you feel choked, suffocating.' He held the exit now, crouching, his beak at the ready. 'It's airless, Mag, stuffy.'

The ferret snarled. 'You'll be *killed*. The regime . . .' She felt giddy. 'You'll pay dearly for this. Owl,' she shrieked, 'come and kill – come and kill them, Athene!'

There was a withering silence. She eyed the sky in the ceiling. 'Athene, come and kill them!'

'She isn't fond of you, Mag.'

'She's pledged,' howled Mag. 'The alliance – the feared alliance of hatred!'

'She doesn't love you,' flung Kine. 'Those who hate die alone.'

'*You'll* die, Kine. Your friends too, they'll die, weasel.' She bowled him into a corner. 'Every *one*,' she screamed, pouncing. 'It's decreed. You'll all perish!'

'Stop her, Bald-ear . . .' Brat lunged. She ripped his head and blood brimmed. He reached her throat and hung on, Bald-ear grappling beside him. Kine rolled clear, jumping up. 'Don't let go,' he cried, charging. They clung to Mag's powerful neck, the three weasels together. 'Keep hold, she's gone mad!'

Jaws locked grimly, they leeched, tossed and pitched against steel, against stanchions and knobs, against Ploughman's thermos, on to levers and handles, in grit, against tools, swiping pedals, blocks, panels. Their backs were lashed, their sides whipped. Like a bronco, Mag bucked then stood trembling, eyes fixed – eyes that focused on marsh, open space, grassy freedom.

She gave a tremulous heave, a climactic leap forward, struck the window and crumpled.

A sudden blob of rain splashed. More came tumbling. The downfall spattered the cab, oddly bright in the sun, over in a few moments.

Kine writhed clear, torn and battered. Brat had crawled from the body. 'She broke her neck,' said the rook. 'Drag your friend out, he's stunned.' Brat and Kine tugged at Bald-ear. He was locked to the ferret. 'Let go, Bald-ear, it's done.'

Bald-ear blinked, his eyes rolling. His beam was beatific.

* * *

The pond reflected the evening. Its swims were smooth and azure, streaked with mare's-tails of cloud. Small fish broke them with rings, some of which interlinked, little carp leaving bubbles. Once a sizable flank, arching brightly, stirred froth, lackadaisical crests, nothing sinister in them.

Even Scrat felt secure. A warm laziness spread, spanning ripples and rings, circumscribed by pond fennel, blue forget-me-nots, crowfoot. Flowering reed raised pink crowns, arrowhead bloomed in shallows. The pond in summer seduced, its dark chasm forgotten.

Looking out from her home, the girl pondered the copse, the gold wheat, the combiner. Other men were at work, her dad banned from the harvest. Ploughman fretted indoors, resting up on doctor's orders. High time, too, the old fool; stumped at last, thought his daughter.

She turned and tucked up her son, his face washed, his hair slick. Bathtime's spell was complete: he was, briefly, an angel. 'Mum, you promised – the story.'

'Yes.' She sat on his bed.

'Flit and Farthing,' the child said.

'Flit and Farthing – where were we?'

The sparrows dropped from the heights past dense spruce woods to heath, a dry and heathery realm resin-scented by pine through which sandy paths trailed, sometimes edging round scrub or by racks stacked with fire brooms. Little lizards ran off and the birds saw a squirrel.

The place was sun-scorched and parched. Where grass

grew it looked dead, the ferns rusty and shrivelled; where vines of bryony drooped heart-shaped leaves had turned brown. A few hazels bore nuts but made thin, straggling bushes. Only the ground growth was dense – wiry stuff, tough and hostile.

'We won't find Wonder in that,' predicted Farthing, descending. They pitched to rest in a fir, the branch crusty with cones. 'We'd never spot her.'

'We'll have to try,' Flit said glumly.

'It isn't much of a land. Let's find food. I feel hungry.'

They watched the squirrel below. It sat erect, tail turned up, pulling scales from a fir cone. In a while it looked round, scraped a hole in the ground and concealed a nut in it. Then, replacing the earth, the beast pressed it down firmly, camouflaging the surface.

Flit said doubtfully, '*What* food?'

'I don't know,' confessed Farthing. He eyed a cluster of toadstools.

'Those are mine,' warned the squirrel. It plucked the largest and scowled, running up the tree with it. Where a branch joined the trunk, it lodged the food in the fork, viewed the sparrows and spat.

Farthing ruffled his feathers.

Flit said, 'Ruffian – let's baste him!'

'No,' said Farthing, 'not yet. Come on, comrade, I'm famished.' He fluttered down to the fungus. 'First, let's eat.'

'*Then* the dust-up!'

They plied their beaks. 'It's not bad.'

'Watch the squirrel, he's coming.'

Headfirst, it descended. The creature came down like lightning, flashed towards them by leaps, reached the toadstools and quivered. Spitting rage and abuse, it hopped round them, tail upright.

'He needs a lesson,' chirped Flit.

'A course in manners,' said Farthing.

There was a lull and they glowered. The squirrel, spotting a nut, had paused to open the shell. Deftly skinning the kernel it gnawed in silence, scratched its chest and resumed swearing. Flit said, 'Right, that's enough.'

148

'Yes, the tike's had his chance.'

They plumped up their gorgets. 'We're not scared of the natives!'

A husky laugh made them jump. 'We're not all quite so vulgar.' It was amused, a calm drawl. 'Push off, squirrel,' it ordered.

'Wonder?' Farthing said slowly.

'You haven't changed, you two sparrows.'

'It *is* Wonder!' Flit ogled. It had been a long time. She was different – older, naturally, grander. The sparkling Wonder had gone, the bouncy Clarylike sprite. This was Wonder serene, almost stately, and handsome.

'Well,' she said, 'I'm surprised, this is quite unexpected.' Her eye was searching, astute. 'So what brings you this distance?'

Farthing blurted, 'It's Hob – the berserker's rampaging.'

Flit said, 'Sacking the valley.'

Wonder frowned. 'Hob – who's Hob?'

'The crazed demon, the night fiend.'

'What of Kine?' It was quiet.

'Safe – at least, when we left. But hard-pressed . . .' Farthing outlined events, going back to the start, and Wonder smiled at Kine's fling, his young mate and the kitts, but grew grave at the outcome. As the story progressed, she sighed, shaking her head, sometimes asking a question.

'You see,' said Farthing at last, 'Kine needs fighters, more help. Without help the vale's lost, Hob will ravage the copse, seize the Life Tree and pond. Soon, he'll spread to the ridge, take his sport – then the orchard.'

'Kine the hero,' said Wonder. Her head rose, age-ennobled. 'He's fought so many brutes. Now he's old, still at war. Well, old fighters die hard – tell him Wonder is coming.'

'We will, indeed!'

'Fly and tell him. Say she'll bring *her* young mate.' She laughed softly, eyes bright. 'Heath's as grey as a squirrel but still has his moments.'

'The old mink fighter,' breathed Flit.

'We'll fly now,' resolved Farthing.

'Wait,' said Wonder, 'first rest. Set out fresh and stay safe. We'll take longer on foot but tell Kine we'll be coming.'

The darkened dyke gave a heave and Hob towered from the water. He had an eel in his mouth and as he mounted the bank it coiled and writhed round his neck. It made his great head more fearsome. He paused to shake, shedding swill, his coarse mane damp and matted, the eel's dance macabre.

From the roof of the pump the small owl watched in silence. She was well out of Hob's reach yet hesitated to speak for, safe or not, she was awed. The sight of Hob stirred her craw, thrilled her cold, perverse heart. They were two – owl and fitchet. Mag was dead, Mag was dead! She wished to blare it out loud but, for now, merely gloated.

Mag had stolen her light, filched the Night Lord's attentions. *Spouse*, the ferret had claimed! There was no spouse in the pact, in the alliance as pledged. Mag had feathered her nest, elevated her station. Well, spouse or not, she was gone – the small witch was Hob's partner.

She nerved herself, peering down. He was a prince of destruction and her high perch was consoling. He would, she guessed, throw a fit when told of Mag's sudden end, and she was not suicidal. He was a messenger killer, a lord of death, crazed, majestic. They were two of a kind. Three had never made sense; why divide the spoils three ways?

'Hob,' she hailed, 'sombre tidings . . .' Did her voice sound triumphant? 'Mag's been killed. It's just us . . .'

'Mag?' She saw it sink in. Hob's head turned and held still. Even the eel seemed to freeze. Then his howl skirled aloft, lashing space in its wrath, whipping clouds into turmoil. In the night, black vaults echoed. 'Killed?' he roared. 'Hob's mate *killed?*' His soused mane stood on end. The eel flailed, Hob's jaws crackling. He tore the thing into shreds.

Then he ravaged the shreds.

On the marsh, the frogs cowed – those of them still alive. Hob's regime had wrought havoc.

'I mourn for Mag,' wailed Athene. Was her dirge too ecstatic? 'Mag the mistress of hate.' Mag the double-faced schemer!

Overhead clouds stampeded, hushed as phantoms; on the hills there was lightning. It cast the fiend in white fire. 'Gone,' he raged, 'my last chance. Hob's last chance to renew, spawn the seeds of revenge, bloat the night with his issue. Gone the night of the brood, the renaissance of terror!'

'It's just the two of us now.' Did the owl sound exultant?

Hob's mouth twisted; he snarled. Dusky winds fled his fury. The brute said suddenly, 'Who? Tell me, night bird, who did it?' The question seared like a claw, made Athene bob quickly. She gave a tremulous hoot, scarcely hiding her gloating.

'Why, the weasels,' she smirked, 'the fool Kine and his friends. A mere trio of sprites and a broken-down rook. I'm surprised they were able.'

'Tawdry goblins?'

'Small vermin.'

'See they die. They are condemned!' Hob's head reared, his eyes blazing. Icily, he declared, 'All they have must be razed, the copse seized, its life wasted. The fallen Tree must be sacked. Every weasel must perish.'

The valley was languid. Showers had passed to the east and the sun glistened on droplets. They hung like gems round the woods, sapphires, jade, rubies, emeralds, some of pure diamond brilliance. It was humid and calm; the corn harvest was over.

Summer's birdsong had waned, the thrush sparing of voice, blackbird's rhapsody frugal. Little music survived as talents rested till autumn. Occasionally, unseen, a jay or magpie struck up, scolding, raucous, but otherwise it was quiet.

Yet unploughed, moist fields stewed, full of dank, bristling stubble. Flocks of birds gleaned the waste or sought groundsel and insects. Here and there, their bills shovelling, small platoons of duck waddled. Hedgerow blackberries ripened. In the sun, ditches steamed, full of tall, wilting stalks.

Spring's cow parsley had died, its thick stems, or gicks, brittle. Banks of willowherb swayed, fuzzy seedheads erupting. Kine peered out at the track then ducked back through the copse. As he moved, he still ached, a reminder of battle.

'*Tchkkk*.' He paused by the brook. The old hollow elm dripped, its sparse leaves gently stirring. It looked normal by day, glowing only at night, but he passed it with caution. It was prodigious, a freak. He held the tree in respect, convinced its power was a sign, a strange and luminous sign. For good or bad, he knew not.

'*Tchk-kkk-chk!*' Something moved. Quietly, Kine crouched and waited. Something skipped though the growth, light of step, drawing closer. With a cry he sprang out, falling on the intruder.

'Kine, it's me!'

He pulled back. Confused, he blinked his delight.

'You've not forgotten me, Kine?'

'Not for a moment,' he yelped, 'not for an instant, how could I?' Aches forgotten, he frisked. 'You've returned – you've been missed! This is wonderful, Clary!'

'Bliss,' she cried. 'And you're safe.'

'We're both safe,' he rejoiced.

'You old war dog.' They romped.

'And the kitts – have they grown?'

'Not so kittenish, Kine, three fine dandies. They're all right where they are, they can cope in the orchard.'

'Where *you* ought to be,' Kine said. It lacked much conviction.

'No,' said Clary, 'not now; my place is with Kine. Look how lively I make you!'

'Kine is always alive!'

'Right,' laughed Clary, 'then catch me . . .' Head to tail, they raced off, daft as kitts, weasel-nimble. Dancing sunrays pierced leaves, flitting shadows disported. Through the wood the sprites chased, under thickets, round dells, over moss and dog violets, leaping serpentine roots, speeding deep through the warren.

'Nothing's changed, Kine,' cried Clary.

'Nothing's going to,' he bawled, 'not while Kine can defend it.'

Side by side they reached the Moon Pond. Water soldiers speared up and great lilypads floated. Clary said, 'It's still perfect. You'll defend it, we *all* will.'

Kine admired her – her verve. She sprang lithely, unstrained, while his own burdened lungs puffed. When at last they drew up, she was smiling, unruffled, the older sprite breathless. 'You know,' he gulped, 'we lost Scoter?'

'Yes, poor Scoter.' She sighed.

'By the stars, we avenged him!'

'So I heard – you fought Mag.'

'Killed her, Clary, for Scoter, overthrew the she-ferret. Brat and Bald-ear did well. They'll be happy to see you.'

'They're fine fighters,' said Clary.

'Mmm,' said Kine, 'they need leading.' He eyed the female askance. 'They had Kine at their head, Kine the hero commanding.' Her smile was fond and he warmed, 'Kine the bold, the accomplished; Kine the dauntless, the legend . . .'

Scrat popped up.

'Not now, scout.'

'Kine, it's bad.'

'It can wait. We've killed Mag. Clary's back,' Kine enthused.

'Let him speak,' said the female.

'The frogs have gone,' blurted Scrat. 'Hob has issued his writ: no one's safe after dark. All the vale will be blood, no one spared the fiend's fury. You never *should've* killed Mag. Every creature is sentenced.'

'Hob is crazed, we know that.'

'D-doubly crazed since Mag perished.'

'So,' asked Clary, 'what now?'

Kine looked grave. 'We must wait, hope the sparrows find Wonder. If she brings Heath, we'll be six. Six against the berserker.'

* * *

A jay had planted an acorn and it had grown near the pump, a fine oak with bright leaves, its height all of twelve inches. Indifferent to its size, a passing gallfly had laid eggs on the tyro. Two had hatched into grubs, each grub raising a gall, a smoothly perfect oak apple.

Amid the growth by the path the young oak showed its emblems. It looked, the engineer thought, like a child – his own son – proud and perky. A young oak, that was apt. A tall tree of the future!

153

He checked the pumphouse, amused. The girl would laugh, he reflected, for he knew nothing of plants. But he remembered oak apples: the kids in town would play with them when hard up for marbles. As he left he bent down, plucking one of the nodules. It was faultlessly round, the engineering of nature.

He revved the van and drove off. He saw his son engineering, following in dad's footsteps, though not a minder of pumps – a Brunel of his era! Dreamily, the man smiled. At Ploughman's dwelling, he stopped and walked to the side entrance.

The kitchen door was unlatched.

Since the mishap occurred the girl had dropped in each day, taking care of her father, but Ploughman's ways were untidy. Dirty crocks lay about, bits of food were uncovered. The gun was propped by the window, a box of cartridges open.

'Anybody around?'

He shrugged, his question unanswered, closed the door and moved on. Ploughman's pleasure was gardening but now the place was neglected. Dandelions reared their heads, a once-shaven hedge sprouted. Down the end, by the huts, the goose hissed, neck extended.

A dull voice challenged, 'Who wants me?' Ploughman sat on a box, shoulders hunched. 'Oh, it's you,' he said glumly.

'Called to see how you're feeling.'

The farm man lowered his eyes. 'Better you than the girl. I can do without fussing.'

'She likes to see you're all right, see you rest. Doctor's orders.'

'Pack up working, you mean?'

'Agricultural work, yes.'

Ploughman said, 'What else is there?'

The younger man dropped the subject. He thought a moment then said, 'D'you want a hand with the garden?'

'No I don't. She keeps asking me that so don't *you* start on me, mister. At least the goose doesn't fuss.' The bird glared as he muttered, its eye unrelenting. 'I can moan to the goose. I can moan all I like here.'

'If it makes you feel better.'

'It does more good than her scoldings.' The veteran glanced up obliquely. He showed a glimmer of interest. 'How's the boy?' he inquired. 'What's he up to?'

'I hope he's home, the young scamp.'

'He'll take some keeping at home, lad, he's a natural explorer. Got the roaming blood in him, like his mother at his age; never knew where she'd get to.'

'We'd better send him up here.'

'I'm no use, son, forget it.'

'Bosh,' the engineer jollied, 'what sort of daft talk is that? You'll pick up, it's reaction. You feel depressed but it won't last.'

'It will, the way that I'm feeling. I reckon this'll get worse. I saw Poacher go this way.' Ploughman paused. 'In the spring. The beggar lasted till autumn, barely autumn,' he grunted.

'Come on, man, that was different.'

'Aches and pains, same complaint. Gone by winter, the sinner.'

'Get along, you're all right. What you need's a good rest. You've got years in you yet.' The young man conjured a smile, the small oak tree remembered. 'You've a grandson to live for.' He turned and said, 'Look, you've friends – two more visitors coming.'

The youths approached from the track, fishing gear on their shoulders. 'They'll buck you up. I'll get on.'

'How's the patient?' They stopped.

'Feeling low, sitting moping. Stay and bolster his spirits, chat to him about fishing.'

'We can do better than that.' They grinned broadly and the big youth said, 'He'll cheer up, we've got something to show him.' He tapped the catch bag he carried. 'We've made a find by the bank where the tractor went over. There's still a lot of smashed glass.'

He held aloft the dead ferret.

Scrat peered upwards and downwards. Either way, the moon glared and filled his pinhead-sized eyes. It blinded him from the pond, dazzled over the trees; flared from bottomless depths and the night's boundless heavens.

Either way his head swam and the midget retreated. Stopping under the trees, he looked back. Their leafy branches were dark, obfuscating the rays so the pool was in focus. He saw its sheen and the reeds, a moorhen's rippling wake, the tight heads of closed lilies.

He saw the great beamy pier, its deck bright in the moon, its bare-fingered arms shining. Atop the pier was the hole and he considered a visit, but Kine had Clary back now and might not thank him for calling.

He watched the moorhen's wake spread. It seemed uncommonly broad, the pond oddly unsettled. The little ripples had grown, become silver-capped waves making ominous sounds, sloshing, plopping, the pool turning lumpy. No fowl alone had done that and Scrat recited the pond law:

Everything has a cause . . .

He felt suddenly chilly. His mini-snout had grown cold. He wished himself somewhere else but was compelled to observe, watch the waves, his feet rooted. An icy spell gripped the dwarf, froze his limbs, every hair on him tingling.

It had all happened before – the mounds, the troughs and the bubbles. Now the lilypads rocked. In tight ranks the reeds swayed, huddling up to one side, scuttling back to another. *Slop!* The pond seemed to heave. Little creeks felt its surge, promontories were jostled. Where the Life Tree stood out drifts of moonlight spume scudded.

'Doom,' moaned Scrat. Warn the weasels! But he was dry in the throat. Something, he sensed, was watching. Gawping up at the Tree he saw two yellow orbs staring, ghoulish in the star-pattern. The witch eyed him fiercely.

'Woe,' groaned Scrat. Wake the heroes!

'One squeak, shrew, and you're dead. Draw one breath and I'll pounce on you.'

Weak with fear, Scrat gulped dumbly. The slap of water was loud. Above, the little owl glowered, squat where planets were whirling. Under her the pond menaced. He saw a great prow wave curve, strike the bank, foam and crumble. Another wave followed.

At last the water curled back, seemed sucked into a trough, and Scrat cringed in stark terror. He shut his eyes, squeezed them tightly. Doom and dread! It was quiet. For maybe four or five seconds he heard no sound, then a crunch – the vile crunch of jaws grinding. Despite himself, the shrew peeped.

A dusky spectre loomed large, shoulders hunched as it gorged, the dead moorhen outstretched. Hob had climbed from the reeds, his kill trickling blood. Coat still slick, the fiend scowled, his grim business offhand, a diversion. Several times the giant snarled, each time eyeing the Life Tree.

On her perch, the owl hissed, 'Kill the weasels, the weasels!' The dumpy witch was impatient. 'In the hole, Hob, the hole!'

'*Silence*,' rumbled the giant. 'No one hurries the Night Lord.'

Scrat was stiff.

'Now!' the owl rasped.

'Let them wait,' returned Hob. The hunched phantom spoke quietly. 'Let them quail till I'm ready.'

The craven midget was mute. If only he possessed courage! Instead fear choked his warning. Kine, run now, his heart pleaded. His tongue would not form it.

He watched the Night Lord rear up. The berserker was monstrous, a spectre of violence. He shook and water dropped from him. Behind a huge skull blazed hate, hate the fuel of his passion. Lips tight, he moved swiftly. He seemed to glide to the Tree, melt like night in its roots, tower again on its topside, fangs exposed. Darts of moonlight flashed on them.

Shout, thought Scrat, shout out bravely – shout or watch the sprites perish! But he kept quiet, valour stifled.

The creature leered. He was grey in the moon, demonically gaunt.

'So,' he sneered, 'this is it? This is hallowed, the Life Tree?'

'In the hole!' cried Athene.

'This old hulk?' the brute cackled.

'Kill them! Think of Mag – kill them! Crush the uppity vermin!'

Hob slid closer.

'Pounce, polecat!'

The ghostly shape rose and fell. Its armed snout closed the gap, its claws scraped the embrasure. Scrat felt sick as he watched. For some moments, Hob toiled then discharged two long snorts. Sitting back, he howled wildly, 'Fool! You imbecile fool!' His eyes blazed at Athene. 'You screeching fool, the hole's empty. *You* brought me here – the hole's empty!'

'I didn't know . . .'

'Curse you, *fool!*'

Heaving quietly, Scrat sighed.

Athene flew with an oath. 'Little cheats,' she exclaimed. 'It's not my fault they've gone. Don't you curse *me*, you fiend. The small vermin have tricked you.'

'They've tricked *you*,' hurled the other. 'Next time, witch owl, I'll flay you.'

'*Aaeeow!*' The bird fled.

When Scrat peered, both had vanished, Athene's hoot distant. 'We'll be back, shrew, tell Kine. Tell the vermin they'll suffer.'

He drew a breath. He was limp, his relief overwhelming. Tiny tremors ran through him. He was alive, in one piece. Kine and Clary were safe. Fear had saved him, he thought, not with pride but correctly. He might have died; might have shouted and died – died a hero for nothing. The velvet mite shuddered.

'*Scrat!*'

He jumped like a frog.

There was a titter above. From dark leaves Kine jumped down, Clary following quickly. 'Scrat,' said Kine, 'you looked anxious.'

'B-but . . .'

'Bear up, we're not *stupid*!'

'It's no shame, Scrat,' said Clary. 'I was scared. We're all frightened.'

'Kine is fearless,' Scrat sighed.

'Pooh,' said Clary, 'not always.'

'He's a hero,' the shrew said.

'Because he's brave,' said the female. 'You can't be brave if you're fearless; only zombies are fearless. Unless you're scared, there's no courage. The more you're scared,' she explained, 'the more it's brave to act boldly.'

158

Scrat looked doubtful. 'I'm *always* scared.'

'Then you could be a great hero.'

'I don't see Kine looking scared. I'm sure Kine's never frightened.'

'Are you, Kine?' Clary smiled. 'Tell the truth,' purred his partner.

'Well, I . . .' Kine said. He frowned.

Brat and Bald-ear reprieved him. Bounding out of the gloom, they rushed into the moonlight. 'We saw them! We saw Hob and Athene heading back to the marsh. Hob passed close, he's immense, a mad monster,' Brat blurted. 'We thought Mag was a giant . . .'

The shrew blinked. 'Were you f-frightened?'

'Frightened?' Brat said. 'I'll say!'

'And you, B-Bald-ear?'

Kine glared. He said, snarling, 'Hear this – enough chat, we're not rabbits; enough idle confessions. I want nerve, resolution; the palpitations are over. We're not mice, we're grown weasels. Pipe down, shrew, you're a scout, you'll *behave* like a weasel.'

'Doom,' squeaked Scrat.

'Pay attention. I want cool, steady fighters. You've seen the foe, you've all gawped; now brace up and think forward. Hob is daunting,' growled Kine, 'so was Mag and she's dead. We stayed calm and outdanced her. Hob's a deadlier threat but Kine's yet to be beaten. Kine does not bow to tyrants.

'And hear this,' he commanded, 'Kine is smart, so take heed. I want boldness and dash but no risks will be taken. First we plan *then* we act – Scoter's wisdom will gird us. I expect reinforcements. Until they come, watch and listen. I want more information. I want to know where Hob rests, want to know his locations. Is he still at the pump? Are there paths the fiend favours?'

He paused. 'The dwarf will report. You'll bask in glory yet, shrewmouse!'

* * *

Kine advanced to the garden. He and Clary were hunting, the air astir from the west blowing straight down the vale. It teased

159

bushes and brakes, loosening leaves prematurely. One or two tumbled past them.

'If only,' Clary was saying, 'the fiend was diurnal. At least, by day we could spot him; at night he's simply a shadow.'

'A lethal shadow.' Kine stopped.

The cottage garden was sheltered. Breath condensed on a window, a small, snub nose squashed against it. Behind the spidery pane, the child's misty eyes widened.

'A deadly wraith,' Kine went on, his partner nodding agreement.

She said, 'Poor Kine.'

'Why poor Kine?'

'You saw the brute before we did, and all that time you kept quiet, kept your fears to yourself.'

'And lied,' he said with a gleam. 'I thought the danger might pass.'

'Well, now you're back in command. That's as it should be,' said Clary. 'We're going to win, just you see. We've got a legend to lead us.'

'Against all odds,' Kine said drily. 'Odds we've got to reduce. We need a stratagem, Clary . . . I wish the others would come. I wish I'd Wonder beside me.'

'Wonder?' Clary said sharply. 'You've got *me*, Kine, why Wonder?'

'And Heath,' he added in haste. 'They're tried and trusty in combat.'

'Aren't *I* trusty?'

'Of course. You're a flame, a bright dancer. You're invaluable, Clary.' Her pout dissolved. 'You're the best, but we could do with more strength, seasoned fighters.'

The face had gone from the pane. They heard the cottage door creak and, ducking into the hedge, pushed on through to the track. Flit and Farthing were dusting, flicking earth with their feathers.

Kine's face brightened. 'They're back!'

'Back last night,' announced Farthing. 'Nothing to it, a doddle.'

'Another mission accomplished,' his comrade chirped smugly.

160

'Would we fail? They don't come cuter than sparrows.'

'Then they'll arrive . . .'

'About now – unless friend Hob saw them coming.'

'No,' said Kine, 'Hob won't stop them. They know the hill paths too well, they know the gullies and clefts. They're old hands, Heath and Wonder.'

'Tried and trusty,' drawled Clary. She mimicked him with wry skill but her mate was not listening.

'Come on, Clary, the wood. They could be waiting,' he shouted.

They were and Clary held back, watching Kine greet the travellers. Their joy was deep but restrained, a touch too sober, perhaps, but then elders were elders. They had an awesome distinction. Heath was quiet and grey-muzzled; his manner was thoughtful. Wonder's poise was – well, wondrous.

She was quite small, very slender; indeed, no larger than Clary. Yet, somehow, Wonder seemed grand, her head high, the gaze daunting. She had a lofty assurance the other resented. Kine was plainly impressed.

'So this,' said Wonder, 'is Clary.'

The brilliant eyes burned a moment with condescension, thought Clary.

Kine said proudly, 'That's her.'

'Can she fight?'

'She's a spitfire.'

'She's very young,' pondered Wonder.

'And you are not!' Clary bridled. 'Does it matter?'

The other stared, the males silent. It had burst out like a bolt, stunned the glade, stilled the wind. Bristling, Clary glared back. She should have bitten her tongue but, too late, stood her ground.

There was a rippling laugh and Wonder bubbled with mirth. 'Good for you,' she exclaimed, 'it doesn't matter a jot. I think you're just what Kine needed.'

Startled, Clary was mute.

Wonder turned from the others. 'I hope it's not your last word. Come, let's talk, I want news: tell me more of yourself, of the kitts, of your orchard. It's time the apples were red; are Kine's scions fine dandies? We'll have our fill of war soon, let's talk first of life's pleasures.'

Heath grinned. 'They'll get on.'

'Yes,' said Kine, his fears gone. 'They've the same kind of spirit.'

'Kia's?' mused Heath.

'Much like Kia's.' Kine regarded him slowly. 'You know,' he said, harking back, 'you've not changed. A bit grey.'

'*You've* not changed.'

'Still Young Heath! It's been a long time, old friend.'

'Too long,' Heath said with feeling, 'since the battle with Rattun. And, before, in the Mink Wars.'

'Always war, my friend, always peril.'

'That's where comrades come in. We're still bold, the old heroes.'

'We're going to need to be,' Kine said.

'It's bad?' Heath asked quietly.

'Worse than anything yet. Worse than Rattun and Gru. I'm not sure we can win, that anyone will survive. That's the truth of it, Heath. Don't let on to the rest. If we fail, the vale's blighted.'

Watchman swooped through the dusk, spotted Scrat and alighted. The shrew had staked out the pump. Hidden near an old spile (long since rotten), he quietly supped on its hoard, ants and slaters abounding. Startled now, the dwarf gasped.

'D-don't do that, rook, at dusk. You could give me a seizure.' He snatched a woodlouse and munched.

'So could stuffing your stomach.'

Pigmy teeth crunched on chitin. 'It's time you roosted,' Scrat mumbled.

'I'm on my way – just a word. He's got you brainwashed, that Kine, you shouldn't be here at nightfall. The marsh at night is a grave. Take a tip from the wise: a bold shrew's in for trouble. A shrew's not made for heroics.'

'Who said that? I'll sh-show them!'

'There you are, that's Kine talking. That's not shrew-talk, that's Kine.'

'I'm a scout. A scout dares.'

'You're a mutt,' grunted Watchman, 'you let them put on

you, dwarf, and they've taken advantage. Let them do their own scouting.'

'I'll show the valley I'm b-brave. I'll soon prove I'm a hero.'

'You prove that, you'll be dead.' The rook scowled down his beak. 'You've a chance as a coward; leave war to the weasels.'

'*You* fought Mag and Athene.'

'I'm a rook not a shrew; I had business to settle. I'm just advising you, Scrat – Kine's no model of caution. You should trust your own instincts.'

As he flew off, Scrat piped, 'Pah!'

'Just a warning in passing.'

'Pah,' said Scrat again, louder. '*Pah*,' with weasel inflection. He grabbed a beetle and chomped. Kine was daring, audacious, everything the shrew envied. 'Now or never,' he breathed, creeping nearer the pumphouse.

It bulked darkly, a dungeon. Bleak brick walls rose above him. Ahead the tunnel's mouth gaped, the black hole to the foundations. Was the Night Lord inside; was Hob using the bunker? If Kine knew *that* ... if Scrat could answer *that* question.

'Now or never!'

He faltered. The bats were up, their wings flitting. Silently, the maw beckoned.

His name would live among scouts in the annals of daring. Intrepid creatures would laud him, speak of him in their haunts, all the valley applaud – if he dared. With a shudder he moved, stopped, advanced to the threshold.

It was fusty and dim. Scrat slipped into the passage. Quivering, he stole on, whiskers stiff in the darkness. It was quiet, the air thick. Doom, the rook had been right! Still, he forced himself forward. Dusky joists flanked his path, murky corners confused. By great bulwarks he crept, over bones, down rank aisles.

'Doom and folly!' he breathed.

He stared; he saw nothing. The labyrinth's entrails were inky. There was a dense, fetid stench. Something brushed the dwarf's snout, something feathery, black – the dry wing of a rook. Watchman's mate. Scrat recoiled. He had an urge to scream out but refrained, somehow passing the relic.

Death, he thought, turn back now. Yet the maze lured him on. Every nerve in him twitched, each pulse throbbed. He must be close to the bunker. He heard a long breath and in a moment another. There was a third and a fourth. The sounds were spooky, unreal, like the drone of swans winging.

Terrified, the shrew listened. Something large was asleep, snoring rhythmically, lewdly. Hob! he told himself, shaking. Hob *was* using the lair; Scrat had answered the question. He felt a thrill of success, of transcendent achievement, then, aghast, heard Hob stirring.

A throbbing snore stopped mid-breath, an appalling grunt echoed. It punched the gloom and rolled on, thundering in the labyrinth. Scrat turned, stumbling wildly. Panic stricken, he fumbled. He was blind in the maze, tripped by refuse and bones, unimaginable debris. He struck walls as he ran, groping where they made corners.

In the dark, the fiend followed.

'Help,' prayed Scrat, 'let me live!' Let him live to reach Kine! Let him gain his reward, bask for once in acclaim. Until then, spare his skin, speed his pin-legs to safety. Already sinew was strained, his minute lungs oppressed. Scrat crashed into a joist. He could hear Hob behind him.

He thought a star blinked ahead. The faintest hint of light glimmered. Let the labyrinth end, the tomb's exit come quickly! Scrat was spent, fit to drop. Then, suddenly, the sky flared, clear air freshened his head and he plunged into grass, a great cool, dewy jungle. A moment later he dropped, too exhausted to struggle.

Eyes closed, the shrew waited.

What had he told the rook? *'I'll show the valley I'm brave.'*

'You prove that, you'll be dead.'

He feigned death in the grass. Not a hair on him moved, the small velvet blob limp. Ages passed, so it seemed; still he waited, inert. Finally, the shrew peeped. Hob had passed in the night – night himself, the night demon.

The last rooks had winged home, drifting down to black castles. Barely visible now, the birds could just be discerned, blotting stars as they turned, dimly circling the covert. A lapwing whirled, crying thinly, then fled.

As Scrat toiled to the wood, horseshoe bats jinked above him. Higher, duck pierced the gloom, flying fast, straight as arrows. A fox barked once, far away, an irascible sound, solitary and cheerless.

By its hut the goose glared, one eye fixed on the house, one regaling the hedge beyond which the night thickened. There was no sign of the man. He should by now have locked up, come to shut in the goose, but Ploughman's habits had changed, grown erratic just lately.

They disconcerted the goose. Food came now at odd times, the hut door was left open – twice all night. The man had simply drowsed off. He seemed no longer himself and the bird was disquieted. Strutting nearer the house, it stood grumbling a while then marched back to its quarters.

Lowering clouds had advanced, the marsh soupy with vapour. From the overcast sprawl, a faint whisper of reeds told that rain was approaching. Carefully the fowl listened. Nearby something moved quickly.

'Who's there?'

It was quiet.

'The night picket!'

From the hedge tumbled weasels, half a dozen, eyes glinting. The force was formed of two sections: one, with Kine, the old heroes, the other Clary's young braves. Amazed, the fowl eyed the goblins.

'We're after Hob,' Kine said crisply. 'We're out to seek and engage.'

With a hiss, the rain reached them. It pounced in over the fields, swift and dark, its force biting. 'Hob?' the goose honked. 'You're mad, you'll never find him at night. Hob's a spectre, a shadow.'

The sprites stood firm in the downpour.

'We'll find him,' Kine said. 'We'll not rest till we find him.'

'He'll find *you* when he's ready!'

'We'll see about that.'

'When you're least prepared for him. He'll catch you, Kine, like the rain in the dusk. Rain at night,' the fowl added. The sprites had gone, slipping off. 'A ghoul,' shouted the goose, but the downpour was deafening.

It came in sheets, like great wings. Battering on the hut, it sluiced down into pools, tearing them into froth. The goose flinched, its eyes stinging. Waddling into the shed, it looked back at the deluge. Water curtained the doorway, streaming darkly to earth. On the roof the rain drubbed, on the walls, clawing round the black chamber.

'Come and talk,' said the fiend, a cruel voice in a corner.

* * *

The dandies ran through the bracken. The orchard was noisy, children squealing and bawling. Mothers talked as they picked, climbing small metal steps, filling baskets with early apples. Freckled faces perspired. Everywhere there was fruit: bulky Bramleys, sweet Grieves, Worcester Pearmains in clusters.

The young weasels ran on.

Near the girl her son pottered, watching butterflies hover. Like the wasps they sought food, drawn to broken-skinned windfalls. The child admired a red admiral, its wings warpaint gaudy. A pale green fly caught his gaze, delicate as a cobweb. He cupped his hands round the insect.

'What's this, mum?' he called up.

She glanced down, her arms raised, plucking fruit as she answered. 'That's a lacewing, it's pretty. They come indoors in the winter. See what else you can find.'

'Mind the wasps,' warned a picker, a large, older woman. She wiped her brow, the work hot. There was a squeak in the bracken. She asked the girl, 'How's your dad?'

'Lost his goose now, poor devil.'

'So I heard, to the fitchet.'

'He's in a state, running wild. He's got the youths out there hunting – as if they'll find it between them! As if,' the girl said, 'it matters; he's no more poultry to lose. It was his own fault, all of it. He should've shut them up safely.'

They took their loads to a crate and returned, baskets empty. The child was munching an apple. 'No more,' the girl said, 'you'll ache.' She wiped his face. 'You've had plenty.'

166

'You can't be careless with poultry.'

'He let the creature get in.'

'The thing's a brute,' said the woman.

'It's only following nature. It could as well have been a fox. They've got to live and you can't blame them. You can't go leaving doors open.'

'He'll get more fowls, I suppose?'

'I don't know – yes, perhaps. He's got to settle to something.'

'He could come out with *me* sometimes,' the child put in, 'to the Moon Pond.'

'You've got that pond on the brain.'

'I could show him the weasel.'

'He wouldn't thank you for that.'

The child peered round through the trees. He looked up, his eyes narrow. 'Do weasels live in the orchard?'

The dandies stopped, listening. The place was getting too busy, too crowded by half. They had a good mind to leave, to find their way to the covert.

'Do they, mum?' asked the toddler.

'I shouldn't wonder,' the girl said.

They came up over the bank, the youths, the dog, Ploughman leading, gun crooked, his face twisted. 'Beat the ditch,' he exclaimed, 'beat the ditch for the fiend!' It was fierce, his voice hoarse, and the terrier panted.

Kine looked out from the reeds. The sun was burning the mist, and there was a hint of autumn about. Soon the leaves would change hue, the whole weasel realm blaze, but for now summer held, though each day warmed more slowly.

Through the steam of the marsh, Kine saw sticks rise and fall, the youths beating and prodding. Their voices floated across and the weasel heard yapping. He told the others, 'Keep down. We'll lie low till they've shifted.'

He watched the dog. It was daft, unpredictably eager. Rushing into the ditch, it jumped out then dived back, all the time its tail wagging. Kine consulted the scout. 'Scrat, you're sure it was Hob? It's pitch dark in the labyrinth.'

Scrat was sure. 'I went in. Kine, I crept to the bunker.'

'You can't see in the bunker.'

'Kine, I *heard*. It took resolute courage.'

'You did well.'

'I excelled!' The shrew jigged, squeaking proudly.

Clary whispered, 'He's brave. Scrat, I said you could do it.'

'I'm a hero, a legend!'

'Pipe down,' Kine snapped, 'they'll hear us.' He viewed the dog; it was listening. 'Now you've done it. Just don't move.' The dog was bouncing with zest, staring straight at the reeds. 'Keep quite still, everybody.'

'It's going to find us,' breathed Brat.

Heath was cool, veteran-steady. 'Stay calm, obey Kine.'

'Dogs are fools,' Wonder said. Her grand scorn reassured, drawing Clary's respect. 'See, the dog has no mind.'

It had begun to advance but, when called, reversed promptly. '*Here*,' the youths bawled, 'the ditch – search the ditch, you daft beggar!' They plied their sticks to the growth, Ploughman cocking his gun. 'Seek, dog, seek!' they exclaimed, tramping on, their sounds trailing.

Bald-ear sprang to his feet. 'Now,' he cried, hot for action, 'no more waiting, let's charge; let's assault the fiend's bunker.'

'No,' hissed Clary, 'hear Kine. Less haste, Bald-ear, be patient. Kine has fathomed the labyrinth, so have Wonder and Heath. Learn from what they can tell us.'

'One thing's certain,' Kine said, 'we can't fight in the bunker. Hob would tear us apart. He's at home in the dark and we couldn't manoeuvre. We'd face him one at a time with no prospect of victory.'

Bald-ear huffed. 'I'd go for him.'

Heath said drily, 'He'd flay you. You'd have the chance of a fly.'

'If we could lure him out,' Kine said, 'we could pull off an ambush.' He eased himself from the reeds. 'We need to survey the ground.' There was no sign of the dog. Stepping on to the path he enjoined, 'Forward, comrades, be wary.'

They slipped in line up the dyke. It was tranquil and rushy; a dragonfly foraged. All the mist had dissolved and the sun flecked the channel. A heron brooded at siege. They passed quietly and the pump reflected ahead, square, grim-walled on the water.

Kine looked at Wonder and Heath. He knew what they were thinking: they had advanced here before, when they were young – young as Clary. They had advanced against odds, against Gru and the minks, fought as heroes that morning. That day One-eyed had died, Kine's old sire; died defending the vale, the ancient birthright, the Life Tree.

Now, they marched the same banks, themselves veterans, young braves at their flanks, sprites unborn in their heyday. All of life was a war, every age, generation. Each new weasel was threatened and none outlived danger. If not Gru, it was Rattun, if not Rattun, the Night Lord. Always evil returned; you could not rest, only fight – fight with weasel persistence.

'It hasn't changed,' Wonder mused, 'the pump was ever an eyesore.' She studied it with disdain. 'Now just think what it harbours.'

Kine viewed the mown grass. 'If we could lure Hob out here.'

'We might,' said Heath, 'if we wait. If can't be done while it's light; Hob won't stir until dark.'

'Then,' said Brat, 'we shan't see him. He's in his element then. It's worth trying it now.'

Heath's grey head expressed doubt.

Brat said, 'Let me go in there.'

'No,' said Kine, 'you stay put. Heath is probably right – anyway, it's my duty.'

'I could lure him,' pressed Brat.

'No,' Kine answered with force.

'I'd be less loss than you would.'

'Do as Kine says,' shot Clary. She cocked an ear, her lips tight. A thin screech reached the weasels.

They swung round to the willow. A vulgar laugh left its boughs, the sound taunting, abrasive. It fouled the air with abuse. 'Kine, you're wasting your time. Hob is gorged. Do you hear me? Hob is sated, you worm.'

Clary bristled. 'Athene!'

'You're the next, Kine, don't worry; you're next for extinction. When the Night Lord bestirs, when the shadows crawl, weasel, when the dusk falls, watch out. And your friends, the whole ragbag of vermin . . .'

'We'll be waiting,' howled Kine. The Blood Fury boiled in him. 'Let him come for us, witch, let him test the death dancers!'

'Kine, ignore her,' drawled Wonder, 'the owl's less than nothing.'

'So stuck up!' screamed Athene. 'All such uppity pests!'

Kine hurled, 'Tell him I'm ready, tell the brute Kine's impatient.'

'Kine, I'll laugh as you perish.'

There was a bark. The sprites froze. 'Quick,' hissed Clary, 'the dog . . .' and Kine, spinning, saw men, the three hunters returning, the terrier leading. It bounded forward full-voiced, charging headlong towards him. There was no choice of command and he bellowed it:

'*Scatter!*'

He heard the little owl hoot, a delirious whoop, then the dog's yapping deafened. Kine sat tall, waiting boldly. At last, convinced he was seen, he ducked into the grass, a tough clump of tall bent, tunnelled deeply and waited. The dog was stupid but quick; Kine did not linger rashly.

As the whelp tore the grass, he skipped out, tantalising. Eagerly the dog followed, led now to a fresh clump. Again, it wrenched at the growth, spitting roots, growling, whining. Again, the sprite shifted. Cunningly, he played tag, bent to sedge, sedge to bent, always one jump ahead, the dog drawn from his friends past the pump to the stream where the goblin turned slyly. 'Come,' he called, 'cool your head, you've got overexcited.' Then he was gone in the current.

He did not wait for the splash that marked the terrier's plunge but submerged, drifting coolly. A dog was only a dog. It was Hob his mind pictured, the night fiend. *'You're next, Kine . . . for extinction.'* The water chilled. *'And your friends . . .'* He surfaced under the bank, climbing out undetected. The dog was still in the stream; he could hear Ploughman cursing.

'Call her out, let's get on; she's blamed useless, that beggar!'

* * *

As the evening returned Kine stole off on his own. He had to think and draw strength, somehow find inspiration. The final struggle was close and, though his will was rock-firm, concentration was lacking, his power to conjure a ruse, his innovatory talent.

Age had dulled his invention. Nerve remained and his pluck – he was still Kine the intrepid. Reserves were there to be tapped; enough, he hoped, for the night, for one last deadly dance. But would his genius rise, his old and consummate cunning?

For all their sakes – Clary's, Wonder's, those of all who stood by him – he had to *think*, rouse his muse. He reached the brook and stared up. Beneath the wood's darkening vaults, the hollow elm cast its spell, its glow strong as light dwindled. Mesmerised, Kine sought help, his head raised to the marvel.

Would the oracle speak? In trancelike silence, he paused, a small figure alone, meditative in vigil. A voice above broke his thoughts. 'Well,' croaked Watchman, 'what's this – in repentant mood, goblin?'

'I came for peace, inspiration.'

'You'll hear no message from *that*.' The rook's squint was sardonic. 'A crop of luminous fungus! You disappoint me, my friend, indulging base superstition.'

'The light's an omen, a sign.'

'Rubbish, shrimp, wishful thinking.'

Kine was quiet, still bewitched. At length he said, 'It brings hope, it illuminates, Watchman. You're just a cynical fowl. The totem's spell is profound, I've been lifted, enlightened.'

'Weasel gibberish, Kine.'

'I feel genius stirring.'

'Bah,' the rook said unmoved, 'you were always a braggart.'

'And never lost for a plan. Rook, my mind is refurbished.'

'Shrimp, you're *out* of your mind; you're a babbling dotard.'

The strange fluorescence winked down, nebulous, enigmatic. Heady, Kine eyed the brook, its dark thoroughfare restful. It reflected the gloaming, a fretwork pattern of leaves dashed with highlights of evening. Its lissom swirl made him sway, dance across then skip back. The irrepressible Kine! 'The old Kine genius, rook! Wait, a stratagem's forming . . .' He glanced again at the elm, thoughtful now, holding still.

'I'm glad you're here,' he intoned, 'I'm going to need your help, Watchman.'

'You'll get no help from *me*, sprite.' The bird shrank from the notion. He had pitched in against Mag and that was all he was doing. Hob was Kine's affair now. 'I'm too old for your wars; there's no end to your problems. I've solved enough in the past, and little thanks I've had for it.'

'I'm in your debt, truly Watchman.'

'In my debt, Kine? They *all* are, all the rooks, all the rest. All the wood's in my debt. Where have *I* got to? A lookout!'

Kine protested, 'Much more.' He gazed up, his voice wheedling. 'A sage,' he said, 'and a friend, a wise head. Without dispute a great mind. More, a prince of the sky.' The paean throbbed. '*A bold flier.*'

'Not at night. Hob's *your* headache.'

'I wasn't thinking of night.'

'Find another.'

Kine sighed sadly. 'You've got it wrong, it's not Hob; Kine must tackle the fitchet. It's something Kine couldn't handle.'

Watchman leered. 'Kine the legend?'

'A task for someone of stature.'

'Oh?' the rook said, suspicious.

'The little owl.'

'Huh!' scorned Watchman.

'She's more than I could take on.'

'You can't fly,' wheezed the rook. 'She's no falcon herself. Why, I've tweaked her tail for her!'

'So you did,' purred the sprite. 'So you did, I'd forgotten. I need her out of it, rook; I need Athene removed before the main operation. She's too much for the sparrows.'

'Them,' the rook croaked, 'they're sprats. What you need is an air ace.'

'They'd be a help, Flit and Farthing.'

'Not to Watchman, my friend, I'd fly rings round Athene.'

'You would indeed,' Kine exclaimed, the triumphant smirk hidden. 'You'd trounce the witch roundly. You'll take her on then,' he urged, 'clear the sky for me, rook?'

Watchman sniffed. 'I suppose, since you're useless without me.'

'Good for you – my plan's formed! Praise the light, we'll prevail.' The weasel ran to the elm. It slanted over the brook, a great trunk, the cleft glowing. It made the goblin's eyes gleam, gave them new, inspired depths. Lustrously, they peered up. 'Rook, the light of good hope, the incomparable beacon!' He gave the bird a sly glance. 'The inestimable fungus!'

'Come on,' Kine churred, 'it's time.'

'He's still preparing,' said Brat.

'Preparing what? It's gone time.' They watched the rook from the track. He was a dot in the tree, still perched high on the covert. 'It's past the time for his takeoff.'

Clary thought of the mission. 'Poor Watchman, it's dangerous.'

'It's vital to us,' rasped Kine. 'If this goes wrong the scheme's threatened. What's up with the corvid?'

'I'd say he's dreaming,' mused Heath.

'I'll give him dreaming! *Go*, Watchman!'

The rook half-stretched his black wings. His gaze took in the vale fondly: the dark green woods, furrowed fields, the broad marsh and blue hills. There were, he thought meditatively, worse lives than a lookout's. He had lost count of his years, the summers passed in that land; the best of lands, he believed, never mind his complaining.

In winter, roosting afield, he had always felt homesick, returning often by day just to stare at its bleakness. Then he would check the old nests, gaze at the pond with nostalgia.

The time had come, he thought now, to stay put all year round. He might not see a new spring – it was, at his age, unlikely. Better die in the copse, be it gale-swept and bare, than away in some lodging. If, indeed, he lived that long. For though he scorned the small witch, he did not underrate her. Athene was vicious.

He closed his wings again, stiffly. They were as creaky as barn doors. He must be mad to have allowed Kine to sway him; he must be getting like Scrat, put upon by the weasel. He had a mind to cry off.

'Pah,' he croaked, 'get it done, give the groundlings a treat, let them see some *real* flying.' He gave a couple of flaps. '*Caw!*' he cried, rising slowly.

'There he goes,' shouted Heath.

'Stout old rook,' exclaimed Wonder.

There was a murmur from Kine. 'Yes,' he breathed with relief, 'do your stuff, rook, don't fail us.'

The corvid wheeled, gaining height. With one eye he looked down, banking over the cottage. The girl was hanging out washing. A little breeze tugged at clothes, blew her hair round her cheeks. He saw the van on the track. Then, with sudden disgust, he caught sight of the sparrows. They rose with brisk, stabbing strokes, Flit to port, Farthing starboard.

'Caw,' he bawled. 'Buzz off, riffraff!'

'We've got our orders,' hailed Flit.

Farthing soared. 'To support you.'

'Support from *urchins?*'

Flit weaved. 'A fighting escort – Kine's orders.'

'I might've known.' The rook glowered. 'I might've known that of Kine. Senseless sparrows! Well, you'd better learn fast – *I'm* giving the orders.' He lurched on grimly, enraged. 'Give me airspace, don't crowd me.'

'V formation,' chirped Flit.

'We're not learners,' cheeped Farthing.

Below the dense wood unfurled, its rolling canopy domed, the glade and Moon Pond encompassed. The pool looked black from above; the man beside it foreshortened. He made a bleak, hunched-up form, desolate and unmoving. Ploughman stared at the depths, seemed transfixed by the water.

The sparrows gave him no thought, struggling now to keep up. The extended V straggled. From time to time Watchman yawed, dipped and rose, wrenching black-fingered pinions. There seemed no haste in his flight yet the sparrows were batting.

'Steady on,' complained Flit, 'we'll have nothing left, Watchman.'

Rhythmically, the rook oared. The great ragged wings groaned.

'Yes, go easy,' gulped Farthing.

'Huh,' the rook rattled back, 'call yourselves fighting escorts!'

'Tatty despot,' winced Flit.

Watchman leered. 'Keep in place. Hold your station. *Work*, urchins.'

Tiny landmarks slipped by, a toy marsh gate, small dykes gutter-sized to the fliers. The levels stretched like a quilt stitched by reeds, rushy cuts, dwarf sheep browsing square patches. A brace of partridge crouched low. Mere brown bugs, they peered up, scrutinising the trio then, on cockchafer wings, crossed the river's bright ribbon.

Watchman rocked, spilling air. 'Going down,' he called brusquely.

Relieved, the two sparrows planed. They were in shallow descent, the rook stiff, a dihedral. Now aligned on the pump he veered slightly and steadied. The only sound was the wind, their quietly murmuring slipstream.

Watchman wheezed. 'There she is . . .'

Flit steeled himself as they swooped. The tree appeared to expand, come towards him at speed, and the rook was not braking. It was a reckless approach, a headlong plunge towards leaves which obscured sturdy boughs. Flit was convinced that Watchman's sense had departed.

He held his breath. The leaves blurred. He felt the foliage part and thought, with fleeting dismay, the next impact would brain him. Then suddenly all was green, a green cave, branches shaving his wing tips. He could see Watchman ahead. The old black fowl swerved and dodged, masterful in manoeuvre.

Farthing yelled, 'Mind the trunk!'

They missed the pole by a scrape, one each side, and Flit blinked. The tree's cavern was dim but he could still see the rook – and there ahead, on a limb, the squat owl, looking startled. Her head cranked round. Watchman struck. Then he was lunging on out, smashing through the far leaves, Flit and Farthing attacking.

They caught Athene off balance. She almost fell as they passed, her eyes blazing. There was a terrible squawk, her flat head spinning fiercely. But they had gone, like the rook, hurtling out of the willow.

As they shot from the tree curses volleyed behind them. At

first, the sun's glare acute, Flit could not see the others. When he did, they had turned. The veteran rook had whipped round, flying back on his tracks. He came close, gaining speed, his glint wicked.

'He's going in again, Flit.' Farthing zoomed. 'Support stations!'

His comrade spun on a wing. So tight was Flit's about turn that the valley seemed to capsize. It reeled a moment then lurched and he had levelled, head swimming. 'I'm with you, Farthing.'

'Let's go!'

A squall of oaths left the tree, vile, cacophonous sounds, Athene's opus of hate, and Flit glanced at his partner.

'Straight in, Farthing?'

'Straight in!'

'Keep together . . .'

They charged the screen, parting leaves; twigs were snapped in their rush. Again, they broached the owl's keep. It was deafening inside, loud with screeches and shrieks, gales of avian rage, and this time feathers drifted. They floated up in a cloud, almost blinding the sparrows. In their midst, owl fought rook, grappling fiercely in space, flapping wildly to earth where the combat continued. There the birds pecked and screamed, the owl plying hooked talons.

Farthing wheeled. 'Flit, she'll kill him!'

'*Dive*,' bawled Flit, and they swooped, threading down between boughs, swirling into the fracas. Athene spat at the sparrows. As their wings drubbed her face Watchman wrenched himself free. 'Get him out,' twittered Flit, 'get him into the open.'

'Quickly,' Farthing agreed.

They hustled Watchman between them.

'Are you all right?' Farthing breathed.

'Bah,' the rook growled, 'I'll live.'

'Flee,' chirped Flit, 'we'll divert her.'

He scurried back to the tree and, with his partner, peered in. They could hear ranting inside, see the foliage swaying. 'She's coming, Flit.'

'Let her come!'

176

'Yes,' yelled Farthing, 'the *crone*.'

They flapped their wings to provoke. 'CRONE,' they shouted and fled. 'Draw her round the tree, Farthing!'

'She's catching up.' They flew faster.

'Where's the rook? Has he gone?'

'No,' puffed Flit, 'look up there.'

Farthing spared a swift glance. There was no time to do more, for he could hear the owl's sails, hear the whirr as she followed. At least the veteran was safe, cruising high, a black speck. 'Jink,' cried Flit, 'zigzag, Farthing!' Farthing hurled himself sideways.

Athene passed, bent on murder. Stabbing air, she turned back.

'Keep evading,' screamed Flit, 'Watchman's not given up.'

In the blue, the speck paused. Like a duck's, the tail tilted. Watchman's wings hugged his flanks. Hawkishly, the rook stooped, falling plumb as a stone. Each split second he grew, streaking down the clear sky, bombing straight for Athene. He shook his pinions at last, splayed his feet and impacted. Like a rag, the owl crumpled.

She struck the ground, looking dazed.

'Mob her!' shouted the sparrows.

The shattered witch did not wait. With a howl she made off, the far hills her objective.

* * *

'We move tonight, the owl's gone.' Kine paced briskly. His fighters lounged in the glade. He paused and cried, 'The plan's on. The birds have won the first skirmish.'

'The *what*?' the rook exclaimed, pained. He nursed himself, preening feebly. He was immensely bedraggled and swayed unsurely above them. 'You call that battle a skirmish? It was a classical air fight, the total rout of Athene. It was masterful, weasel.'

'I'm glad you coped without loss.'

'Without loss?' Watchman howled, almost falling. 'I've lost the best of my feathers! I gave my all for you, shrimp, I'm enfeebled. Now I'll probably die. Not that *you'd* care, you ingrate.'

'Come,' cooed Clary, 'Kine cares; we all care for you, rook. You excelled. No one else could've done it.'

'Hmm,' the rook grunted, preening. He scowled peevishly. '*Skirmish!*'

Kine returned to the point. 'We've cleared the sky, thanks to Watchman – thanks to Watchman's *great* skill, not forgetting the sparrows – and now we wait until dark. Everyone knows the scheme. Clary leads the young braves; Kine will lead the old heroes.'

Bald-ear grinned. 'We can't fail.'

'Can't wait,' Brat cried, 'we're ready.'

'We'll teach the berserker . . .'

Wonder's tone was less sanguine. 'You'd better rest,' she said calmly. She eyed the Life Tree and pond. The glade was busy with insects. They had gathered for autumn, their last sun-hallowed feast: glistening flies, dopey wasps, hairy overgorged bees bent on life's final binge. Wonder pondered the throng. Who would be there tomorrow?

Wars did not respect plans. She had taken part in them, seen their death and confusion. Like the grey, subdued Heath, she was far from complacent.

Kine had found his old swagger. She watched him stomp the Tree's deck, leap ashore, strut the bank. Kine the killer of giants had always beaten the odds but this struggle was different. Kine had tussled by day, never fought a night battle, let alone against Hob. She feared a lot would be learned, much of it from the fitchet.

'Until dusk,' said Kine, 'we'll relax. Wonder's right, get some rest, take some food, conserve strength. We meet here – meet to conquer!' His eyes were bright. 'Till then, comrades.'

'Huh,' sniffed Watchman, 'brave words.'

'You'll see braver deeds, Watchman.'

'Not me, shrimp, I'll be sleeping.'

Kine smiled and went to the pond. A water vole made a splash and Clary joined her mate quietly. They watched the vole as it dived, its fur silvered by bubbles. A moorhen loped by the reeds, three-quarters grown, brown and leggy. 'You love the pond, don't you Kine, for all its dangers?' said Clary. 'For all the sadness it's brought you?'

'He's perverse,' the rook grunted.

Kine shrugged. 'I've always lived here. The sadness strengthens the tie.' The traumas, grief and the fears. Happiness there had been but somehow now, looking back, it was the bad times that inspired – the bad times overcome. Such was being a weasel!

He contemplated the pool. 'The wood's my birthright,' he said. 'My first steps were here, Clary.'

'Kine, be careful tonight. You're taking all the worst risks.'

He laughed. 'We're all taking risks. I've had plenty of practice.'

'Don't do anything rash. I'd have nothing without you.'

'You would indeed – the whole copse.' He tried to jolly her, adding, 'I've got more lives than a cat. When they expire, this is yours; my territory is yours. So speaks Kine the survivor!'

She did not smile.

'Let's stroll, Clary.' They ambled on round the bank, a white duck paddling near them. It took to the air with a quack and two wildfowl rose with it.

'Kine, I don't want to lose you.'

He shook his head, lightness gone. 'Nor I you, but war is war. In any case,' he went on, 'you know we'd have to part soon. The days are shortening and there'll be a frost any night. You do realise, Clary, that summer partnerships end?' He could see she did not. 'That's the way of the weasel. It doesn't last,' he said gently.

'But it must . . .'

'It's the law – that's the law of the vale.'

'Are you *sure*?'

He smiled gravely. 'We hunt alone again, Clary. The weasel way is solitary.'

'It makes no difference,' she cried, the words abrupt, almost savage. 'I want you safe and unharmed. The spring will come, a reunion.'

Kine was touched by her passion. 'No,' he said, 'I'm too old. The spring will bring you new suitors. I've one more battle to go . . .' He evaded the future. 'I've had the last of my flings, a most bountiful summer. I couldn't ask for much more – youthful mate, thriving offspring: three dandies from Clary! The line of Kine is replenished. In time they'll come to the wood, fight its enemies, breed here.'

'Stop it, Kine, you're not ancient! You'll not dismiss me so easily. Just you wait till next spring.'

He said, flattered, 'We'll see.'

'And just be careful *tonight*.'

He showed a line of bright teeth. 'Careful? Kine the audacious?'

The sun sank slowly, bright red, an immaculate circle. It lurked a while in the trees like some far away fire, then was gone, the sky lurid. Small white clouds became pink, others salmon and orange. In the west, long and flat, strands of mauve hung in space. As the afterglow waned, they turned grey and gulls winged in dark waves.

At the set in the wood a striped face quizzed the evening. Since the lea was still light brock withdrew for a moment. A chary pheasant was honking, making much of retiring. There was a luminous pause, a strange hiatus in time while the gleam tricked the eyes, casting haloes on fields, then small creatures stirred quietly.

Woodmice moved, rabbits twitched. Down the length of the hedge half-glimpsed shapes crouched and nibbled, sloppeting close to holes, sitting up on pale diggings. It was the hour of alarms; at a thump they would vanish.

A mighty roar filled the sky. It grew black and in a dense, screeching cloud a host of starlings swept past, then, once more, it was silent. The dome had drained of its flush. A single heron sailed home.

Beneath the eaves of the cottage, the child's night-light glimmered. Sparrows settled nearby, twittering as they roosted. Below the garden was dim and a tiny form scuttled. 'Hey, Scrat,' exclaimed Farthing. The dwarf stopped.

'It's getting dark, shrew, take care.'

Scrat blinked up.

Flit said, 'Time you were gone. It's the night of the violence, the night the weasels wage war.'

180

'Doom,' piped Scrat.

The birds fluffed. There was a thrill in their voices. 'The night of Hob the crazed, pigmy, the night all sane beasts take shelter. A night to cover your eyes.'

'Nowhere's safe,' wailed the mite.

'Time's short, midget, beware!'

'Nowhere down on the ground.' Scrat was shaking. 'It's c-cold.'

'As a corpse, shrew, a corpse.'

'There's a f-frost on the way.'

'Scenes to freeze the blood, pigmy.'

'Doom and dread – *you're* all right.'

'We're not daft. We've done our bit for the cause, now it's up to the others.'

'I've done *my* bit,' the shrew protested.

'Like a hero,' Flit granted.

'Nobody cares.'

'You have to fend for yourself.'

'It's not right, not f-fair.'

'That's the way of the world, dwarf.'

'*Eeow*,' squeaked Scrat, running on, 'the world's cruel'. He bumped his head and sat down, his eyes smarting. Through tears he viewed the obstruction, the dark and overgrown shape of his old hide, the flowerpot. It would give *some* protection. Wriggling in, he cowered, quaking.

The pot was gloomy and cold, a chunk knocked from one side, the growth in it anaemic. The drainage hole made a draught which, in time, became raw as the ground's temperature fell. Fear and frost numbed the pigmy.

He felt faint. Suppose Hob came his way? Suppose the battle raged round him? He gave a whimper of dread. The pot was fragile and cracked. From time to time the hole moaned, the air whiffling in it. Eerie sounds reached his ears, sounds he could not interpret: murmurs, scuffles, a snap.

Abruptly, someone said, 'Wait . . .'

A second voice said, 'The pot.'

'It reeks of fright,' said a third. 'Something's there. Let's find out.'

Rigid, Scrat held his breath. A snout appeared at the hole, a couple more at the base. With sudden speed, the shrew ran, a blind dash, to be tripped and lie kicking.

'It's Scrat the shrew!' He heard squeals. 'We're in luck, it's the dwarf. Scrat, remember the kitts? We teased you once, by the pond. Clary's dandies, remember?'

'Ugh?' he breathed, scrambling up.

'We're from the orchard – got lost. Are we home? Where's the copse?'

'Doom,' he gulped.

'Scrat, don't fret, we're only playful. Cheer up!'

'P-playful?' Scrat sobbed. '*Tonight?*' Further words failed the midget.

Kine advanced to the pump. In the twilight it churned, lowering the dyke levels. The channels slithered and swirled. Water sloshed and turned white, snatched into the impeller, slammed through to the valve, hammered out to the river. It roared and foamed, chucking spume; all the marsh heard its throbbing.

It would be heard at the copse, which Kine could barely make out, a vast ghost in the gloaming. There his comrades were waiting, each a sworn fitchet fighter, each briefed and now posted. They would be listening and anxious. Would his stratagem serve? If not Kine had misled them.

He watched the spluttering froth. Above, a noctule flew high and the Eve Star was shining. For a moment he stopped, contemplating the valley. Its sweep was silvery-grey, the marsh broad, to Kine noble. He knew its hunt paths, its keeps; it was Kine's kingdom, his frontier.

'*Tchkkk!*' He entered the labyrinth.

The motor's pulse shook the earth, rocked the fusty foundations. His heart was cold, his head cool, every movement determined. He knew just what he must do and remembered the martyrs. Pitch darkness engulfed him. In the depths of the maze, he paused short of the bunker. '*Tchkkk*,' he bawled, 'this is Kine; this is weasel land, fitchet!'

He heard it echo and die. The pump had suddenly stopped; an uncanny hush settled.

It seemed to last for an age before the chamber erupted.

There was a snarl from the gloom, a rumbling thunderous oath, and Kine shouted, '*Kine rules! Kine the fitchet despiser!*' Then he turned, running back, the snarl blasting behind him. It rolled and blared at his heels. Racing into the dusk, he glanced round.

Hob burst out of the labyrinth. Monstrously, he reared up. 'Kine, you'll scream like a rabbit. I'll tear the guts from you, vermin!'

Kine did not stop to listen. In no doubt of pursuit, he gained the marsh gate ahead, caught his wind and streaked on. Up the track his lungs laboured. Quick enough in the sprint, he now began to lose ground, his age telling. Rabbits bolted in panic. Hob was closing the gap. Kine could hear him behind, great claws scrunching on grit, every raking bound powerful. By the time the copse loomed, the brute's breath was hot on him.

The dusky monster was swift, a neck's stretch from the weasel. With a life-saving twist, Kine plunged left off the track, gained the trees and was dodging. In thicket and brush, he possessed the advantage. He knew the twists and the kinks, picked the narrowest places. Being small had its points. As he came to the brook, there was time to look back. Then the ogre was charging.

Kine careered down the bank. At the base of the elm, he took off with a leap, landing on the old trunk. It slanted up, the bark dead, soft and crumbling above. Snarling, Hob reached the bottom.

'Sprite, you're trapped. No escape.' The loury shadow stretched up. Its dark mane stood on end. Slowly, leering, Hob climbed. 'Your last scamper is over.'

Grimly, Kine climbed ahead. The trunk was rotten and powdered; he sent small dust cascades tumbling. At last he clung to the cleft, peering into the hollow. The fungus shimmered within, on the walls and the floor, glimmering as he entered. It was eerily light; he could see up the funnel.

Climbing on in the hole, he stopped where its gape narrowed. He had a moment to wait then Hob entered beneath him. The awesome brute filled the hollow and, as he did, Kine squeezed out, slithered back down the trunk and took stock at the bottom. Heath should be in position.

'Quick,' hissed Heath from the bank, 'in the brook – wash it off!'

'Do I shine?'

'Like a star, Kine!'

As Kine rinsed in the brook, the fungus particles glowed, drifting swiftly downstream while Heath urged him to hasten. 'He's coming out, Kine, be quick. He's searched the hollow, he's leaving.' The weasels hid in the bank growth.

The wood was dim, its roof black. In the half-light ahead a gleam broke from the elm tree. Hob appeared in the cleft. Kine was suddenly cold; he could feel his coat dripping. He scarcely dared to look up. The Hob that climbed from the hole was like no natural creature.

From head to tail, the brute shone. He was a torch in the gloom, every hair incandescent. Kine had banked on a glimmer; instead the beast coruscated, winked and flared in the murk, an incredible spectre.

'We've done it, Heath, we've a chance; we've made darkness *our* ally. Hob's no longer the Night Lord!'

'Caution, friend, he's still deadly.'

'A luminous fitchet! He's revealed, Heath, uncloaked. All the valley can see him.' The glowing prodigy snarled, moving down the tree slowly. Kine said, 'Back to the track – the second phase of the plan, Heath!'

They ran swiftly, in silence. The air was still in the trees and Hob's stench hung about, dense by buries and scrapes where the damp earth was pungent. Beneath the skirt of the wood a soft and husky voice stopped them. 'Is that you?' Wonder challenged.

'It's us.'

'Are you safe?'

'Yes, yes . . .'

'Kine, you look spent.'

'Hob's the one who'll be spent – don't waste time.' Kine glanced round. 'We can't talk, take your stations.' He watched them fade on the field, ghosting over the clod where the beans had once grown. The land had been ploughed and moist furrows were dark. Looking back, Kine drew breath. 'Hob, I'm

184

here,' he announced, 'Kine the slayer of giants. Come and dance with me, fitchet!'

'Kine, you've danced your last dance.'

There was a rustle of leaves. Kine heard a grunt in the dark then a glow lit the thicket.

Quietly Kine quit the path, skipping furrow to furrow. At the voor, he bobbed down, spying over the ledge. On his nape, the hairs tingled. All he saw was the copse, cast in gloom, growing darker each moment. Then a light left the trees and came on, strange, macabre, pulsing weirdly. 'Kine, your time's up. Where are you?'

The fitchet stepped on the soil. There was a frost in the air and the ploughed land was slightly tacky. It clung to Hob's hairy feet, clogged the claws as he prowled.

'Over here.' Kine moved on.

The brute charged.

'No, not there, Hob, I'm here.'

'Not *where*, Kine? You can't see me.'

'Oh, I can see you, berserker!'

The monster shone like a beacon. 'At night,' he roared, '*no one* sees me.'

'*I* can see you,' called Heath.

Hob swung sharply, surprised.

Behind him, Wonder proclaimed, 'So can I, you've just moved. I can see you quite plainly.'

'You're clear to all,' shouted Kine, 'you're no longer the Night Lord. It's no good charging about.' Hob was lunging at sounds, chasing this way and that. 'You'll exhaust yourself, Hob.'

'You're condemned – you lie, weasel!'

'Careful, Hob, the land's heavy. So are you. You're no sprite. A sprite floats on the plough; Hob sinks in, his claws burdened. You're getting nowhere,' mocked Kine. 'Try the voor.'

'Try the ditch,' shouted Heath.

Wonder laughed. 'Try the hedge. Wrong again, Hob, you're lost. You've got feet of clay, fitchet; you've lumpen limbs and tired lungs. You're out of breath, your tongue's lolling.'

'I'll fight the three of you, Kine.' Hob stood still, breathing deeply. 'On the track, where it's firm. Do you hear me, small dancer?' They saw him start for the path.

'Yes, I hear you,' called Kine.

'Where I can see you,' snarled Hob.

'You'd like that!'

'On the track . . .'

It was quiet, the sky clear. The last of twilight was dim and there was a round moon on the ridge, the shadows dense by the wood under elder and thorn. Leaves of ash fringed the path in black fans; a large burdock had drooped, its expiring growth mildewed. Clary crouched by its stem, Brat and Bald-ear beside her. 'Ready?' Clary asked quietly.

Hob hauled on to the track. Sullenly, he traversed, glaring back at the furrows.

'Right,' cried Clary, 'attack!' And the braves flew like arrows. They took the fiend in the rear and, for an instant, he froze, mystified by the impact. Then, with a shriek, he swung round and the weasels clung to him.

Clary leeched, her head giddy. Askance, she saw Bald-ear fall, hit the path and bounce up. He gave a shake and charged back. There was a grunt and Hob reared, hurling Clary through space, the fiend's muddy claws flailing. Bruised and shaken, she rallied. So it went for a while, the young braves persevering.

Brat and Bald-ear fought close, harrying the berserker. Clary joined them with verve; she was reckless, a spitfire. Enraged, she stove at the giant, shouting on her companions. 'Keep it up, don't give in! The old heroes are coming!' She caught a glimpse of the field, her mate leaping the furrows.

'Dance,' cried Kine, 'a tight ring!'

He was beside her, concerned. 'Are you hurt?'

'No. Are you?'

'Save your breath,' grunted Heath, weaving past. 'Faster, comrades,' he urged. Wonder whirled beside Brat. As Hob thrashed, she ducked in, snapped and twirled away, spitting. The weasel circle revolved. It was a singular scene, the six sprites round the foe, round a luminous giant, raising dust as they darted. It was like something unreal, like a scream in the night, a small beast on a gibbet.

186

'Dance faster! Close in!'

Hob looked dazed.

As he lashed, Clary dodged. 'Careful, Kine . . .'

The crazed fitchet wheeled round. Suddenly, he had lunged, sending Kine and Brat reeling. Heath and Wonder were skittled. The monster towered in two minds, howled, then broke for the trees. They interrupted the glow, its gleam snuffed by their boles, shining fitfully, fading.

Kine was back on his feet. 'Surround the wood, keep a watch!'

'He took the pond path,' churred Heath.

'He's mine,' cried Kine, 'I'll go in.'

'Not alone.'

'*Alone*,' Kine said.

The sparrows heard the door open. It was closed quietly, with stealth, and someone sat on the step. They could make out the child's back, bent down over his legs. He pulled his shoes on and rose. Then, with scarcely more sound, he shuffled off to the hedge, a squat shape in its shadow.

The boy paused. There was no stir in the house. The parlour curtains were still, brightly lit from inside; no one moved. A few minutes at most and he would slip back upstairs, would have fathomed the mystery. They would not know he had gone.

He crossed the track to the barn. From the front of the pile, he could see down the dark field and *it* was there, moving round. It had looked smaller before, from his room, but had grown none the clearer, still distant and vague, still hypnotically puzzling. An elfin lantern, perhaps?

At all events, thought the child, it had no human connection. There were no tractors at work, nor was it some kind of hand torch. It had no beam, just a glow, and that teasingly puckish. Indeed, its frisk on the field – who would frisk on ploughed land? – was eccentric. He stood bewitched in the dark, oblivious of the cold.

Behind the boy the barn's hulk, black and huge, seemed to nudge him. He took a step on the path to where its edge met the clod, then, unsurely, another. The dusky furrows were yielding; the light on them flitted. He lurched towards it and stopped. Earth had balled on his shoes and that would mean a cross mum.

Prudently, he retreated, kicking mud off his feet, and watched the phantom change tack, heading now for the woods. He could approach round the track; that way he would keep clean. But barely had he set off before, again, the light moved, this time into the covert.

'Wait,' he shouted, 'keep still!'

Contrarily, it gained speed and as he started to run it reached the brushwood and vanished.

The boy scrambled into the copse. It was much darker inside. Thicket snatched at his arms, mighty columns loomed dimly. The youngster's confidence faltered. There were no stars in the vault, only grey and gnarled limbs, malign caves, witches' nooks. Black boughs creaked, fingers plucked. He heard sighs, eerie rasps, and imagined strange whispers. They made him long for his bed; he felt cold and alarmed.

He was lost, the murk thick. Then, ahead, the light glimmered. And shuffling on, he kept track, deeper now in the wood, following the bright lure. He was no longer intrigued; the glow had ceased to enthral. He did not know why he advanced – perhaps because the light lived, one live thing in a tomb, in a nightmare of ghouls, spectral trees, spooky reeds . . .

Something chill gripped his feet. His shoes were heavy and squelched. Faintly, out in the dark, he saw a great masted pier and, stiff with fright, tried to shout. He had no voice. His shoes oozed. There was a dank, pondy smell. He tried to shout for the weasel.

Kine flew into the wood, bounding high, streaming forward. The time of truth had arrived, the hour of Kine the giant fighter. The weasel's gallop was proud, for was his name not renowned? Was Kine not peerless in war? Was not his fame forged in battle? Tonight the legend would live – if he must die to assure it!

Courageously he advanced, small in size, big with challenge. Thus had Kine charged the minks, braved the lists with the Rat

188

King. Valiantly he pranced, style and self-esteem blending. Kine's conceit was intact; age had not drained his bounce. The arch-devil himself, if such was Hob, would not shame him.

'*Tchkkk!*' he flung as he sped. 'Kine is small but supreme!' For was he not still unbeaten, a champion in his realm, rich in guile, skilled in strife? There was a fire in his step and a weasel wrath in him. Kine would fight to the death. Live or die, fame would fête him.

'Hob, it's me. Are you ready?'

'You've come then, worm?'

Kine drew up. There was a glow by the pond and the giant turned towards him, head low, shoulders heaving. A great tail swished, coarse and bristling. 'I thought you'd come on your own. So your friends have packed it in? You're the offering, are you?'

'We fight on hallowed ground, Hob.'

'Hallowed?' Hob sneered. 'It's squalid: puffballs, toadstools, dead wood. A rotten tree in a pond, fit for earwigs and weasels.'

'Kine's domain. I was born here.'

'Then here you'll die, Kine, that's fitting. A tawdry glade in the gloom; an execution's in order. You see,' drawled Hob as he stretched, 'you're far too cocksure to live – *Kine's domain, hallowed ground!* You're smug and tricky and vain. And, like the rest, you'll die squealing.'

'Dance, Hob, join the dance!'

'You think you're clever. You're *small*.'

'Learn the steps.' Kine advanced.

'You're old,' rasped Hob. 'Kine, you're stiff.'

'Try me,' Kine said, alert. 'Join the dance of death, fitchet.' He feinted, swinging his neck, and as the brute struck, dodged nimbly. '*Tchkkk,*' he mocked, 'Hob is clumsy.'

He waltzed away, his step light. There was a gleam in his eye and, when the berserker pounced, Kine had skipped to the flank, darting in to nip sharply. It stirred the fitchet to rage.

'Calmly, Hob, keep your head!'

Crazed, the monster hauled round. 'I'll have *your* head, Kine, you wait.' Frenziedly, the fiend charged and Kine reeled. Driven back by sheer weight, he was thrown to the

bank, scrambling clear by a hair. Hob whirled viciously.
'*Ha*...'

A claw-tipped arm raked Kine's brow.

Dancing off, the sprite laughed, but it stung and he could
feel the blood welling. He shook himself, taking stock. The *old*
Kine would have ducked; he had to fight with more caution.
The battle rested on guile, weasel cunning.

'Bah,' a voice croaked, 'the fool.'

Watchman yawned, squinting down. Kine's blood dripped
and the rook, roused from sleep, despaired for him. Tackling
Hob on his own – Kine had asked for it this time!

The weasel blinked through a veil. It was opaque, a red haze.
He saw fangs, looming jaws. Something pale caught his eye, a
white sphere in the grass. As Hob sprang Kine kicked out. The
puffball burst with a gush, its spores choking the fitchet.

Overhead, the rook gawped. 'Run, shrimp, run!'

Kine stood still, semi-blinded. There was a flint in his
breast, a chill nub of raw hate that numbed fear, disdained
safety.

Hob defiled Kine's domain. Hob abused the sprite's copse,
desecrated its sanctum. Hob was a blight on the vale, a foul,
murdering presence. The weasel glimpsed a great head. As it
spluttered and sneezed, an ear turned and Kine seized it.

Spinning round, the fiend howled, thrashing grass. The
hold tightened, tormenting. Maddened, Hob whirled and
bucked, his tail lashing. In a storm he reversed, tearing turf,
scything swaths in the frost, his mouth twisted, froth rising.

Thumped and flailed, Kine hung on. With each swing his
strength ebbed, with each knock the pain stabbed. Then, with
a rip, Hob's ear tore and the weasel was sprawling.

Watchman groaned. Kine was flat. In the trees by the rook,
roosting wood pigeons bolted. 'Move – get up, you small fool!'

Kine lay motionless, gaping.

'Kine, you fool . . .' The rook froze.

As the fiend curled his lip, Watchman saw the blebbed
fangs, caught a crazed glint and shuddered.

Kine looked up at cruel eyes. This, then, was the end; he had
given his best. The last steps had been danced. He tried to turn
from the blow then, absurdly, heard prattling.

'Look, it's Kine . . .'

'Kine, it's us!'

'Clary's kittens, remember?'

He raised a horrified gasp. '*Go* – clear off!'

'We can fight.'

'*Go, I say.*' Half-grown brats!

'If you say so . . .'

Kine winced. They were imps, barely fledged. But they had startled the fiend and, as they vanished, the pummelled weasel lurched up, saw the Life Tree and ran, somehow reaching the roots, then the deck where he flopped. It seemed to roll and his head swam. A brittle film glazed the pond. He would go through if he slipped, drown, held down by the ice. Close behind him Hob grunted.

* * *

She needed comforting, holding, it was that kind of night: cold and haunted, she thought, snuggling up to her husband. That he kept watching the box, smiling absently, riled. The programme got on her nerves and, when he failed to respond, the girl's sigh was impatient.

'There's nothing else,' he observed.

'Well, we could just watch the fire.' Ash logs burned in the hearth. At least the fire had some life: dancing flames, sizzling sap. 'You can't be bored by the fire. It's lively and cheering.'

'Yes,' he said without looking.

'It can tell tales,' the girl said. 'Better ones than the box. All Poacher had was his fire and he used to sit and dream by it. Poor old Poacher.' She sighed, less theatrically this time. 'He dreamed magical stories.'

'He told some whoppers, all right.'

'D'you think he sometimes comes back?'

'I wouldn't know.'

The girl leaned nearer the hearth. 'It's cold tonight,' she complained. 'It's very early for frosts. Don't you feel that it's cold?'

'I'll fetch more wood when this ends.'

'I feel shivery suddenly.'

'A few more minutes.'

'*What's that?*'

'What was what?' The man frowned.

'Turn the sound down,' she said. '*Murmuring* – can't you hear it?'

'Nothing. Maybe the wind.'

'There's no wind.'

'Don't be daft, there's a wind. You little bumpkin,' he teased. The girl had curious moods. 'It's the wind in the drainpipes.'

'Quiet, I'm trying to listen.'

'Perhaps a window is open.' He dragged himself to his feet. 'I'll look round.'

'No,' the girl breathed, eyes large. They were telling her something. The cottage spirits were troubled. They had to be, she surmised, to come when *he* was about. They were afraid of the townsman; she only sensed them alone – until now. 'No, you'll scare them.'

'Scare who?' he inquired. He gave a tolerant smile. 'Come on, love, settle down.' But she had gone to the stairs, staring up, then he could hear her ascending. He shrugged. He was no match for intuition. He was born with mere reason. She was a child of the marsh.

She came back down with a rush, her face pale.

'He's gone,' she blurted, 'come on!'

'Gone?'

'He's nowhere upstairs.'

They threw the downstairs doors open. The boy was not in the house. 'Outside . . .' the man said, dismayed, and flung the girl's jacket round her. The night air snatched at their breath. He had been right, there was a wind, a chill draught from the east. It stirred the hedge, drove thin clouds. Dark shapes circled the wood, pigeons wheeling, unsettled.

'Dear God,' the girl cried, 'the pond!' and they ran side by side, shouting.

As the fiend climbed the hulk, Kine backed up. The monster's rage had declined and turned to sneering contempt, an almost indolent malice. With evil relish, he paused. The weasel could not escape, for icy death hugged the pier. All Kine could do was retreat, crawl the length of the Life Tree. The other savoured the prospect.

Trunk to limb, limb to twig, a slow and lingering drag. Limb to twig, twig to – nothing! Twig to *death*, thought the giant. Ahead the deck stretched out coldly, its width inexorably shrinking. Frosty gleams streaked the pond, dimmed as clouds hounded swiftly. The great glazed pool made small creaks; around it, the reeds huddled.

'Your final journey,' rasped Hob. 'Make the most of it, weasel.'

The sprite stopped by the hole. A host of memories filled it. It was the lair of his forebears, of his siblings and Kia; the home of Clary, their offspring. The hollow was sacred.

He said, 'Keep off, the hole's charmed.'

'A slug hole, vermin, stand back.'

But Kine stood fast, his spine humped, while overhead the rook muttered. The sprite was bloodied and striped and Watchman pondered his folly. The shrimp deserved all he got. And yet the bird gave a gulp, beset by mutinous stirrings: he felt compassion, respect. He was admiring the braggart. He blinked the mist from an eye. The fool had earned no such feelings.

'Back off, shrimp!' wheezed the corvid.

Instead the weasel attacked. From seeming spent, he sprang up, fuelled by wrath, the Blood Fury. Once more he danced, his head high, and the monster, caught off guard, flinched. Kine was reckless, despairing. For several seconds he pranced then, worn out, stood and glared. With cruel contempt the fiend pounced and the sprite was flung to the deck.

Staggering, he withdrew, barely conscious. Each side of him the pier sloped, the Tree's frosted bole glassy. He had to dodge, somehow dance, but his feet slipped and skidded. He saw his foe through a fog and the woodland reeled round him. Gingerly he skipped sideways then backwards. Below the pond seemed to tilt, glazed and bleak, very slowly subsiding.

'Dance,' sneered Hob, 'while you can. It gets narrower, cockroach.'

The fiend came on with sure steps. The shuffling lope was

remorseless, hustling Kine to the brink, dogging him as he lurched. Frantically he back-pedalled. A foot trod air and he froze. A gulf had opened behind him, the trunk dividing in two, its limbs flanking the chasm. As he dithered, Hob struck, an armed forepaw descending. The crushing blow left him pinned, gawping down into shadow.

The daunting gully was deep; far beneath him ice glinted. Slowly, clawing and sharp, the huge foot forced him downwards.

'Feed the fish, weasel, drown! The sprite's grave has no bottom.'

'Stop!' An inky shape fluttered and Kine saw black pinions. There was a dissonant *caw* and Hob snapped, twisting upwards, then cursed and spat feathers as Watchman's wings beat his head until with rickety strokes, they bore the corvid to safety. In the fray Kine broke loose.

Free, he scrambled on weakly. He had to drag himself now, choosing one of the limbs, crawling painfully on it. The path was steep, thin, decayed. Stripped of bark, it was smooth, treacherous underfoot. Hearing Hob in pursuit, he turned, facing the danger.

'*Tchkkk!*' he spat. His eyes blazed.

'Too late, Kine, it's the end.'

'Others fight if I die. Hob, the covert's surrounded.'

'They'll die, too, they're condemned.'

'There'll be more. Clary's dandies. They'll soon mature, soon be fighters. The line of Kine won't give up.'

'Vermin, Kine!' Hob advanced.

Kine withdrew, crouching grimly. The perch was mean, pale as bone, the wood crumbling and rotten. The second limb rose nearby, as infirm as its twin. The sprite measured the gap. If he jumped, would he make it? Would it break if he did?

Teetering, he inched back. The fitchet's breath fouled his lungs. So close was Hob's gaping mouth that Kine could see past the fangs to the black throat behind. He felt faint. Flakes of wormy wood tumbled. He clutched the frail spar and swayed. The monster's weight made it shake. Kine saw Hob stop and stiffen.

194

There was the faintest of sounds, a low and ominous creak, then a crack like a gunshot. It brought a gasp from the giant.

Wildly, Kine vaulted sideways.

Curling out through the murk, he had a glimpse of Hob falling, going down with the branch, then something hard struck the weasel. In desperation he clawed, all four feet seeking substance. The object rocked and he leeched. Unlike its unmasted twin, the limb held and he dangled.

For what seemed ages, he hung, scarcely daring to move, then eased on to the Life Tree. Below the pond's roof was dim. There was a hole in its glaze. A flattened bubble dispersed. He thought he saw a limp shape, ghostly under the ice, but the pond kept its secrets.

Clary crouched beside Wonder, the females close to the track. It was quiet in the dark but for the odd frosted leaf falling. Down the wood's edge lurked Heath, Brat and Bald-ear beyond him. Clary fretted, tail twitching.

'It's been too long. I'm going to look for him, Wonder.'

'No,' breathed Wonder, 'hold on. We must try to be patient.'

'I've tried. I'm going to find him.'

'You have to heed what he said.'

'I don't care what he said. He could be injured – or *dead*.'

'Then we must wait here for Hob,' the older weasel said firmly. 'That is our task,' and she added more gently, 'Have hope. Kine's a doughty old rogue, don't despair for him, Clary. He might not be all he boasts but he *is* a survivor.'

'He's obstinate.' Clary frowned.

There was a crunch in the wood.

'Down,' called Heath, 'someone's coming.' They could hear footsteps approaching, heading slowly towards them. The sound was loud in the frost; twigs and frozen growth crackled. Alarmed, the small creatures ducked. The mounting noise chilled their hearts, heavy steps unpropitious.

'That's not Kine.'

'No, keep down.'

Ploughman trudged from the copse. He had the child on his back, the boy's arms round his neck. The moon came out and the sprites peered. There was a rush down the track. A voice was shrilling, 'He's here!' and the girl stopped, out of breath. 'Is he safe?'

'Safe enough.'

'Oh, thank God! Give him here . . .' She snatched the child and embraced him. The engineer loomed. 'Is he all right?'

'Aye, no harm,' grunted Ploughman. 'I found him down in the wood.'

'How?' the girl asked at length. 'What were *you* doing in there?'

'That's my business.' Ploughman shuffled his feet. 'It's no business of yours. I was thinking – aye, thinking.'

'In the dark?'

'Can't I think? There's no law against it.'

'By the pond,' piped the youngster.

'Well yes, all right,' Ploughman sighed. 'It was a mood, a fool notion. It was a black sort of mood; I wouldn't never have done it, not like Poacher's old man.' He forced a hesitant smile. 'Just as well I was there.'

The boy smiled.

'Aye, we'd best get us home.'

'Yes,' the girl said, 'indoors.'

'By the fire,' said her husband. 'Hot drinks for us all. Let's get warm, can't talk frozen . . .'

As they moved off, the sprites stirred.

The sound of voices grew faint; small, bright eyes gleamed in shadows. 'They've gone,' breathed Wonder, 'it's quiet.' She cast round and said, 'Clary?'

Clary sped through the wood.

She scarcely saw the great boles, barely noticed the brush. Scabrous briars raked her coat, coiling vines looped and snared. Past dark tangles she raced, past the burrows and stumps, under grappling thorn, one concern on her mind, one thought driving her forward: she must, at all costs, find Kine.

As she burst to the glade she saw the dandies before her. They were at ease by the pond.

'You!' she cried.

They beamed fondly.

'But you should be . . .'

'It's all right.' The imps laughed. 'It's quite safe.' They

skipped round her, delighted. *'The monster's dead, Hob is dead! We watched the battle of battles. We saw them, Kine and the giant; Kine the bold, the giant killer.'* They danced with glee. 'Kine's unbeaten!'

'Where?' gulped Clary.

'The Tree . . .'

She saw his form on the hulk, bloodied, huddled, unmoving. 'Kine!' She flew to him, trembling. In fear she paused. He was limp.

'Fast asleep,' chimed the dandies. 'Just collapsed, started snoring.'

'Oh, poor Kine.'

The imps grinned.

'Fetch the others,' she told them. Then, nursing Kine with her tongue, she gently tended his lesions. His eyes half-opened, approving.

'Kine, you did it,' she purred.

'Yes, of course,' he said, yawning.

Epilogue

It was again almost Christmas, the countryside silent. The vale was frozen but bright, a pale winter's sun precious. It drew glints from bare trees, picked out colours in hedges. Hips and haws came alight, mossy roofs were made golden. For a spell, around noon, the pond gleamed, azure fire in its icecap.

The weasel climbed from the hole. His mate and friends had dispersed, each alone for the season. Such was the law of the species. His path was cold, solitary; his coat the hue of dead leaves but in the sun of tiger lilies. He reached the wood's edge and sniffed.

By the copse pheasants fed, a few acorns still present. A robin trilled, the sound wistful. It seemed to echo past springs, poignant, thin and nostalgic. The next few months would be hard and Kine, gritting, pressed forward. Winter preyed on the old.

Distantly the marsh sprawled, its dykes stiff. Drooping reed tassels shivered. The weasel turned up the track, passed the barn and cocked his head. With a twist through the hedge, he was facing the cottage. The parlour window framed warmth, flaming logs. Girl and husband were kissing, the mistletoe hoisted.

'*Tchkkk*,' churred Kine, moving on. There were no hearths in the wild, no snug, fire-cosy nooks. He looked up as duck whirred, flighting south in dark skeins. Some fled winter's harsh reign: Kine the weasel fled nothing. When death caught up, as it would – he could feel its chill in him – Kine's remains would stay put, where his ancestors rested.

He crossed the lane to the field. On its margin he paused, near the huts Hob had plundered. The child and Ploughman were working, putting up some new fencing. The boy was happy, red-nosed, a small fist round a hammer.

'That's the way!' Ploughman beamed.

Pullets watched as they toiled and young geese stood in a

gaggle. The farm man's stock was replenished. He said, 'You're learning, my lad, you take after your grandad. We'll give them plenty to scratch. Don't ask much, doesn't hens: bit of land and a perch, nice clean nest. Not much brains but they'll thank you.'

Kine continue his prowl. His wounds had healed and he looked sleek, but fighting Hob had left scars, scars inside, aches and creaks. He could feel the joints stiffening. He forayed slowly, resigned, seeking out sunny patches. The sun would go, ice would follow. There was a promise of snow and Kine worried for Clary. But she was young and would live; it was Kine who would perish.

'Doom!' The shrew joined the weasel. 'The snow is coming.'

'Shut up, Scrat.'

Scrat was cold. 'You're all right. *I'm* afraid.'

'Scrat the scout?'

'Just a dwarf. Not like you, Kine, you're brave.'

'Yes, well . . .' Kine raised his snout.

Scrat said, 'You're a *real* hero.'

'Right, but you did your bit.'

'You're a giant killer, Kine.'

'True,' the weasel agreed, a bounce quickening his step. 'A fitchet fighter,' he mused. 'It's a flair, Scrat, a gift.'

'You've no fear, you're a legend.'

'So they say.' The sprite strutted.

'You've a mate waiting for you – all the valley is waiting. Come the spring they'll all hail you.'

'Spring?' said Kine. 'Yes, why not?' His jaw set in defiance. The old braggart was stirring. No one put down a legend; he was Kine the determined. He knew the art of survival, knew the trails, the deep places. He knew the hunt paths and warrens, the vole's retreat, the mole's fortress. He could interpret the signs, could take care of himself.

He skipped on lightly, head high. He was unbowed; none was bolder. He was Kine the death dancer. He knew the ways of the fox and was wise to the barn owl. Let the winter blow cold – he had a trick or two waiting.

He said, 'There's life in us, Scrat – keep your tail up, don't weaken.'

Author's Note

According to a newspaper, Kine has changed the popular image of the weasel from that of the loutish vandals at Toad Hall to one of an enviably athletic hero.

But the former view was always countered in the countryside itself by a more favourable attitude. One man's pest is another's ally and, while the weasels of *The Wind in the Willows* may be caricatures of the old-fashioned gamekeeper's 'vermin', to the traditional farmer the weasel was a welcome rodent catcher.

As a country child I saw life from the farmer's viewpoint. My early impression of weasels was of small, bouncy creatures of great agility – indeed, of the athleticism then a common attribute of boys' heroes, a breed who tended to extricate themselves from danger with easy bounds.

Once, hunting rats in a blocked-up culvert, I was so startled by the agility of a weasel that the memory is vivid after fifty years. As I poked round with my stick, the animal suddenly leapt from the pipe, flew clean over my shoulder and disappeared. I suppose its leap approximated to a human high jump over a lofty building. Such is the stuff of superheroes.

Of course, in a wildlife context, heroes and villains are only fantasies. As a conservationist, I am urged to emphasise that Kine's opponents, not least the polecat which is now very rare in Britain, are deserving of respect and protection from persecution. Given the chance, however, the polecat is sometimes a wasteful killer, possessing a 'berserker' instinct when confronted by an abundance of captive prey.

It is also, as a matter of fact, capable of breeding with its domesticated relative the ferret, though the male (hob) polecat is considerably larger. Both fitchet and foul-marten were common alternative names for the polecat when the species was widely known.

As for the dormouse, I have used a name I heard applied to that charming animal in my youth, in Hampshire: chessel-crumb, or chestle-crumb. I know nothing of its familiarity elsewhere, or its derivation. If, as seems likely, it comes from chessel, which means cheeseboard, it would appear more appropriate to the house mouse than the dormouse. Perhaps dormice, kept as pets, had a taste for cheese?

The little owl is a neighbour I rather like. Introduced to Britain in fairly recent times, it was soon unpopular in the country for its alleged 'devilry' as a killer of songbirds and others. Doubtless, its strangeness told against it. Now accepted as a naturalised character, Athene remains conspicuously bumptious and bellicose.

I remember one little owl on the farm that includes, in reality, Kine's territory. At dusk the creature would chase all the blackbirds from their evening song perches, replacing their melody with a series of catcalls while bobbing excitedly up and down.

Finally, Kine's ruse of the glowing fungus is not all fantasy. Luminous or 'ghost' owls are a documented, if puzzling, ornithological phenomenon. The most satisfactory explanation, according to Bunn, Warburton and Wilson, authors of *The Barn Owl*, Poyser 1982, is that the birds roost in tree hollows containing luminous bacteria or honey fungus, itself sometimes luminous. The rest follows . . .

A.R. Lloyd
Kent, 1989